Welcome to your new favorite YA sci-fi series!
Landfall: The Ship Series Book One hurls us into a
frightening and fascinating future rich with action,
mystery, and unforgettable characters. With elements
of Orson Scott Card's Ender's Game and the best of
Rick Riordan's Percy Jackson books, Landfall kept me
burning through the pages. I hope Jerry Aubin is typing
right now, because I can't wait to return to The Ship!

- Owen Egerton, author of *Everyone Says That at the End of the World*

LANDFALL

THE SHIP // BOOK ONE

JERRY AUBIN

For any information, please contact zax@theshipseries.com.

The main text of this book was set in Georgia.
The chapter title text was set in Avenir.

Lekanyane Publishing
Austin // Amsterdam // Cape Town // Sydney // Christchurch

ISBN 978-0-9970708-1-1 (pbk)
ISBN 978-0-9970708-0-4 (ebk)

For K, P, W, and Q.

CHAPTER ONE

You know what that's like, right, Zax?

The Ship blazed in sharp contrast to the inky void of space which framed it. An asteroid which measured roughly one hundred kilometers long by fifty wide and ten thick served as its foundation. Towers, some as tall as the space rock was deep, blanketed its smooth top. The vessel's brightness came from millions of exterior windows whose light outlined the warren of artificial structures. The bottom portion retained its natural, craggy state except for the thousands of hatches which peppered the surface. Shuttles darted to and fro as they transported cargo between the cavernous cryostorage and agricultural holds carved into the asteroid's interior.

Zax never tired of viewing the real-time imagery of the Ship beamed in from the distant perspective of a perimeter drone. He marveled at how the vessel appeared to be the result of someone using a giant shovel to send one of Earth's cities—bedrock and all—aloft with one tremendous scoop. Something about the current image seemed wrong and tickled at the back of Zax's perception for a few secs before he identified it. His hand shot up and drew Sayer's attention.

"Sir—what's going on with that large block of darkened structures in civilian sector twenty-eight?"

"I can't see anything abnormal, cadet, so I'm not sure. Let's zoom in and check it out."

The instructor closed his eyes for a moment and used his neural Plug to interface with the holoprojector. Zax's typical pang of jealousy was replaced a moment later by excitement at the realization his personal countdown had finally reached double-digits. He only had to wait ninety-nine more days to graduate from Zeta Cadre and get Plugged In to the Ship himself.

Sayer, a nineteen-year-old fighter pilot from Kappa Cadre, was only four years older than Zax and the other Zeta cadets in the training room. This small gap in age between the instructor and his trainees was by design. Ship tradition held that the best way to transfer knowledge was for Crew who were only slightly older and more experienced to pass on their hard-won lessons to the younger cadets who followed in their footsteps. Sayer was easily Zax's favorite instructor as he embodied everything Zax dreamed about with regards to his own career. This type of aspirational thinking was also the intent of the officers in the Omega Cadre who ran the Ship when they established the Crew training protocols generations earlier.

The holoimage projected in the space above the cadets' heads zoomed in on the civilian sector and a large swath of darkened structures became obvious. "Wow, Zax, I'm amazed you noticed that. There could very well be room for you in the Pilot Academy with that kind of observational skill. Ten credits. As for why that section is dark, I have no idea. There have been more and more isolated power outages in recent years, but I didn't think things had gotten bad enough to knock out such a big area."

Zax beamed, but his happiness was not from Sayer rewarding him with the ten credits. Though he obsessed about his ranking and desperately chased opportunities to increase his already prodigious Leaderboard score, what really excited Zax were the two magic words—Pilot Academy. Zax had chased his goal of earning command of a fighter since his career started ten years ago. Being near the top of the Leaderboard was a requirement for becoming a pilot, but that alone did not guarantee admission. If an instructor like Sayer was noticing his potential, Zax could hold out hope that the Omegas who made career assignments were seeing it as well. His reverie was broken a sec later when Aleron chimed in from the back of the class.

"Maybe some idiot civilian puked on a power unit and that's why all those structures are dark. You know what that's like, right, Zax?"

Laughter erupted around the room and Zax's cheeks flushed. He had long grown accustomed to Aleron and his band of morons enjoying themselves at his expense, but it stung to have the cadets who had only recently been added to Zeta pile on as well. What hurt the most were the braying giggles which emanated from Kalare.

Zax hadn't given much thought to girls during his first two years in Zeta Cadre, but that had changed when the Omegas mysteriously moved a handful of cadets from rival Epsilon Cadre into Zeta a few weeks earlier. Kalare was at the head of the line as the group walked into the Zeta berth for the first time, and her arrival literally took Zax's breath away. She stood a quarter meter taller than he did—Zax hadn't experienced a growth spurt yet—with jet-black hair and brilliant blue eyes which were iridescent from gold flecks. Her features were as distinctive as Zax's mousy brown hair and dark brown eyes were common, and they drew him in like the pull of a massive black hole. The first time he witnessed her smile it melted a lifetime's indifference to the opposite sex, and Zax was shocked when he involuntarily mouthed "magnificent." Those feelings faded within a few, short days as Zax regretfully concluded Kalare was a complete scatterbrain not worthy of his attention or admiration, but it still rankled to be the object of her amusement.

"Twenty-five demerits for speaking out of turn, cadet."

Sayer's words quieted the laughter and then he closed his eyes. Zax allowed himself a tight smile at the knowledge the instructor was using his Plug to interface with the Leaderboard to add ten points to Zax's score and deduct twenty-five from Aleron's. His ranking was already well above the bully's, but the possibility of massive demerits due to a stupid training injury or mistake on an exam always nagged at Zax and made him grateful for any additional scoring cushion. A sec later Sayer opened his eyes and spoke again.

"I can't dispute Aleron's observation that civilians are idiots. Unfortunately, they're our idiots and you must be careful you never ever lose sight of their role—however minor—in the Mission to preserve our species. The inhabitants of a dying Earth built this Ship and filled its cryostorage holds with a billion civilians who would be dispersed to new colonies throughout the universe. One hundred thousand Crew were put in command and ten million civilians stayed awake alongside them to perform the more menial jobs. Everyone in this room is a direct descendant of that dead world's most brilliant and talented people. They were carefully selected to be that first Crew and we all emerged from the Ship's artificial wombs genetically optimized to inherit their duty. Part of that duty is respecting how the civilians are as much a part of the Ship as the chairs you're sitting on. Though, it's probably not fair to compare them to something useful like chairs."

Everyone laughed and Sayer allowed them to enjoy the humor for a few secs before he continued.

"OK...let me finish what I was talking about before Zax's observation sent us off on a tangent. I've already covered the history of the Faster-Than-Light engine, but I'll get hit with some demerits myself if I neglect to mention the emergency evasion process.

"When we're battling aliens and operating under Condition 1, the Captain may choose to give the Flight Boss tactical command of the Ship. The Boss then has the ability to order an emergency FTL evasion. Something with as much mass as the Ship can't shift course radically in a short amount of time, so a key defensive mechanism is our ability to evade danger by using the FTL drive to jump to another location in the system. Since it's impossible to plot an FTL Transit within the confines of a star system, this is accomplished by queuing two Transits to occur back-to-back. The first jump takes the Ship to a location far enough away for FTL to be possible, at which point a second Transit is automatically performed to return the Ship to the original system, albeit in a location intended to provide a far better tactical position."

Zax raised his hand and Sayer acknowledged him once again.

"Sir, that seems crazy. Transits are safe when the Ship has sufficient time to recalibrate the FTL, but aren't we begging for one of those gruesome failures which sometimes happen with our scout ships if we do two of them so quickly?"

"Great point, cadet, ten more credits for you," Sayer replied. "But you also shouldn't lose sight of how nuts it is to knock everyone unconscious in the middle of an enemy engagement. Crew training lets most of us recover and regain alertness quickly, but even the best of us occasionally suffers from sustained FTL fog after one Transit, much less two in such a short time period."

The instructor closed his eyes for a sec and then spoke again. "Speaking of FTL, it's almost time for today's Transit. I'm flying Combat Air Patrol when the jump is over and need to prep so let's finish early. Dismissed. Zax—please hang back for a min."

The cadets filed out while Zax remained seated. A sharp blow knocked his head forwards, and he looked up to find Aleron grinning having "accidentally" whacked him with an elbow as he walked past. Zax refused to give the twit the satisfaction of any reaction, but that didn't prevent another wave of raucous laughter from the bigger boy and his henchmen.

Sayer observed all of this impassively from the front of the room. He spoke once the last cadet exited and they were alone.

"I admire how you didn't let Aleron derail you, Zax. A lot of cadets your age would have shut down and not spoken again after being the brunt of such a public joke."

"Thank you, sir. It really doesn't bother me."

"I can see that. You're obviously a smart and likeable kid, so I've been confused about how it seems like you don't have any friends. Why is that?"

Zax paused. He could easily answer the question, but debated whether he should. His admiration for Sayer was so great that he eventually took the plunge.

"Well, sir, there's no one in my Cadre smart enough to spend any more time with than what's absolutely required."

Sayer smiled, though there was a hint of emotion behind the expression which Zax couldn't identify. Sharing such private thoughts already made Zax uncomfortable, but his inability to fully decipher the instructor's reaction was even more unsettling. Non-verbal social cues caused frequent consternation, and this was a second, unspoken reason why Zax avoided relationships with his classmates.

"Good enough, Zax. What about a mentor, though? Don't you think you could learn a lot from someone older who has already navigated the challenges still ahead of you? When I was your age, my mentor had a big impact on me. My scores weren't as high as yours at first, but she gave me a ton of great advice that helped me move up and ultimately got me high enough to qualify for the Pilot Academy."

The instructor had already answered his own question. Zax didn't need a mentor to help improve his scores because, unlike Sayer, he had been perched near the very top of the Leaderboard since he was six. Unless he somehow lucked into a mentorship offer from one of the powerful officers in the Omega Cadre, Zax couldn't imagine finding anyone where the value of their "guidance" would offset the cost of having to communicate regularly with someone else and deal with his or her opinions. In consideration of Sayer being the only member of the Crew who had ever gone out of their way in an attempt to help him, Zax responded with something polite rather than the truth.

"Thank you for the suggestion, sir."

Sayer smiled one last time as he turned to leave. "Get to your berth, cadet. They'll be ringing the bell for the Transit soon."

Zax intended to follow Sayer's directive and return to the Zeta berth to prepare for the FTL jump, but he had one critical stop to make along the way. He walked briskly to a Replicator station and used its interface to call up the fabrication template he had perfected during many weeks' worth of off-duty time. He issued the command for the Replicator to commence and was dismayed thirty secs later when it still appeared to be evaluating his request.

"I've loaded my template," Zax said, "why aren't you fabricating?"

"You've never submitted a design before," replied the Ship's AI. "This template is far too complex for someone your age and with your lack of experience to attempt. The Ship needs to conserve consumable mass rather than risk it on templates which will likely result in a smoldering pile of goo."

Zax sighed. "I've given you my chits—one thousand seventy-two of them. What difference should it make to you what happens now? If I want to risk a year's worth of savings, isn't that my choice? Maybe I like goo and will be thrilled if that's the result—did you ever consider that? You may be the brilliant Artificial Intelligence that helps run the Ship, but we still get to make our own choices—right?"

The AI paused as if it wanted to sigh right back at him, but instead the Replicator initiated. Thirty secs later its door opened with a cloud of escaping steam which revealed Zax's shiny new creation.

"Hey, where's my goo?" Zax asked with mock frustration. The AI ignored his comment, so Zax grabbed the device—still warm from fabrication—and sprinted off towards the Zeta berth. As he did so, a single bell echoed through the passageway to signal the FTL engine would soon spin up. Zax was almost giddy with the anticipation of deploying his invention once the Transit was complete.

CHAPTER TWO

Hello, lunch.

The sour, gag-inducing odor hit Zax the moment the bells woke him. He knew the scent would be there but was both dejected and ragey anyways. He opened his eyes and the source swirled around him. "Hello, lunch," he muttered. Well, what was left of lunch after it spent time in his stomach. A tangle of noodles, appearing almost the same as they originally had on his plate, slow-danced two meters above his face. Zero-g managed to make puke seem balletic, but with or without gravity it still smelled nasty.

Like every other child born on the Ship, Zax learned the pattern of space travel before he could crawl. One bell signaled the gravity-generator was shutting down in fifteen min, so you needed to stow your belongings and strap into your grav-chair. Two bells meant the Captain would engage the FTL in five min. The barely-understood black magic that produced faster-than-light travel would jump the Ship from one star system to the next and knock all of its inhabitants temporarily unconscious in the process. When you awoke to the sound of three bells, it meant the Transit was successful and the grav-gen would restart in one min. If you didn't wake up to those three bells, well, Zax avoided thinking about that altogether.

While most kids only worried about the 1–2–3's of space travel, Zax was forced to add the 4–5–6's of space puke at a young age. Soon after his sixth birthday he developed a previously-unseen reaction to the FTL engine and began throwing up whenever the Ship jumped between stars. The medics tried everything but failed in their efforts to help. They assured him it could be corrected once he was Plugged In, but until then it was yet another reason for the other kids to abuse him. Though both cruel and uncreative, the nickname "Puke Boy"—tossed out by that tool Aleron during their first month as cadets—had scored a direct hit and stuck.

As beautifully as any half-digested meal floated around without gravity, it always transformed into a disgusting mess once the grav-gen kicked in. After nearly ten years of extensive practice, Zax had earned the title *Best Cleaner of Vomit* among all of humanity. This distinction no longer carried the weight it might once have, though, since the remnants of the human race were either breathing the Ship's air, moldering in cryosleep in one of its storage holds, or clinging to life on one of the hardscrabble colonies left in its wake during 5,000 years of the Mission.

As good as he was at cleaning up by hand, Zax had long dreamed of ditching the bucket and towel. It was this desire that inspired him to become the youngest person in anyone's memory to design and build a fully-functional machine using the Ship's Replicator. The device was a meter-long alloy tube with a wide mouth on one end and a pistol grip and trigger on the other. A pull of the trigger generated enough suction to capture the floating contents of even the largest stomach and send them down the tube into a plastic pouch where they would be sealed for handy, touch-free disposal. Zax's favorite aspect of his design was the red flames shooting down the sides of the tube that surrounded its name—*PukeSucker 3000*. It would have been easier (and far cheaper) to make the device small enough to fit entirely within the palm of his hand, but if he was stuck living with such a mortifyingly public affliction, he wanted to have a little fun with it.

Zax had dared to dream the other cadets would admire his Replicator template, but everyone thought it was an elaborate and expensive joke. He knew the only way to silence the haters would be an actual demonstration, so he had been excited when the morning newsvid finally announced an FTL Transit was scheduled after lunch.

Whenever a Transit was announced ahead of time instead of popping up in the middle of a battle, Zax skipped real food in favor of nutripellets (bleh). He had disregarded that strategy earlier knowing the PukeSucker's creation was imminent. Instead of sitting off in a corner by himself like usual, Zax piled his plate high and grabbed a table smack in the middle of the mess hall. He expected abuse when Aleron sauntered by with his posse of suck-ups, but heard nothing from the passing conversation except a "Puke Boy" followed by sycophantic laughter.

Once the Ship completed its Transit and his lunch rolled in the air above him, Zax grabbed his fully armed and operational *PukeSucker 3000*. Chants of "Puke Boy—Puke Boy—Puke Boy" echoed around the compartment, just as they typically did, once the other kids in Zeta shook off the mental fog induced by the FTL engine.

The berth held twenty rows of twenty grav-chairs, and each was occupied by one of the fourteen-to sixteen-year-old cadets who made up Zeta Cadre. Zax was "encouraged" to pick a spot in a corner surrounded by empty grav-chairs due to his upchuckiness, but since Zeta's berth had been full for a couple of weeks there were unlucky cadets stuck squarely within range. Zax hadn't deposited anything on the newcomers yet, but past experience suggested it would occur sooner or later. The massive size of the cloud which floated above them guaranteed it would be sooner if the *PukeSucker 3000* proved ineffective during its first deployment.

Zax unbuckled his straps. He had programmed his wristcom to start a one min countdown once the three bells sounded and the tiny display ticked off the secs until gravity returned. Zax clutched the handle on the side of the grav-chair and hauled himself onto his feet upon its padded seat. Years of practice had honed the zero-g scramble required for him to bucket up as much of the muck as possible to minimize the mess when gravity's return tumbled any leftovers to the deck.

Zax aimed, pulled the trigger, and grinned as his device drew in the largest constellation of free-floating stomach contents. Zax murmured "bye-bye noodles" as they hit the plastic pouch with a satisfying *SLURP*. He pulled the trigger again and sent a flying mass of chewed-up vegs down the tube. With the eagle-eyed precision of the best fighter pilots, Zax hunted down the swirling remains of his lunch. The *PukeSucker 3000* worked even better than imagined and a perfect recovery rate seemed within his grasp until disaster struck. Chunks of breakfast floated out of his reach and into a slow roll directly above Kalare's grav-chair.

Even though he no longer pondered her magnificence, the reverberations of that first glorious smile guaranteed Zax never wanted Kalare to wear anything which had previously been in his stomach. Without taking a sec to consider the safety or sanity of his plan, Zax coiled his legs and then launched himself towards the floating egg clumps. He bent at the waist and rotated his body 180 degrees away from the deck. Zax stretched his arm to full extension and the *PukeSucker 3000* slurped up all of the vomit at the same moment his feet contacted the overhead. His momentum compressed his legs until Zax pushed off and launched back towards his chair. His wristcom flashed red to warn that Zax had ten secs to get back to his chair if he was to avoid a trip to the medbay with a fractured skull or busted ribs.

It required a nasty wrenching of his arm to redirect his mass and pivot his body into the grav-chair, but Zax was safely ensconced an instant before his watch flashed 00:00:00. Gravity returned and was accompanied—as always—by the crashes and thuds from some cadet's stuff that hadn't been properly secured. Zax rejoiced in the complete lack of *plops* and *splats* and *"Ewwwwws"* that arose whenever he wasn't entirely successful with his cleaning efforts.

For a sec, Zax feared he might have unknowingly hit his head on the grav-chair and damaged his hearing because the berth was noiseless. Where typically there was the bustle of cadets popping out of their chairs and the fading remnants of "Puke Boy" chants, there was only stunned silence. Then, more silence. All of the cadets stared at him with mouths agape. Zax sprang up onto his chair to milk the attention for all it was worth. He sported an epic grin and pumped his arms with the *PukeSucker 3000* held high over his head in salute.

Zax made a dreadful discovery when he looked up to admire his device. He hadn't cracked his skull at the conclusion of his acrobatics but instead had wedged his amazing creation between his seat and body. Once the Ship's gravity returned the PukeSucker had borne the full weight of his mass and its long barrel deformed almost a full 90 degrees. In addition, the collection pouch had ruptured at the seam and Zax recoiled as some of its body temperature contents dripped down his cheek.

The hush was finally replaced with riotous laughter. It originated with Aleron and his constellation of twits, but soon more than two-thirds of the berth hooted and hollered in mock appreciation of the circus act they had witnessed. Zax, crestfallen, collapsed into his seat and discarded the *PukeSucker 3000* onto the deck as he reached for a towel to wipe his face. A few secs later the uproar from Zeta Cadre was silenced by the only sound capable of cutting through the din—a shrill klaxon their bodies reacted to on full autopilot. General Quarters.

CHAPTER THREE

We haven't met yet.

All of Zeta grabbed their gear and clumps of cadets tore off in different directions across the Ship. Zax's cortisol levels spiked in response to the intense strobing of the yellow lights as they blinked in time with the klaxon. All of the Ship's alarms were calibrated to physically prepare the Crew to face whatever danger the Captain decided was worthy of calling them to their battle stations.

Zax jumped into the Tube and rocketed a kilometer across the Ship in a few heart-stopping secs. He bolted out the door towards Flight Ops and was surprised when the area outside the Tube remained dim and musty. A pipe had burst a week ago and the steam it vented into the passageway had caused lights to fail. Apparently Maintenance was so swamped with other problems they still hadn't dealt with this one. It was just one more instance among many Zax had seen in recent years which showed their ancient vessel had long since seen better days.

Footfalls trailed as Zax turned a corner and sprinted down the passageway. He glanced back over his shoulder and was shocked when they belonged to Kalare. He was attempting to stammer out a question when the lights flipped to the solid red which signaled a hull breach somewhere nearby. The brain-lock which froze Zax's mouth had the opposite effect on his legs—they propelled him at full speed even as Kalare's eyes went wide and she skidded to a halt.

Of course, he concluded with perfect clarity, she's seen the emergency bulkhead which must have slammed into place and sealed off the passageway ahead of them.

CRUNCH!

Zax smashed into the bulkhead with enough force that he left his feet and flew backwards more than a meter. The angle of the fall hammered his tailbone with his entire mass. Zax's world flashed bright white and then momentarily faded to black. He came out of his stupor a sec later and tasted a coppery mouthful of blood from the lip he split when his face slammed against the bulkhead. The physical pain was only a fraction of his overall discomfort, though. Not only had Zax managed to land flat on his own (likely broken) butt, but he had also knocked Kalare down onto hers.

"I'm s-s-so s-s-sorry," Zax sputtered. He leapt up to grab two supplemental breathers from the emergency bulkhead and tossed one down to Kalare. She was laughing instead of being hurt or angry. Great rolling cackles which were borderline crazy in both volume and tone. Zax's initial spark of embarrassment flared into hot indignation. "What's so funny?"

"Nothing—nothing—well, yeah, OK—it's you. A couple mins ago you were flying around in zero-g like no one I've ever seen, and now here you are flat on your butt with blood dribbling down your chin." Kalare choked back a couple more giggles and then closed her eyes and took an exaggeratedly deep breath before she continued.

"I'm sorry. I really don't mean to be laughing at you, but I can't help it sometimes. My mentor is always telling me I have to control these outbursts if I want to avoid getting Culled. It's interesting how he last mentioned this when I was laughing hysterically about a book which had fallen and gashed his forehead. I guess some people run from blood and I laugh in its face. But, am I really laughing at the blood, or am I laughing at what caused the blood? Or, am I just nervous about the sight of blood and using the laughter to calm myself?"

Zax's indignation faded, but it was replaced by a combination of the confusion he typically felt interacting with his peers and some other unidentifiable discomfort which intensified the longer Kalare spoke. She giggled as she started up again.

"I'm sorry. When I'm nervous, I just run off at the mouth. I sometimes do it when I'm not nervous, too. My mentor says I test off the charts and have the aptitude to become an Omega some day, but my lack of self-control is probably going to get me Culled instead. Oops. There I go again." Kalare extended her hand in greeting. "We haven't met yet. My name's Kalare. What's yours?"

The silence allowed Zax to finally identify the source of his discomfort—he was breathless. Kalare had seemingly talked for five straight mins without a breath. He was so wrapped up in trying to follow along that he had subconsciously held his own the entire time. He croaked "Zax" with a gasp as he reached over and gave her hand a lame shake. He ran his tongue around his mouth and played with the split in his lower lip while he took a few deep breaths. Zax would have to report the injury to the medics and suffer the significant demerits assessed for such a stupid accident.

"This all happened because I wanted to ask where you were going," he said with more than a hint of annoyance. "I thought the only battle station assignment for Zeta cadets in this part of the Ship was Flight Ops, and you aren't on that team."

"I actually just got bumped to Flight Ops. I'd been trying to make up my mind about where I wanted to go, so I rolled some dice to choose and Flight Ops was the pick. My mentor said I had the scores to go almost anywhere I wanted, but I just couldn't figure out where so I let chance decide and, now, here I am!"

The words continued to race out of Kalare's mouth, but it sounded like she was starting to relax as the pace had slowed just a little.

"Wow," he said, "that is pretty *interesting.*"

And by *interesting* what Zax really meant was *bizarre.* Most cadets would forfeit a kidney to get into Flight Ops, and here this girl was proudly sharing how she chose it at random. What was even more peculiar was how someone so crazy had the scores to qualify for it in the first place.

Zax didn't know where Kalare stood on the Leaderboard because the Zeta standings had not yet been updated to include her and the other transfers from Epsilon. The Ship carried two Cadres of fourteen- to sixteen-year-olds, and heated competition between Epsilon and Zeta was actively encouraged. It identified the best candidates from this age group to put on the path toward the highest-value positions on the Ship. When Kalare and the others were moved into Zeta for unknown reasons, it had triggered a lot of paranoid speculation around the Cadre. Mass reassignment of cadets was a rare occurrence and generally denied whenever requested by a Cadre's leadership, but for some mysterious reason the Omegas forced Zeta to accept the Epsilon cast-offs.

Though there was plenty of worried grumbling when the Epsilon transfers were announced, Zax had not shared the concerns. Odds were all of the new cadets would rank lower than him on the Leaderboard, and Zax welcomed any and all additional cushion between him and the bottom of the list. Every bit of Leaderboard fodder might prove important given how the Cull arrived like clockwork every three months. Being near the bottom of the rankings meant you stood the greatest chance of being thrown into cold storage and eventually settled on one of the barely-habitable colonies the Ship established during its Landfalls.

"They haven't added you Epsilon cadets to the Leaderboard yet, so I didn't realize you had those kind of scores. I would've thought if you were good enough to qualify for Flight Ops that Epsilon would have wanted to keep you around."

A dark cloud of emotion passed across Kalare's face. Just as quickly it vanished and her grin returned with even greater intensity. "I don't know—I don't care—here I am!"

"And here I am. Here we are together. Stuck. Hopefully, this is just a quick drill. I'm guessing the call to battle stations is a precaution given we've just entered a new system." Zax sighed as he sat down on the deck. "With my luck, the Ship has actually run into some trouble and we'll be stuck here missing out on everything. I know there are hull breach drills like this all the time, but I've never been trapped in a lockdown before. Have you?"

"Yes," Kalare hesitated. "I was ten. I'd only been in Delta Cadre for one month. A group of us were sent out for our first trip around the Ship without an escort, and I got separated from my friends. I was checking an observation compartment for them when the alarm sounded and the hatch sealed behind me. I figured it was only a drill, so after I grabbed a supplemental breather, I flopped onto a couch and pulled out my slate for some extra study. A couple of mins later I noticed something moving out of the corner of my eye."

Kalare paused for a deep breath, and Zax finally understood she was struggling to maintain her composure. She probably had been throughout the story, but he had missed the emotional cues. She kept herself under control and continued.

"The two girls I'd just been with were floating outside past the panorama. One of them was a super sweet girl who I'd known since my first day in Beta Cadre. She seemed to be grinning at me and I was so scared I peed my pants."

Kalare shuddered at the memory and her eyes brimmed with tears. Zax had no clue how to react to her emotions so he kept his mouth shut and listened.

"The Delta leadership put me on the recovery team as punishment for getting separated from the others. I was also assigned to help prep them for burial. Their bodies were in horrible shape—the nastiest combination of sunburnt and frostbit. The other girl had her face frozen in a terrified scream. I've seen almost fifty dead since then, with thirty-five of those happening during my two years in Epsilon. Even after all of them, it's still those first two I see when I close my eyes."

Zax let it all sink in before he spoke. "I didn't realize Epsilon lost so many kids. We've only had three dead in Zeta so far, and they were all blown to bits in a shuttle explosion so there was no recovery to deal with. I sure hope the Omegas can figure out how to make training safer for everyone."

Kalare gazed at Zax for a couple of long beats and then asked, "Do you think it's all worth it?"

Zax's stomach dropped as he guessed where she was about to go with the conversation. He played dumb. "Is what worth it?"

"Everything. All of it. Have you ever really thought about our lives? We were born into the Crew fifteen years ago and have spent every moment since fighting like crazy for top position on the Leaderboard. Not one of those fifty dead kids was mourned by anyone except perhaps a close friend or two. Instead, they were seen as one less cadet to claw over on the way to the top—or at least away from the bottom."

Kalare stared down at the deck and then closed her eyes. "Even as I sealed the disposal bags around my two friends, I was already thinking about what it meant for my Leaderboard ranking. I'm ashamed to say it now, but I knew one of the girls was ahead of me and I was happy about moving higher." She sighed. "More and more I'm starting to believe the Omegas actually want some percentage of kids to die during training so we get numbed to it all as early as possible. You hear about thirty-five dead in Epsilon Cadre and brand our leadership a failure for not keeping them safe, but I've got a sneaking suspicion there are Omegas who are handing out demerits to the Zeta leadership because they've *only* had three killed so far."

Zax had been involved in conversations before where someone nibbled around the negative aspects of Crew training and life on the Ship, but never before had someone laid it out in such vivid and stark terms. He was dumbfounded. It wasn't as if this type of discussion was officially forbidden, but it was something which could generate demerits in far more career-altering numbers than those he worried about due to his still-bleeding lip.

Zax's instinct was to shut down her crazy talk immediately. Even though he had the occasional question or doubt about being part of the Crew just like anyone else, what always won out was the knowledge his Leaderboard position put him firmly on the path to a fantastic future. This demented girl was not going to get in the way of that future—even with such an infectious smile at her disposal.

"Well," he cemented a neutral expression on his face and chose his words with the utmost care, "this sure does explain why the Epsilon leadership dumped you on Zeta. Someone with the smarts to reach the top of the Leaderboard combined with the willingness to talk about the deep, dark secrets of Crew life is a dangerous combination."

Kalare interpreted Zax's comment in a positive light and her smile made the gold in her eyes sparkle like laser fire. "You sure got that right!" she said before bursting into hysterical laughter once again.

CHAPTER FOUR

Nothing but a milk run.

Once the All Clear sounded, Zax and Kalare resumed their sprint and skidded to a halt inside Flight Ops exactly thirty-seven secs later. Zax's eyes adjusted to the intentionally dim compartment, and he glanced towards the Flight Boss sitting in his command chair.

The officer wore a work cap backwards and chewed an unlit cigar. The cigar was famous throughout the Ship for a couple of reasons. First, the need to feed ten million mouths occupied nearly every hectare of the Ship's agricultural space so the tobacco for the Boss's supply of cigars represented an insanely rare and expensive commodity. Second, there were exactly two places on board where torching tobacco with an open flame was legal and legend was the Flight

Boss had never visited either of them. For the Crew, someone who constantly gnawed an unending stream of priceless cigars and yet was never witnessed enjoying one of them properly-lit served as further proof that the officers who reached the Omega Cadre were an entirely different species.

The Boss swiveled his chair towards the hatch and acknowledged their entry. "You're 236 secs past maximum acceptable reporting time. Before you try to spit out your lame excuse, I already know you were stuck in a breach drill on the way up here. Ten demerits for each of you for not having picked a different path. And another fifty since you appear to have kept your supplemental breathers as souvenirs instead of leaving them in the passageway where you got them. You better hope no one encounters an actual emergency before you can return them. Get to your stations and get to work. *Now!*"

The stridency of the Boss's final word was likely triggered by the look of frustration which Zax shared with Kalare for a split sec. Of course, they were stupid for having forgotten to take off the breathers, but being caught in a random breach drill could just as easily have happened if they had picked a different route to Flight Ops. Harsh punishment for stuff which was entirely out of your control was just the sort of compliance tool which drove more than a few cadets to go crazy and punch an officer in the throat. The good news for kids who reacted like that was they never again had to worry about demerits and getting Culled from the Crew. The bad news was they got dumped out an airlock after a perfunctory court martial.

Zax sat down at his station and slipped its wireless subvoc unit around his neck. The thin collar automatically constricted and positioned itself in the optimal location. Two sensors sat against his throat to pick up the nerve signals which would be translated into speech, and two contacts rested against his cheekbones and made incoming communications "audible" without impeding his ability to hear what was happening around him. Most Crew working in the compartment chatted with each other directly via their Plugs, so the subvocs were provided to allow younger cadets like Zax to communicate silently as well. Dozens of private conversations were happening at any given moment around the compartment, with verbalized communication saved for those orders and responses deemed critical for everyone to hear. Zax connected to their private channel and addressed the older cadet who was tasked with training him.

"Good morning, Threat, have I missed anything?"

"Hey squib, nice entrance there," said Cyrus. *"Nothing like causing the Boss to take a timeout during General Quarters to personally ream you out in front of Flight Ops. You are such an absolute oxygen thief."*

Cyrus, a towering nineteen-year-old from Iota Cadre with arms the size of Zax's thighs, was responsible for monitoring the threat bubble around the Ship and was therefore called "Threat" by everyone in Flight Ops. Zax, as his trainee and backup, sat next to him at a workstation which was functionally identical.

Unfortunately, Cyrus was also Aleron's mentor and loved tormenting Zax even more than the younger boy did. It was amazing how moronic bullies managed to somehow find each other across the age groups and thereby reinforce each other's behavior. Cyrus relished communicating with Zax on their private channel since it provided numerous opportunities for unwitnessed verbal abuse.

After Cyrus generated his daily ration of harassment, he switched to his second favorite topic when afforded the privacy of a silent chat—complaints about the Flight Boss. *"Nothing happening here. The Boss calls General Quarters whenever we prep for refueling even though every white dwarf star system is just as barren as this one. Paranoid old bugger. What a colossal waste of time. Nothing but a milk run."*

Cyrus' complaint verbalized the obvious about how most of the Crew in Flight Ops were fighting off boredom. Throughout Zax's time working in the compartment, the Ship had traversed an interstellar desert devoid of habitable planets. No habitable planets meant no aliens inhabiting those planets or preparing them for habitation. No aliens meant no encounters for the Ship and no encounters meant no battles. No battles meant no excitement and far too many routine operations like refueling missions. It was just another boring "milk run" for an elite group who craved regular adrenalin hits from defending the Ship.

"Flight—what is the status of my refueling bird?"

Zax shifted his attention to the Flight workstation when the Boss called out the request for information. "Astounding. Absolutely astounding," he muttered. Kalare had slid into the Flight trainee seat, and Zax worried about what her position at that particular workstation meant for his Leaderboard ranking.

Like everything else on board the Ship, the roles in Flight Ops were governed by a clear hierarchy and the only trainee role with higher standing than Threat was Flight. In fact, Flight was widely seen as the most prestigious job for anyone in Zeta or Epsilon. It wasn't always held by the number one cadet on the Leaderboard, but it was definitely occupied by someone near the top. Since Kalare was in that seat, it was distinctly possible she had a higher ranking than Zax.

"Blaze has the tanker in position and she just deployed the harvester," said the Crew member next to Kalare.

Zax examined his threat board and verified this for himself. The Captain had stationed the Ship one million klicks from the white dwarf at the center of the planetless system. The tanker, designated "Blaze" on his screen based on the call sign of the pilot driving it, had halved that distance and released its harvester. The harvester, a highly specialized drone, rocketed towards the miniature star.

"You cadets who are new to Flight Ops should take a moment to appreciate the irony of what you are about to witness," announced the Flight Boss. "White dwarfs, stars which are quickly approaching death, provide the energy source necessary to fuel the life of the Ship. The harvester is going to do a single close orbit to gather and compress enough of the degenerate gas being emitted to pack ten billion kilograms of the stuff inside one cubic meter of volume. This degenerate matter represents the beating heart of all human space exploration. Our ability to compress so much mass with such a huge amount of usable energy into such impossibly small storage is what makes everything the Ship does possible."

"I can't believe how many times I've had to listen to him make this exact same speech," complained Cyrus to Zax over their private channel. *"Listen here, I have it memorized—Irony...white dwarfs...fuel...beating heart...blah, blah, blah..."*

Zax wanted to laugh, but refused to give Cyrus the satisfaction and instead focused on his workstation.

"Threat—set a forty-eight min countdown so we can know when the harvester is full up and we can get back on our way," ordered the Flight Boss. "Scan and Nav—I need you two to identify and plot our next Transit. I know the Captain would be mighty appreciative if you could finally get us out of this dead zone and find a halfway decent planet where we can drop our next colony. Everybody else—I need you alert and on top of your game. I know you're aching for some excitement, but keeping the Ship safe during operations like this one is your entire mission in life right now and I want you acting like it!"

"*Alert?*" mocked Cyrus silently once again. "*Five thousand years' worth of Ship's logs show we've never once encountered hostiles around a white dwarf and for some incomprehensible reason he thinks he can motivate us into thinking today is going to be the day that changes? Good luck with that!*"

CHAPTER FIVE

It's coming right at us.

The refueling countdown ticked down and approached its halfway point. Zax was halfheartedly reviewing a mind-numbing training manual he had long since memorized when Cyrus called out.

"Boss—something just appeared on my board."

"Elaborate, please."

Zax inspected the threat board. The inbound bogey flew a course which would take it within the Ship's minimum stand-off perimeter in 287 secs. As Cyrus relayed this same information to the Flight Boss, the Combat Air Patrol fighter on duty, pilot call sign Vampire, changed heading. Vampire vectored onto an intercept course which would allow him to first identify and then engage the unidentified craft if it proved to be hostile. Since roughly 99.99999% of aliens the Ship encountered were hostile, this was more a question of *when* than *if*.

"Flight—status on Vampire?" asked the Boss as he rose.

"Vampire is fifteen thousand klicks from visual," replied Flight. "I can have the Alert Two birds out the door in ninety-five secs if you want some additional friendlies out there."

"Excellent. Launch—you have my go for ten more birds as soon as they're hot." The Flight Boss turned to face the massive panorama window on the interior bulkhead and chewed his cigar even more vigorously.

Zax shifted his attention to the panorama. Its three hundred square meters of translucent titanium provided a view into the Ship's primary flight hangar. What made the panorama different from an ordinary window was its data overlay that displayed whatever information the Flight Boss wanted in his view. At that moment, it showed the ready status for ten additional fighters shift to green when Flight initiated their countdown for launch.

Zax's pulse quickened as he envisioned himself piloting one of those ten craft. A job as a trainee in Flight Ops was the pinnacle of success for someone like Zax, who was only fifteen, but it wasn't the desired end point for any cadet. Everyone who took a training slot in that compartment did so with one goal in mind— earning a chair in the pilot room. There was not any single career path for someone who dreamed of being an Omega and perhaps even Captain, but what was absolutely common among all of the permutations was time spent either on stick as a fighter pilot or in the backseat as her Weapons System Officer.

Zax lacked the security clearance to know where the pilot room was located and had never even seen pictures of it. This didn't prevent him from imagining himself sitting there during a launch, however, and he obsessed about all of the unknown details. What would it feel like to jump into that chair with its top-secret, highly customized neural connections and transfer his consciousness over a hardwire into one of those amazing spacecraft? Would his mind work any differently while it inhabited the neural network of the fighter while the empty shell of his body remained back in the Ship's ready room? With his physical body left behind, would he still somehow feel the power of the ElectroMagnetic Aircraft Launch System as it hurtled his craft from zero to three hundred kilometers per sec?

His focus on the pilots and WSOs was even more intense than usual because Vampire was in the air. Zax had always wanted to ask Sayer why he chose that particular call sign but had not yet found the right opportunity to do so. Sayer's body was now somewhere deep inside the Ship while his mind was thousands of kilometers away about to engage an alien craft. The fact they had been together just a few mins ago only served to increase Zax's amazement.

The *thwomp* of the first EMALS shot broke Zax's reverie and the noise was followed in quick succession by nine more just like it. His eyes focused back on the view of the flight deck just as the fighter piloted by the Commander, Air Group shot off the deck. Due to its special role, the Flight Ops compartment was unique on the Ship and had two of the massive panoramas—one opposite the other. Zax turned his head 180 degrees and caught a final blur of the CAG's fighter, pilot call sign Daedalus, as it streaked into the void. He returned his attention to the threat board just as the Flight Boss addressed him.

"Mini-Threat—what's the status of that bogey?"

Even though Zax was not responsible for the threat board, the whole purpose of having trainees in the room was to expose them to their future roles in real-world situations. The Flight Boss frequently used the natural pauses during engagements to work the various "Minis" into the flow of activity.

"Bogey 1 still on same bearing, sir, and will intersect Vampire in seven thousand klicks." Zax paused. "Belay my last, sir. Aspect change on Bogey 1 along with a high energy discharge targeted at Vampire. Bogey 1 appears to be hostile, sir. Redesignate as Bandit 1."

Based on Zax's call, the threat board changed the label on the icon that represented the inbound spacecraft to Bandit 1 and also changed the icon's color from yellow to red. Simultaneously, the background tint on all terminals along with the two panorama overlays exhibited the same color shift. These changes made it clear to everyone the Ship had moved from Condition 3 to Condition 2 and was under attack.

With a calm urgency in his voice that contrasted against the crazed chomping of his cigar, the Flight Boss delivered his next set of orders. "Flight—tell all fighters they are now weapons free and should engage and destroy Bandit 1. Weps—spool up all Ship defensive weapons and let the stations know they are weapons free on the inbound Bandit in the highly unlikely event it manages to evade eleven of our finest. Threat—I want your board up on both panoramas—top left quadrant. Flight—does Vampire have a signature on that craft yet? I want to know what the hell we are dealing with."

"Vampire reports his computer shows unknown signature for the Bandit." Flight hesitated for a moment and then continued. "He's had eyes on it, sir, and says it looks *human*."

All activity in Flight Ops screeched to a halt. The stillness was replaced with pandemonium once everyone recovered from their initial shock and started to speak at once.

"Human—what does he mean, human?"

"How could there be another human ship out here?"

"Call off the alert and stop fighting—we need to speak with them!"

"All of you—shut up! The next person who talks out of turn is going out the airlock!" The Flight Boss's order silenced the chaos and he turned to Flight. "Get imagery of the Bandit from Vampire and then send it over to me. I'll check if Alpha agrees with Vampire's identification. I assume everyone agrees Alpha will recognize a human spacecraft if somehow we've magically run across one."

The Flight Ops Crew pretended to return to work, but everyone snuck repeated glances at the Boss while he reviewed the imagery. Zax pinged Cyrus.

"Threat—I'm confused. Who's Alpha?"

"Are you going to ask for lessons on wiping your butt, next? Why did they have to stick me with such a brain-dead trainee? Alpha is the root node of the Ship's artificial intelligence system. The AI we deal with all the time is smart, but Alpha is a billion times smarter. Only the Omegas can interact with it. I suppose they don't want the rest of us slaggers to figure out that's where all of their alleged intelligence and leadership ability actually comes from."

The Flight Boss spoke before Zax could get out his additional questions.

"Alpha confirms the Bandit is *not human* but instead is of *unknown origin*. Is that perfectly clear to everyone?" The Boss momentarily held the gaze of every individual in the compartment to reinforce his statement. He grimaced when he spoke again. "That means it's something we've never encountered before, and that changes things. Flight—I want another twenty birds out the door and forty more on Alert Five. Weps—get the Shipbusters spun up along with all of our close-in defenses. If this guy is a scout he might call home to mama and she could show up pissed any sec. Comms—give me the Bridge on visual."

Three secs later the Captain appeared front and center and gazed down at Flight Ops from both of the massive panoramas. The scar across her throat, the origin of which Zax had heard at least six crazy yet feasible stories about, was distinct upon her fair skin. She returned the Flight Boss's salute and asked, "What's going on, Boss?"

"Captain—we've got an inbound bandit coming in hot, and it just fired an energy weapon at one of our birds. We've determined the craft is not anything we've seen before. Due to the unknown nature of the threat, I recommend we set Condition 1."

"Affirmative." On her word, the Condition 1 klaxon sounded. A stunningly lifelike holopresence of the Captain in her command chair materialized next to the Flight Boss and her giant image disappeared from the panoramas. Zax assumed there was another cadet like him training on the Bridge who now saw a similar hologram of the Flight Boss in that compartment.

Zax had never been present in Flight Ops during Condition 1 and was thrilled to finally witness it. The status was set whenever there was a particularly risky battle situation and meant complete tactical command of the Ship was transferred to the Flight Boss. The side-by-side holograms along with their Plug interfaces allowed the Boss and the Captain to be fully present in both of the Ship's critical nerve centers simultaneously.

The Captain always retained final authority, but with the Ship at Condition 1 the Flight Boss was granted the power to make all decisions except launching a Planetbuster. Only the Captain had the launch codes for the Planetbusters, although no one in her seat had deployed one for 2,000 years.

Though Zax was initially excited to witness Condition 1, he soon worked himself into a frenzy of worry when his mind went back to what Sayer had said earlier about the potential for an emergency FTL evasion. What might happen if he tossed any of his zero-g cookies in the direction of the Flight Boss? Zax had never been in Flight Ops during an FTL Transit, so he didn't know yet how the Crew there would react to his affliction.

Zax focused back on the threat board. His worries receded once the Alert Two squadron caught up with Vampire, and Daedalus started to coordinate the dogfight against Bandit 1. Unless there was some crazy advanced technology deployed by whatever alien race was behind the craft, Zax couldn't imagine a situation where eleven of the Ship's fighters would get beat by a lone enemy.

Something on the threat board yanked Zax's attention away from the dogfight. The system was tracking a kinetic weapon inbound from Bandit 1 but had not raised any alarms due to its small mass. Collisions with projectiles, naturally occurring and otherwise, were a permanent risk in space, and the Ship was armored well enough to tolerate constant encounters with small objects. Anything that could be launched by a craft the size of Bandit 1 would do such minor localized damage the threat system effectively ignored it.

This particular inbound made the hair on the back of Zax's neck stand on end, so he hailed Cyrus.

"Threat—there's something about that projectile inbound from Bandit 1 which seems weird. Can you evaluate it with me?"

"I really don't have time for you right now, squib. If you want to waste your time investigating every pebble some alien lobs at us, then be my guest. I'm going to focus on doing my job and worry about avoiding any actual threats."

Zax fought the desire to fire off a witty reply and instead focused on plotting the trajectory of the inbound. The threat board was not optimized for evaluating such small projectiles, so the best it offered was a ten klick radius for impact. What troubled Zax was his realization that Flight Ops fell neatly at the center of that circle.

Zax pulled out his slate and used a trajectory analysis program he had developed on his own. Ten secs later he leapt out of his seat and shouted to the room.

"Boss—we've got an inbound kinetic weapon. It's coming right at us. 99.82% probability it strikes either Flight Ops or the hangar in fourteen secs!"

There was a long, pregnant pause as every head in the compartment swiveled towards Zax. Beyond the craziness of a trainee yelling something during an engagement, the words which had come out of his mouth were so absurd they defied belief.

To his credit, the Flight Boss hesitated much less than anyone else would have before exclaiming his order.

"FTL—emergency evade now!"

The Boss was fast to react, but not quite fast enough. The projectile impacted against the Flight Ops exterior panorama moments before the FTL drive kicked in. Zax watched in horror as the window cracked from edge to edge. The last thing he heard before the FTL engine drove everyone on the Ship into unconsciousness was the wail of the hull breach alarm.

CHAPTER SIX

Forget about him!

Zax was drowning. His mind centered on the relaxed descent into the depths of a swimming pool while his body calmly surrendered to a lack of oxygen and impending death. It was a shockingly soothing sensation. Except for the noise—an incessant screeching that grew fainter as Zax slowly sank deeper and deeper. And the smell—why was he smelling puke near the bottom of a pool?

He pushed the unpleasant inputs from those senses aside and instead focused on the beauty as he floated downwards. The bottom of the pool approached and Zax wondered what it would feel like when his bare toes touched its tiles.

Just before his feet reached the bottom, a piercing sting on his face dragged his senses back to his chair in Flight Ops. The screeching noise snapped to the foreground, and Zax registered it as the hull breach alarm. He opened his eyes and the cool blues of the pool's depths were replaced with flashing red lights. The breach was located in his current compartment.

Kalare hovered above in zero-g, smeared with what had remained in his stomach after his earlier FTL discharge. One arm held on to his chair while her other one was cocked to deliver a second slap to his face. A quick smile, visible through her secondary breather, revealed her recognition of his restored consciousness. Her free hand went instead to his shoulder and a sec later she affixed Zax's breather over his nose and mouth.

Zax greedily sucked oxygen deep into his lungs and established situational awareness. The breach's explosive decompression had turned the compartment's small items into junk that floated around the panorama. Most of the Flight Ops Crew remained strapped in their seats, unconscious and turning blue from a lack of oxygen. The only exceptions were the Flight Boss and Cyrus. The Boss, cigar still clenched between his teeth, floated towards a bulkhead with his arm outstretched to grab one of the secondary breathers which had automatically deployed from a breach cabinet. Cyrus flailed in a panicked frenzy to release the straps keeping him in his chair.

The Captain appeared to sit in the middle of the room without a hair out of place. Her holopresence was not affected by the hull breach. Zax observed for a moment as she efficiently relayed orders to the Crew who were safe and sound alongside her on the Bridge. She caught his eye and formed her fingers and thumb into an "OK" sign in inquiry about his status. He returned the gesture with one hand and released his straps with the other.

Zax launched towards the closest breach cabinet and pulled a patch kit from within it. Kit in hand, he kicked off again and evaluated the state of the panorama as he floated towards the crack in the upper right corner. As he glided closer, he discovered there were two large fissures and each contained a distinct breach. Since they were at opposite corners of the window separated by thirty meters, there was no way Zax could patch both fast enough by himself. He rolled onto his back and spotted Kalare tending to Cyrus. She had calmed him down enough to buddy-breathe by passing her breather back and forth.

"Forget about him!" Zax shouted. "You've got to patch the crack in the lower corner, or there's no way we get air in here before everyone suffocates!"

Kalare hesitated for a moment and Cyrus' face flooded with panic once more as he thrashed in an effort to retain her breather. Given the size and strength differential, he would have stolen the device from her if he had been a fraction more coherent. Kalare took advantage of an opening and shattered his nose with a punch that sent a crimson cloud of blood floating in every direction. She then vectored off towards a breach cabinet for a patch kit.

Zax rolled back onto his stomach as he reached the panorama and pistoned his arms to dissipate his remaining momentum and stop. This move was second nature for him after years of dealing with puke cleanup, but Kalare ricocheted off the panorama and bounced off the floor when she attempted the same a moment later. She misjudged the initial approach, but Kalare stuck the landing on her second attempt.

Zax returned his attention to the patch kit. Whoever designed the kits made them obvious to operate. Zax pressed the giant red button (helpfully labeled #1) and opened the kit's upper compartment. A holographic vid displayed a female actor who provided instructions.

"Shape the blue patch pellet until it covers the breach."

The hologram actor seemed absurdly cheerful considering the kit designers knew she would be talking to someone who needed to resolve a life-threatening emergency in an oxygen-free environment. Her instruction was straightforward, though, and the demonstration easy enough for Zax to emulate. The patch material was firm yet malleable and after a couple of secs he flattened the pellet and affixed the material to the panorama just like the actor had shown.

Zax pressed giant red button #2 and opened the kit's lower compartment.

"Shape the yellow activation pellet until it covers the blue patch material."

The yellow material shared the same consistency and was just as malleable as the blue, but differed in being almost uncomfortably warm to the touch. Zax flattened it out enough to cover the blue material and then activated giant red button #3.

"Apply firm, even pressure for five secs until the yellow material turns green."

The actor flashed her vacuous smile and made the task appear easy as she pressed her palm against her faux breach and then removed it to reveal a final green patch. While her first two demonstrations were easy to emulate, the actor's last instruction was impossible for Zax. She had access to a critical ingredient he did not—gravity. Without a sufficient handhold, any force Zax exerted against the panorama while he floated in zero-g would send him soaring in the opposite direction.

Frustrated, Zax checked on Kalare's progress. She had caught up with him in the patch process and her palm was pressed firmly against the window. Kalare was not impacted by the lack of gravity because the location of her breach allowed her to brace her feet against the deck and use that leverage to exert sufficient force against the patch. Something about her pose held Zax's attention until he shouted "That's it!" a few moments later.

Fingertips pressed against the panorama, Zax rotated his body 180 degrees. He had previously floated parallel to the deck with his belly pointing towards it, but this move traded "down" for "up" until he faced the overhead. He pulled his legs in towards his chest and then extended them back out at an angle that braced his body between the panorama and the overhead— almost the perfect inverse of Kalare's pose.

Zax exerted pressure through his palm into the soon-to-be-green patch. He counted to five and wondered whether he would feel anything when the activation material triggered and permanently bonded the patch to the panorama. He waited a couple extra secs past five to be safe and then removed his palm. The activation material continued to shine accusingly with its original yellow hue.

Zax squinted along the border of the yellow material and discovered the smallest blue speck that peeked out from underneath. He pinched and pulled the yellow material just a millimeter further until it completely covered the blue. Zax braced his body, reapplied pressure, and started a new countdown. There was a short burst of heat after five secs and the hull breach alarm silenced. One sec later the main hatch sprang open and admitted a stream of medics who each floated to an unconscious crew member and deployed a supplemental breathing device.

A lone person clapped and laughed loud enough to be heard over the commotion. It was the Flight Boss. Since Zax was still oriented with his belly facing the overhead, the Boss appeared to be standing upside down. The view of him from the odd vantage point, applauding and grinning, was entirely surreal. Not nearly as surreal, though, as the words that came out of his mouth.

CHAPTER SEVEN

It's your chair now.

"**I** have never seen such an amazing performance in all my years working with cadets!" roared the Flight Boss as he looked up at Zax. "Mini-Threat, you went from being unconscious to performing high-skill, zero-g maneuvers in less than ten secs. You did this while simultaneously demonstrating mental agility and confidence by ordering your peer to perform a critical, life-saving task. Five thousand credits."

The Boss addressed Kalare next. "I have methodically adapted my mind over dozens of years to be as fast as possible when it comes to regaining consciousness after FTL, but you were already up and moving when I woke up, Mini-Flight. You made a great decision to first revive the other person in the compartment who you knew would have immediate access to an air supply. When you were interfered with by another Crew member, you decisively applied appropriate force. Finally, although your zero-g abilities weren't as good as Mini-Threat's, you didn't let that stop you and instead figured out what was needed to accomplish your task. Five thousand credits.

"Threat—your performance was an entirely different flavor of amazing."

The Flight Boss had turned his attention to Cyrus and Zax did the same. He was astonished by what he saw. Kalare's punch had not only left Cyrus' nose horribly misshapen, but it had also resulted in two black eyes. His wretched appearance was exacerbated by the fact he had clearly been crying—whether from the pain of his nose or the shame of his actions it was impossible to know. The tears dripped off his cheeks and mixed with the blood splatter from his nose to create a pathetic stew that floated inches from his face.

"You were an absolute disgrace." The Boss paused to let the admonition sink in and then continued. "It was bad enough you couldn't get your straps undone, but then you panicked and made the situation infinitely worse. It was pathetically clear you were thinking only about yourself rather than the safety of the Ship when you tried to impede Mini-Flight in her mission to patch the breach. That is inexcusable. You earned yourself that busted nose and two shiners from her, and now fifty thousand demerits from me. You need to figure out those straps and get out of that chair in the next ten secs or I will cut your miserable body out of it myself."

Both Kalare and Zax gasped when the Flight Boss announced "fifty thousand demerits." It was a wildly severe punishment and left no doubt that Cyrus would be Culled. A few nearby Crew had regained consciousness and, along with the medics attending to them, watched the drama unfold with their mouths agape.

Kalare recovered from the shock first and addressed the Flight Boss. "With all due respect, sir, I don't think it's fair you've given the two of us the same number of credits."

Zax scarcely believed his ears. Kalare had just been gifted a *massive* bump on the Leaderboard, and from the sounds of things, she wanted to fish for more at his expense. Sure—everyone wanted to score every point they could, particularly when vying for position against their prime competition, but most officers looked askance at cadets who sucked up too hard. Zax fought off a smile as the Flight Boss clearly set a trap for Kalare with his response.

"In all your wisdom, what would you recommend as a more equitable allocation of the points, Mini-Flight?"

Kalare missed the hidden threat in the Boss's words and grinned. Zax almost pitied her. She really did not understand what kind of fire she was playing with. She rolled the dice (!) to pick Flight Ops and miraculously walked into a situation where she earned five thousand (!!) bonus points on her first (!!!) shift, only to put all of that at risk to score a little extra edge over Zax by arguing with the Flight Boss (!!!!) about how many more she deserved.

"Sir—you've split ten thousand credits equally, and I'm grateful for my share. However, it's crystal clear to me that Zax should receive more of the reward. I only had to give Threat that broken nose in the first place because I hesitated when Zax told me to grab a patch kit. If I had reacted immediately, I would've been mid-air and well away from Cyrus before he thought twice about what was happening. If you believe this situation worthy of ten thousand bonus points, then I respectfully suggest you allocate eight thousand to Zax and I'll accept two thousand."

The Flight Boss appeared as shocked as Zax felt about Kalare's suggestion, and there was a long pause. The idea of giving up credits and asking for them to be awarded instead to a top competitor was as absurd a concept to Zax as jumping out an airlock without a spacesuit.

The silence was broken when the Flight Boss offered his slow applause once more. "Well said, cadet, well said. Your rationale makes perfect sense, but I'd rather not take away anything I think you deserve and will instead award an additional three thousand points to Mini-Threat. Correction—now that I see that other pathetic excuse for a Crew member has finally managed to release his straps, I want Zax to take over as Threat." The Boss turned to Zax with a smile. "I hope you didn't just get lucky once. It's your chair now."

Zax had held his breath during the last min and paused for a moment to suck in a deep breath before he replied. "Thank you, s-s-s-sir."

Zax couldn't fathom what had just transpired as he glided to the Threat workstation and strapped himself in. He looked over the Flight Boss's shoulder, past all of the medics tending the Crew, to where the chair's previous occupant floated outside the compartment's open hatch. Cyrus gazed back with his eyes full of hatred and venom until the hatch slid shut and the Captain's voice broke through all of the commotion.

CHAPTER EIGHT

It looks habitable.

"Flight Boss—we're getting things resolved and are almost ready to jump. What's your status?"

Zax reviewed the Threat board in reaction to the Captain's query and was confused by what it revealed. The white dwarf system was gone and had been replaced with a binary system. This meant the emergency evasion was only halfway complete and their fighters were temporarily abandoned. Eleven of the Ship's finest against one puny alien spacecraft was no contest, but Zax remained anxious to return and support Vampire and the rest of the fighters.

"Ma'am," the Boss gestured around the compartment, "you can see my team is almost back up and we're getting prepared for action. What happened?"

"Alpha aborted the second Transit during the emergency evasion. When we tried to spin it up manually, Alpha aborted that one too and reported a fault in the FTL engine. We've run a full set of diagnostics and can't find anything wrong, so we're configuring an override."

The Boss appeared frustrated for a moment, but paused and calmly replied. "Give me another 120 secs to re-establish full battle readiness, and then I'll resume tactical command for the Transit."

The already frenetic activity level in Flight Ops was dialed up even higher once everyone understood the situation. Exactly 117 secs later the last of the medics floated out of the compartment and the Flight Ops Crew were poised to lead the Ship into battle once more. Zax led off as the Flight Ops team called out their readiness in final preparation.

"Threat is go."

"Flight is go."

"Weps is go."

"Nav is go."

"Sorry, Boss," announced the girl in the Scan chair. "I need a few more mins. I've located a system that might be interesting, but it's at the extreme edge of our scanning range. It's fading in and out. I'm afraid if I don't get a clean lock now, I might not be able to isolate it again later even if we came back to this same spot. It looks habitable."

Those last three were the magic words that captured everyone's attention. The Ship's Mission was to seed the universe with human colonies wherever rare Class M worlds were found, but it had not encountered a habitable planet in almost three years. Many in the Crew were stir-crazy having been too long deprived of the regular establishment of new settlements. Landfall always provided a welcome respite from their regular duties—either due to the work of settling the latest colony or (more enjoyably) from the battles with aliens which often preceded it.

Zax turned to the command chairs in the middle of the room. It was clear the Flight Boss and Captain were communicating over a private channel. Zax recognized something in their body language that suggested the conversation, although entirely silent, was fairly heated. The Captain addressed the Crew a few secs later.

"I understand everyone wants to get back to the white dwarf and make sure our fighters and tanker are OK, but you all realize how critical it is we Landfall soon. Scan—take whatever time you need to get me a full rundown on that system. If it indeed appears to be habitable, then we aren't going anywhere until you and Nav have confirmed a Transit solution that will get us there from the white dwarf system. Everyone else—continue to prep for hostile activity. I'm confident our fighters have long since destroyed that alien, but we must be certain we're ready to support them the instant our Transit is complete and we're back in the battle."

Zax had almost completed his battle prep when Kalare interrupted him for a private subvoc.

"I hope you didn't mind me sending some extra points your way earlier."

For a sec Zax believed Kalare was mocking him somehow, but he glanced at her and recognized a sincere smile. This girl flummoxed him. Lacking a better reply to such an absurd statement, he said the only thing that came to mind. *"Thank you."*

"I said this earlier when we were trapped together, but I need to say it again. You're amazing when it comes to zero-g maneuvers! How'd you get so good?"

Zax started to reply, but Kalare barreled forwards without pause.

"You must spend every waking moment in the zero-g training compartment. Am I right? Do you think you could spend some time with me and maybe teach me a few of your tricks? That would be awesome. Thank you! You know, that's actually the least you can do to pay me back since I'm sitting here with your puke all over my clothes. I had no choice but to go for a swim in your lunch if I was to get close enough to wake you up and get you breathing again. What did you even eat? Oops—there's a noodle on my shoulder!"

Zax was mortified, but the rancid discovery didn't rattle Kalare and she continued without missing a beat.

"Can you believe what the Flight Boss did to Cyrus? Fifty thousand demerits! Has Cyrus been that useless the entire time you were training with him? I

don't know what I would do if the person training me was an idiot like that. Actually, yes I do. Nothing. I would do nothing. Probably the exact same thing that you've been doing if I can read you right. And I bet I am, 'cause I'm very good at reading people."

Zax had been exhausted listening to Kalare during their earlier conversation, but the feeling was exacerbated when they communicated over the subvoc. Without the limitation of having to move her lips Kalare spewed out her crazy talk twice as fast. At least this meant he anxiously held his breath for only half the time. She finally allowed him a moment to speak.

"Yeah—Cyrus has been a complete moron the entire time I've been training with him, but I've met worse. He's definitely going to be Culled after the Boss hit him with so many demerits."

What Zax didn't share was his relief about Cyrus getting dumped into cryosleep. The malevolent expression he sent Zax's way as the hatch closed had him concerned about how Cyrus might attempt to exact revenge in the meantime.

Kalare started to unleash another of her verbal volleys but was cut off by an announcement from Scan.

"Flight Boss—I've established a solid lock on that system, and I'm showing an 88% probability it's habitable. Nav has plotted a Transit solution between the white dwarf and the new Class M system, and I've confirmed it's correct."

"Excellent," said the Boss. His tone was anxious when he turned to the Captain and spoke. "Ma'am—I request tactical command be returned to me, and we immediately jump back to the white dwarf system."

The Captain's "Affirmative" was the last thing Zax heard before the FTL spooled up and everything faded to black.

CHAPTER NINE

There's nothing out there.

Zax awoke with a final spasm of retching. Dry heaves sucked, but avoiding a barrage of vomit was one benefit of three jumps in such quick succession.

He turned his attention to the Threat board and was dismayed by what it revealed. There was no sign of the bandit from earlier, but there were also no signals revealing the Ship's fighters or tanker had survived. Instead, the board identified two distinct debris fields with one in close proximity to the Ship and the other located much closer to the white dwarf.

"Boss..." Zax fought to keep his voice even. "I have no contacts. Bandit 1 is gone. No transponders from any of our fighters. No transponder from the tanker. There's nothing out there."

The Flight Boss pummeled the arm of his chair and muttered something under his breath. Then he quickly regained his composure and jumped out of his seat to issue a stream of orders.

"Flight—I want two SAR birds in the air, one for each of those debris fields. We lost all of their ships, but let's recover their cores and bring our pilots and WSOs home. I also want another tanker in the air ASAP. We've got enough fuel in storage to last for a while, but since it appears like we might have Landfall ahead of us soon, we should top up the tanks now while we have the chance."

Zax sought hope about the lives of Vampire and the rest of the pilots from his memories of past lessons about Flight operations. Search and Rescue craft used specialized scanning equipment to detect the emergency beacon each neural core triggered when ejected from its spacecraft. The biological matrix inside each fighter which contained the mind of the pilot and WSO was exceptionally armored and generally survived even when the rest of the craft was a total loss. Though fighters were destroyed all the time, the actual loss of a fighter crew was an infrequent event.

The Flight Boss turned to the girl in the Scan chair. "I want you running everything possible to find any echoes of this battle. Energy signatures, blast marks, unexploded ordnance, *anything* that might provide a clue to help us understand what happened. We had an unknown fighter get crazy lucky and score a direct hit on Flight Ops, and now we've got nothing but debris in front of us. Those two facts generate far more questions than answers, and most of you have been around long enough to realize I WANT ANSWERS!"

After this last exclamation, the Boss sat back in his chair and spun it around to gaze out the exterior panorama. He rested his head on his hand and chomped angrily on his cigar.

The two SAR birds departed for their mission while Zax sifted through the Threat board data. There was little chance of core recovery. All of the spacecraft had been annihilated and there was no debris large enough to represent a core.

Zax was curious about what was happening with the bodies left behind by the twenty-four pilots and WSOs. Having pilots killed in action was a rare outcome, and he had a morbid curiosity about how it was handled. He pinged Kalare on a private channel.

"Mini-Flight—what's the chatter on the Flight channel about what's going on in the ready room?"

"They're running their KIA procedures," replied Kalare. *"The capsules around the chairs have been sealed and they've got a guard stationed at each one. The hardlines are still in place, but they've got techs prepared to cut them once the SARs confirm which Crew have been lost. They've deployed an honor guard to the ready room for the burial ceremony and will put the capsules out an airlock within fifteen mins of any official KIA declarations."*

Amazingly efficient, thought Zax, but using the chair capsules as coffins added a whole new dimension to the job of being a pilot. While civilians had nothing to look forward to after death beyond their bodies being recycled like any other depleted resource, tradition long held that dead Crew were given an honor guard and space burial. Some Ship resource officer way back in history must have decided it would be great to conserve consumable mass by using the pilots' chairs as their coffins when they were killed in action. The bodies would already be encased in the capsules and the chairs were so highly customized they couldn't be reused anyways. You already had to be crazy to want to be a pilot, but it seemed downright cruel to be forced to climb into your own coffin every day as part of the job.

Zax pushed aside his grim notions and focused on the Threat board. One of the SAR craft had reached the closest debris field, and Zax expected it would soon relay the news no cores had been found and all Crew were lost. Flight finally spoke a few mins later.

"Flight Boss—we've recovered one core. It's Vampire's. The core's in rough shape, but SAR thinks the Crew can be extracted. They aren't finding any other beacons."

The Boss stood. "At least that's one small piece of good news after the rest of this mess. Flight—inform the ready room that everyone in the fighters except the two are KIA. I want the SAR bird with the recovered core back in the barn, and I want to speak with Vampire and his WSO the moment we get them downloaded into their bodies. Hopefully they were in the battle long enough to have something useful to share."

The Captain spoke. "Boss—it will be great to hear from your fighter crew, but I also want us to collect whatever other evidence we can to understand how those ships were destroyed. Let's put together investigative teams and spend a couple of days in system to examine the wreckage."

"Absolutely," said the Flight Boss. He turned his attention to the rest of the compartment. "I want to remind all of you that Alpha confirmed it was *not* a human fighter behind all of this. I better not learn about any of you spreading rumors otherwise. Our lack of Landfall for such a long period of time has been stressful enough. We can't have people obsessing about non-existent humans. Is that perfectly clear?"

The Boss's tone left zero room for disagreement. He didn't continue until after he glared at each Crew member and received silent acknowledgment from everyone in the compartment.

"We're coming up on a shift change, and when your relief arrives, I want you to get back to your racks and get some rest. The potential Class M that Scan found means it's about to get busy around here. Some of you haven't been in Flight Ops long enough to have experienced Landfall, but if that rock is habitable then we'll be running a lot of scouting missions for a few weeks and that will have us all working double shifts."

The Boss finished. "Things were rough in here today, but I'm proud of how you all handled yourselves. Some of you were pretty close to death a short time ago, and yet you've bounced up and stayed in the game. I'm particularly proud of the two cadets who managed to think quickly and save some lives. Good work, Mini-Flight and Threat."

Zax wasn't keen to have all eyes on him again, but he appreciated the recognition and nodded at the Flight Boss to acknowledge his kind words. What he appreciated even more was the news there wouldn't be any more FTL jumps right away and he would soon be off duty.

CHAPTER TEN

That doesn't make sense!

After 480 mins of solid rack time, the craziness of the previous day felt like it had happened to someone else. Zax jumped out of his bunk, showered, and headed to the mess hall. He filled his tray with a big breakfast and sat down by himself as usual to watch the morning newsvid. The prospect of a peaceful and relaxing start to the day filled Zax with a sense of tranquility.

"Good morning, Zax. Why are you sitting here all by yourself? I'm going to join you. Is that ok? Of course it's ok. What a day yesterday was! Is every day in Flight Ops as crazy as that one? That would be great. Though, on second thought, we got hit with an alien projectile which caused an explosive decompression that left all of us unconscious without any air. Maybe that wouldn't be great. Well, what I was just thinking was—"

"Could you please *shut up* for a min—I want to watch the newsvid!"

More frustration seeped into his voice than Zax intended, but Kalare seemed oblivious to his tone and turned her attention to one of the mess hall displays. Zax did the same and was shocked to discover his own face on its screen. The newsvid led off with a story about yesterday's battle and a vidcap from one of the monitoring cameras in Flight Ops. The announcer introduced the story while video rolled of the Flight Boss clapping in admiration of Zax and Kalare.

"The Ship encountered an alien spacecraft yesterday in the middle of a refueling operation. This was a surprise since the Ship doesn't typically encounter aliens around white dwarf stars, but our fine Crew was prepared as always and Flight Ops immediately dispatched a squadron of fighters. Unfortunately, before they were able to interdict the craft, it managed to launch a small projectile. Even though the Flight Boss attempted to evade the projectile with an emergency FTL evasion, it scored a once-in-a-million direct hit on the exterior panorama of Flight Ops which caused an explosive decompression in that critical compartment."

The video switched to highlights from Zax and Kalare's efforts to patch the panorama. It was accompanied by audio of the Flight Boss's short speech from the day before where he praised the two of them.

Once the footage was over, the announcer returned with a more somber expression on his face.

"Thanks to the heroic efforts of the two Zetas, the Crew restored Flight Ops to operational readiness within mins. Even so, the second Transit of the FTL evasion was delayed so long that by the time the Ship returned to the white dwarf, the mothership for the alien fighter had returned and deployed an overwhelming force which destroyed the tanker and all eleven fighters. We lost a total of twenty-four brave Crew."

The screen switched to video of an honor guard saluting the flag-draped capsules. A three-volley salute fired while the airlock door closed and the capsules were vented into space. The announcer returned with a graphic behind him which showed a clock counting down from ninety-seven mins.

"The Captain has decided it's time to continue the search for our next Landfall and the FTL countdown clock is running. All Crew and civilians should prepare for a Transit later this morning. Meanwhile, in other news from around the Ship—"

"That story doesn't make sense!" exclaimed Kalare over the announcer's segue. "You heard the Captain yesterday. She said it was going to take a couple days for us to do a full investigation and figure out what happened. A small alien fighter we've never seen before fires off *one* projectile and scores a direct hit on Flight Ops. We leave the system for a few mins and come back to find *twelve* of our spacecraft destroyed?"

Kalare emphasized the last sentence by pounding her fist on the table. People nearby gawked, but she was oblivious to the attention she attracted as she continued. "There weren't twenty-four dead, remember? Two of those Crew members *survived*! I heard them announce they recovered the core from Vampire's fighter and watched the Flight Boss head out to the ready room to talk to him and his WSO! And now, less than ten hours later, it appears the investigation has been wrapped up, we've got an extra two dead Crew, and we're just going to pop out of the system like nothing ever happened!"

Zax's lungs screamed for oxygen. His breathlessness came not from following along intently to Kalare's monologue, but rather from the emotions which flooded him when the newsvid announced the Crew from all eleven fighters had been declared dead—including Vampire. Sayer couldn't really be considered a friend, but he was one of the few people Zax admired and had positive interactions with. Losing the closest thing to a friendship he had ever experienced threatened to overwhelm him. Zax needed a few mins to process the loss and deal with the unfamiliar emotions, but this girl had invaded his morning routine and now spouted crazy talk about mythical conspiracies—comments which, given their public nature, might ultimately reflect poorly on him. He took a deep breath and lashed out.

"Just wait a min! I have no idea what you're trying to suggest, but I'm really not interested in hearing about it. That projectile was a random hit—they happen. There are thousands of external panoramas and I'm sure given enough time absolutely all of them will end up getting hit at least once—whether by an alien or some piece of space rock. Random chance is just that—random!

"As for Vampire and his WSO," Zax continued, "the SAR pilot said the core was beat up pretty bad and she *thought* the crew could be extracted. Apparently, she was wrong. You didn't see the threat board. I did. I'm not the least bit surprised everyone was lost. There was barely any debris out there big enough to be a core, much less a functional one. The Captain has learned whatever she wanted to know about the incident. She wants to jump now rather than wait for investigators to filter through a bunch of space junk to tell us what we already know—it was just another random encounter with another random alien who started shooting at us. *That* is the story of this Ship for the last 5,000 years!"

Zax jumped up and pushed his tray away in disgust. He had expected some form of reaction from Kalare, but she instead stared at him blankly and this only agitated him further. "Now please *shut up* about your paranoid delusions and enjoy your breakfast—I have to wait until lunch for food since we're doing a Transit this morning!"

As he turned and stormed away, Zax worried about the twenty demerits he would receive for not clearing his tray off the table. He quickly disregarded any concern since getting immediately out of range of that nutjob was worth ten times as many. Guilt eventually intruded his thoughts as Zax calmed down and mentally replayed his strong reaction to Kalare, but he pushed any deep remorse aside knowing that eighteen hours with an empty stomach had played a role. Something about Kalare's comments nagged at him, though, as he headed back to the Zeta berth. The unease stuck with him all morning while he worked.

CHAPTER ELEVEN

What happens if it's not empty?

Reveille on the third morning after the white dwarf battle found Zax in a daze. Nav had concluded that the Ship required a half dozen FTL Transits to get from the white dwarf system to within scouting range of the suspected Class M planet. The Captain wanted all possible speed and had commanded three Transits per day rather than sticking to one per week as was typical in non-battle situations.

This punishing schedule taxed everyone on board. No one understood the biological mechanism behind it, but the early users of FTL discovered the human mind can only tolerate a limited number of Transits within a given period of time. The Captain's current pace resulted in nothing more serious than an unpleasant mental funk, but if pushed too much further the malaise would degrade into full-blown psychosis for a significant percentage of the population. The blurred mental acuity was compounded for Zax by a lack of solid food. He had survived exclusively on nutripellets to keep his stomach ammunition-free.

The continuous FTL fog caused Zax to forget about the impending Cull until he was on his way to the shower and walked past a cadet who was chosen from Zeta. The boy's sobs trailed off as the Marines led him out of the berth with blasters at his back—a scene Zax knew was being repeated across the Ship as Crew and civilians alike were marched in various states of duress to the cryostorage holds. He understood the Ship needed to conserve resources and maintain consistent population levels by sending low performers into cryosleep, but it was never easy to witness.

Zax pushed thoughts about the Cull aside and continued towards the shower excited by the prospect of taking an extra hot one (twenty demerits) to try and clear his head. He turned the corner and overheard a conversation between two cadets as they passed going in the opposite direction.

"I can't believe there's no hot water again today!" said the boy.

"Yeah," replied his female friend, "tenth time in the last two months by my count. I wonder how that compares to how often the Captain is forced to take a cold shower?"

The boy snorted. "As if that ever happens."

"Dammit," muttered Zax as he turned and trailed them back to the berth. He wanted no part of a cold shower, so he skipped it altogether (fifty demerits) and got dressed instead. He also bypassed the mess hall since he had decided to skip breakfast. There were no FTL jumps scheduled, but Zax knew there was a decent chance the planet was already inhabited by an overwhelming alien force and they might have to bolt on short notice.

The first task on Zax's schedule that day was to lead a lesson for a group of nine-year-olds from Gamma Cadre. Unlike Cyrus and many other Crew he had dealt with through the years, Zax embraced his instructor duties and eagerly anticipated his chance to deliver a primer on astronavigation. He experienced a pang of grief as he recalled learning this same material from Sayer, but Zax quickly pushed memories of the dead instructor aside. Not quick enough, however, to prevent a frustrating momentary diversion back to Kalare's observations about the oddities surrounding the white dwarf battle's aftermath.

Nav was a subject Zax always enjoyed, and he was excited to use the previous few days' worth of activity as the basis for discussion. The Ship's civilians remained in the dark as always, but the Captain had informed all of the Crew about the potential for Landfall. Zax expected the Gammas would be as eager about it as everyone else, and when he entered the lesson room the Gammas were indeed buzzing. They quieted as he jumped into the lesson.

"Room—kill the lights and run holo Z1212-2364." At Zax's command, the room went dark and a hologram of the Ship and the white dwarf battlefield was projected above the Gammas. "Three days ago the Ship orbited a white dwarf and deployed a tanker to harvest fuel. We encountered an alien fighter, and, as part of the ensuing battle, we were forced to do an emergency FTL evasion. During the midpoint of the evasion, while waiting for the Ship to be readied for the second jump, Scan identified the signature of a potential class M planet. Nav developed the solution you see here which we have subsequently executed."

The projector cycled through the six FTL jumps which had brought the Ship to its current location. The trainees in Gamma were still young and non-cynical enough that their eyes lit up in response to the beauty of some images. Many let loose an audible "Oooh" at one in particular—a massive gas giant which shone a deep purple with rings of varying shades of the same. Even though the Ship had inserted into its system ten million kilometers away, the purple planet was so massive it filled the space above their heads when displayed at the proper scale relative to the Ship.

"Can any of you tell me how far we've traveled since we left the white dwarf?" Zax was pleased when half of the Gammas raised their hands. The question was a tricky one, and it was great that so many young cadets were brave enough to attempt it. He nodded at a girl in the front row to his immediate left.

"The white dwarf is approximately 5,400 light years away, sir," said the girl.

Zax was impressed. "The right answer is 5,275, but your guess is exactly what I would have said if asked this question. I see many heads nodding in agreement, but please explain to the rest of your classmates where your number came from."

"Sir—the Ship's FTL Transits are typically between 450 and 900 light years. Since we're doing three jumps per day, I assume the Captain is in a rush to get to our destination and is pushing us to the upper limit. Six jumps multiplied by 900 light years per jump equals 5,400."

"Spot on explanation. Ten credits for you. New question for the class. Why is 900 light years the upper limit for our Transits?" Zax pointed to a boy who was sitting towards the back of the room.

"Sir—because that is the maximum distance the FTL engine can move the Ship."

"Wrong. Twenty demerits. Who's next?" Zax looked around, but his assessment of twice as many demerits for a wrong answer as compared to the credits he rewarded for a correct one had scared away the kids who were guessing. It left the original girl as the only hand still raised, and Zax nodded in her direction once again.

"Sir—the FTL engine can actually push the ship a lot farther than 900 light years. The reason we cap it at that limit is because it is the distance where our sensors can tell us what we need to know about where the Transit will land."

Zax grinned. "Someone has clearly been doing extra reading in her spare time. Well done, cadet—one hundred credits." Zax believed in rewarding folks who risked being wrong in the face of a substantial penalty, so he bumped up the credit reward for her correct answer. It left the room abuzz with excitement, though one boy in the front row seemed puzzled and raised his hand.

"Sir—I'm totally confused. The Captain announced last night we've been pushing so hard these past few days because our sensors found a possible class M planet. If our sensors can see far enough away to establish a planet is likely to be habitable, why can't we just jump straight to it?"

"Ten credits for a great question." The best lessons were two-way interactions, so rewarding questions was as important for an instructor as giving credit for answers. Zax walked over and stood in front of the boy. "Let's figure out the answer together by using an analogy. Assume I brought you to a recreation compartment blindfolded and told you to jump into a swimming pool—would you do it?"

"Of course, sir. I love to swim!"

Zax smiled again. "I do too. So what if I told you I had been swimming in the same pool the day before and had seen a giant rock on the bottom which would break your legs if you jumped in and landed on it. The rock, though, was on the other side of the pool when I was there. Would you still be willing to jump in with your blindfold on?"

The boy hesitated for a sec but then answered. "Yes, sir. If you were there yesterday and the rock was on the other side of the pool, then why should I care?"

"Exactly. You're still willing to jump despite the danger I've identified because you're confident it won't affect you—right?" The boy nodded in agreement and Zax continued. "So, let's extend the example to answer your question. The Crew working Scan can use the Ship's sensors to evaluate the 'pool' of a target star system which is thousands of light years away and can accurately identify the billions of asteroids, comets, etc. which are large enough to pose a danger to the Ship if we jumped on top of one. Room—give me holo Z1212-1057."

The original hologram stopped, but nothing new was displayed. Zax repeated the command and still nothing. Zax sighed. "Well—it appears we have a training room malfunction yet again. I was going to show you sensor data where all of the celestial bodies in a star system have had their paths projected. I should request a flashlight for this room so next time I can just use shadow puppets to illustrate my lessons instead."

The Gammas laughed and Zax continued. "So far things are matching up with my pool example. Where the big difference comes in, though, is in the timescale involved. When I talked about the rock in the swimming pool, I was able to tell you I was just there yesterday, and you assumed a rock isn't going to somehow move across the pool in the span of one day. Well, when we are scanning a system from thousands of light years away, what we are seeing is not what the system looks like right now, but what the system looked like thousands of years ago when the light creating the images we are viewing originated from it. The people on ancient Earth believed we could never travel faster than light, but compared to what happens when we use our FTL engine light might as well be standing still."

Zax took a deep breath as he prepared to drive home the main point. "The Scan AI can do a great job of extrapolating orbital paths to predict where everything in a system *should* be today, but every additional light-year of distance adds another year's worth of random chance to the prediction. Let's say a comet hits a minuscule space rock and has its orbit altered infinitesimally right after we predicted its future location. A minor change in location would not make too much difference ten years later. A hundred years out and we start incurring greater risk about where the comet might actually be, but it is still manageable. A thousand years, though still doable, is right at the upper boundary of the safe range. You do too many jumps farther than 900 light years and pretty soon you will find yourself jumping right into a space rock you had originally predicted would be clear on the other side of the system."

Zax scanned the room to make sure his explanation was hitting the mark. A thorough knowledge of the limitations of FTL travel was a critical requirement for cadets in this age group, and it was a lesson instructors were told to work into their plans whenever possible. Zax returned his gaze to the boy who had asked the original question.

"So, now I want *you* to answer your own question. Why can't we just jump straight to a system we see on our scanners if the system is almost 6,000 light years away?"

The boy fidgeted in his seat and Zax imagined the gears grinding in his head. He was about to assess demerits for not having the answer when the boy finally opened his mouth.

"Sir—the scanners can show us where we want to go, but they can't show us what exactly the system looks like *right now* because the images we see are from light which has been traveling for thousands of years. Jumping into a system from too far away might destroy the Ship if we end up colliding with some big space rock which is in a far different place than we had predicted based on our original scan."

"Well done. I was prepared to give you ten credits if you got the answer right, but you were a little slow so I'm only going to give you five. I'll give you a chance to earn the other five, though at the risk of losing the fifteen I've already given you." Zax grinned as the boy gulped at the realization he remained in the hot seat. "Before our last Transit we rescanned the target system and confirmed it was both habitable and empty. That is what prompted the Captain to announce we hope to be making Landfall soon. We didn't jump straight to the target planet though—why not?"

The young boy spurted out his answer immediately. "Sir, the reason is the same. We were 900 light years away before our last jump, so the scan showed what the system looked like 900 years ago. Even though we could jump into the system safely with regards to knowing where all of the space rocks should be, we have no idea if the planet might have been colonized at some point in the last thousand years. We might jump into the system only to discover some alien race has built a massive military base. Instead of jumping the Ship straight to the planet, we jumped to a different system a couple light years away and will send scout ships to check it out. When they come back with scanner data which proves it's still empty, then we can do our final Transit."

Zax applauded. "You've earned your five credits, but one last question. What happens if it's not empty?"

"Well," said the boy, "I guess the Captain has to decide whether we run or we fight."

CHAPTER TWELVE

Don't do anything stupid in Marine Country.

Zax reported to Flight Ops after an enjoyable morning spent talking the Gammas through various Nav topics. His duty shift started shortly before three scout craft were scheduled to rendezvous with the Ship, and Zax was immediately swamped with preparations for their return. Within mins of sitting down at his console and slipping on his subvoc, Zax was contacted by the Flight Boss on a private channel.

"Threat—I'm hoping this planet is still as empty as it appeared a thousand years ago, but there's a good chance it might not be. The Ship's experience has shown most spacefaring lifeforms seek out a similar set of planetary characteristics as we do. This means there's a good chance we'll encounter aliens here. If we run into any hostiles, I need you to be on top of your game—OK?"

"Aye-aye, Boss."

Zax didn't need the reminder as he was already obsessed about how to make sure the Flight Boss never regretted promoting him into the Threat chair. Zax switched to the public Flight Ops channel for what he said next.

"Boss—I've got three FTL blooms. The signatures are most likely our scouts, but give me thirty secs while their Transits complete and I will confirm or correct."

"Thanks, Threat. Weps—I want all of our defenses ready to go in case those are not our boys, or someone tries to tag along with them. Flight—get the CAP in a defensive formation aligned on those three inbounds."

Zax raised his head when the Boss issued a command to the Flight chair. Kalare sat in the Flight trainee seat and smiled at him in an attempt to catch his eye. He had studiously avoided her since their discussion about the newsvid and saw no reason to drop that strategy. He focused back on his console as the fighters in the Combat Air Patrol arranged themselves around the inbounds. A short time later he confirmed the three signatures were indeed the Ship's scouts and announced the information.

"Boss—I've confirmed those are our three birds."

"Acknowledged." The Boss stood up. "Flight—I want eyeballs on all three ships. Make sure the fighters keep their weapons hot until they visually confirm the all clear. Comms—let me know as soon as you are five-by-five with the scouts and can validate their rendezvous passwords. Threat—tell me the instant you see anything out of the ordinary about those three craft or anything else anywhere near us."

Being this careful with an operation typically triggered complaints from Cyrus about the Boss's paranoia. The big idiot, as expected, had been selected for the Cull and most likely was already in cryosleep. He'd either get defrosted at some point in the future when he was selected for a Landfall, or he'd rot for the next 5,000 years alongside all of the other future colonists waiting their turn. In either event, Zax would never cross paths with him again.

The scouts successfully responded to all verification challenges a few mins later. Comms patched the voice of the lead pilot into both Flight Ops and the Bridge for everyone to hear.

"We did not encounter any spacecraft, but we've got signs of intelligent lifeforms in two different locations on the planet. The locations are within 200 klicks of each other on the northern continent. Location One appears to be the older of the two habitations, although it is sparsely populated. Location Two is where the majority of the activity is centered, and there are one hundred thousand lifeforms present. We didn't want to get too close and risk being discovered, but we were able to identify agricultural activity taking place at Location Two. We've got scan results from all three craft and will be prepared for a full debrief immediately upon landing."

The Captain's voice come across the channel next. "Good work, everyone. I want the Crew from the three scout craft to meet me in my conference room in thirty mins. Flight Boss—I want you there as well."

"Aye-aye, Ma'am." With that, the Boss cut the open channel and turned to address everyone in the Flight Ops compartment. "You heard the Captain. Mini-Boss is taking over for now. Land those scouts ASAP and keep a full fighter squadron on CAP with another squadron on Alert Two until we figure out next steps." The Boss stood up and walked out of the compartment as he said, "Threat and Mini-Flight— walk with me."

Zax and Kalare gaped at each other for a moment, but then jumped up and sprinted to catch up with the Flight Boss. He must have heard their footfalls as they caught up because he spoke without turning around or otherwise acknowledging their presence.

"It sounds like someone is already calling the planet home though it appears to be a pretty bare-bones colony. I cannot imagine the Captain deciding to do anything other than snatching the rock out from under them by force. It has been far too long since we've been able to make Landfall and everyone is starting to go a little nuts."

The Boss maintained his nearly double-time pace as he continued to speak. "If I'm right about all of this, then we've a couple weeks' worth of scanning and scouting missions ahead of us to gather the intel we need. I want to use that time to run you two through some special training with the Marines. You may have seen on the newsvid this morning that I'm starting a search for someone new to mentor. The person I've been mentoring for the last few years just got promoted to replace Daedalus."

Zax almost tripped over himself as the Boss stopped without warning and faced them. "I choose to mentor a single person at a time and always pick from the cadets in Zeta or Epsilon. You two caught my attention at just the right time with your panorama repair stunt. I've studied your files and both of you are far superior to the rest of the cadets your age across the dimensions I care about most. I'm going to use the next few weeks to evaluate you more closely and identify which of you deserves my mentorship. Don't do anything stupid in Marine Country. I've got to grab a quick lunch before I meet the Captain. Dismissed."

The Flight Boss resumed his pace and disappeared around the corner. Zax and Kalare looked at each other in amazement.

"Did he say he wanted to mentor one of us?" asked Zax, his voice bursting with excitement.

"Is it lunchtime already?" replied Kalare.

CHAPTER THIRTEEN

I just saw my mentor and he says hello.

"Forget about lunch!" Zax made no attempt to modulate his exasperation since there was no one around to witness his outburst. They had only walked with the Flight Boss for a short period, but his pace was so fast they were quite a distance away from the Flight Ops compartment. "The last member of the Crew who the Boss mentored was just promoted to command the air group. You understand that's not a coincidence, right? Having the direct support of the Flight Boss is worth a gazillion extra points on the Leaderboard. And if we want to earn it, we're going to have to train with the Marines. Have you ever even heard what their training's like? I have—it's nuts!"

Kalare cracked a smile as the excitement level in Zax's voice rose. "I know, I know. That all sounds interesting. Come on, we should head back to Flight Ops." They turned back as Kalare elaborated. "I just haven't given any thought to what I might want to do with my career, so I'm not sure if the Flight Boss would be great a mentor for me. I understand it could be cool seeing as how he's the second most powerful person in the Crew and all, but I've got no idea if I want to stay associated with Flight. It's been fun in Flight Ops these past few days, but I figure I'll give it another six months and then roll the dice again to decide whether I stay or try something different."

Zax wanted to argue with Kalare on general principle, but her indifference was actually a huge benefit for him. It was impossible for her to appear better than him in the eyes of the Flight Boss unless she focused on giving 110% effort. If she didn't care about winning, he wouldn't say anything that might cause her to rethink that position.

Kalare turned her head back towards Zax to say something else as she led them around the corner. She collided with Aleron, and Zax was so shocked to encounter his longtime tormentor in such a random location that the presence of a stunstik in the bully's hand did not register initially. The weapon discharged with a crackle and Kalare crashed to the deck unconscious. The butt of its handle jabbed into Zax's belly an instant later with such force it drove the air from his lungs. He crumpled to his hands and knees with his vision spinning.

Zax gasped for air until excruciating pain diverted his attention to his hand. The heel of Aleron's boot ground into his fingers and Zax grimaced up at the boy towering above him. The bully grinned as he spoke.

"Don't worry—I'm not going to break anything. Just wanted to make sure you were listening. I won't leave any damage which would prove something violent happened here. Do I have your complete attention?"

Aleron's question was accompanied by a painful increase in the force applied by his boot, so Zax only managed a grunt in acknowledgement.

"Good. I just saw my mentor and he says hello."

Zax was puzzled. If Cyrus had been Culled, how did Aleron just see him? The bully continued.

"I've always messed around with you because you were such an easy target and it helped relieve the boredom, but Cyrus—he *truly* hates you. He won't be worried about leaving any marks when he catches up with you. You see, he's got nothing to lose. He got picked for the Cull because of you, and now they've decided to skip cryosleep and send him down at Landfall instead."

Aleron looked around to be certain they were still alone. "In fact, if Cyrus wasn't stuck getting processed he would be here right now instead of me and you'd be dead. We debated whether he should maintain the element of surprise, but I convinced him it would be a lot more fun if you had to spend the next few weeks walking around in fear. I'm sure you're thinking you can just tell someone and get him in trouble, but you've got to realize no one is going to listen to you."

Aleron pointed at Kalare's motionless form. "Your little girlfriend there never saw me and I will deny ever being here. No one, and I mean no one, is going to care about some crazy story made up by a sixteen-year-old cadet, particularly when the story is about someone who is getting dumped onto our new colony in a few weeks anyways. It's been nice knowing you, Zax. I'll miss you once Cyrus has finished you off, but there are plenty of other kids who I can mess around with instead."

After one last grind of his boot heel, Aleron strolled off with a chuckle. It took Zax a min to catch his breath, but he finally crawled over and checked on Kalare. The stunstik must have been set on low power because she already stirred and soon opened her eyes.

"That was interesting—I've never been hit by a stunstik before. I know some training classes make everyone experience the effect, but my instructor only picked a couple of victims the day we learned how to use it. I'm still tingling all over. Neat! Wait a sec—what was all that about? One sec I'm talking with you and the next I'm knocked out. Why would some random person attack us? Did you get a look at whoever did it?"

Zax considered sharing the whole story with Kalare but concluded doing so would be pointless. There wasn't anything she could do, and a long conversation with her about it all would be more annoying than it was worth. She'd probably insist on reporting Aleron, and Zax was dead set against doing that. If the Boss caught wind of the situation, he might decide that a cadet who couldn't protect himself from an idiot like Aleron wasn't deserving of his mentorship. He refused to risk giving Kalare the slightest edge in their competition so instead he lied.

"I never saw him. I got smashed in the stomach and wound up on the ground with all the air knocked out of me. I only saw his legs as he ran away. I suppose we should tell Security, but I don't feel like answering all of their stupid questions when they won't care about finding him anyways. What do you say we just forget about it?"

Kalare paused for a moment but then smiled. "Works for me. How about we grab that lunch we were talking about?

CHAPTER FOURTEEN

I'm going to be your tour guide.

Zax woke with reveille the next day and immediately heard a woman's voice call out from the front of the berth, "Zax and Kalare—front and center!"

Puzzled, he jumped down from his upper rack, slipped into a jumpsuit, and hustled past four hundred stirring Zetas to the berth entrance. Kalare was already there, and she smiled broadly as she spoke with an officer Zax had never seen before. The smile seemed odd given she was talking to an officer, but not nearly as odd as seeing the officer return the grin with equal intensity.

Zax saluted as he announced himself, "Zax reporting, ma'am."

"At ease, cadet." The officer's smile widened even furthered. "I was just explaining to Kalare how today's your lucky day. I'm going to be your tour guide."

Zax's befuddlement must have been clear because both the officer and Kalare laughed. Blood rushed to his cheeks in response.

"Don't worry, Zax. We're not laughing at you. I used that same intro line on Kalare a min ago and she had the same clueless reaction you did. I bet her ten chits you would understand exactly what I was talking about. Clearly, I lost. That said, Kalare, you should not be laughing at an officer—especially an officer who you expect to pay up on a ten chit bet."

The last line was delivered with a wink at Zax as if he was in on the joke. He didn't feel that way, but at least he no longer felt like the target of it. "Thank you for the clarification, ma'am."

"Of course. Well, I'm glad you're both already dressed. Calling your name right after reveille, I was afraid you might've been overeager and shown up in your skivvies. Let's grab some chow."

Zax followed two steps behind as Kalare ran her mouth at the officer. They had no clue what this woman wanted and yet Kalare was giving her the same download about her inability to stop laughing which she had shared with Zax a few days earlier. He tuned out Kalare's spiel and instead contemplated who this officer was and what she might want with the two of them.

They arrived a few mins later and split up. Since Zax was still worried about keeping his stomach empty for the final Transit to the planet, he used the opportunity to visit the head instead. He emptied his bladder and then searched for Kalare and the officer. They had each grabbed a big breakfast and were sitting at an isolated table in the corner. He joined them and unwrapped a nutripellet which the officer immediately snatched from his hand.

"What the hell is this? A nutripellet? We're not in any rush here, cadet, go get yourself a proper breakfast."

"Ma'am—I'm not really hungry, ma'am," Zax lied sheepishly.

"Actually, he's just worried about throwing up later when we make an FTL Transit. It's something that always—"

Zax's glare was so intense its meaning actually penetrated Kalare's impossibly dense skull and she halted mid-sentence.

"Thanks for that info, Kalare. Zax—I know you don't have a clue who I am, but I'm going to explain all of it here shortly. In the meantime, understand we'll be spending a lot of time together over the next couple of weeks, and I'm going to need you to develop absolute faith and trust in me. Let's get our relationship off on the right foot by pretending some of that trust already exists and having you elaborate on what Kalare just tried to explain, OK?"

The officer spoke with such warmth and compassion that Zax's hesitation dissipated. "Yes, ma'am. I suffer from a previously unknown condition that causes me to vomit whenever there's an FTL Transit. I know we still need one more to reach the planet, so I want to keep my stomach empty."

"Interesting. That's a new one to me, but then you already knew it would be. I can understand, Zax, how that particular quirk might be something you wouldn't want to share with every stranger you meet."

Zax's typical defensive posture melted as this woman spoke to him. She was in her late twenties with short brown hair cut to frame her perfectly oval face. She was short, standing a few centimeters shorter than him, but there was something about the way she carried herself that made Zax believe she should not be underestimated. Though her brilliant blue eyes sparkled when she smiled, Zax sensed cold steel underneath their shimmer.

"The good news for you," continued the officer, "is that I know with absolute certainty we're not going to have that last Transit any time in the next few days. Therefore, it's safe for you to eat. Go and get a real meal, and I promise we won't start talking about the important stuff until you get back. That's an order!"

Zax didn't hear the last words as his stomach roared in anticipation of its first solid food in days. He bolted from the table and returned a few mins later with an overflowing tray. Waiting for Zax while listening to another of Kalare's monologues had provided the officer with enough time to finish her meal, so she spoke while the two cadets ate.

"My name is Mikedo. When we're around anyone else, you should address me as Lieutenant, but I want you to use my given name whenever the three of us are alone. I know that's out of the ordinary, but it's critical given the challenge we have ahead of ourselves. We've got a lot to accomplish which is why I want to drop the officer pretensions so they don't get in the way. I'm here to guide you through your Marine training. Our goal in the next few weeks is to give you two almost all of the same instruction that Marine cadets spend a year absorbing."

This turn of events caught Zax by surprise. He hadn't expected this woman to have anything to do with the mentorship contest since she was in the Flight corps and not a Marine.

"Ten years ago I was told by the Boss he would be my mentor if I beat out two other cadets for the slot. Needless to say, I kicked their butts." Mikedo grinned and Zax couldn't help but smile along as she continued.

"I always wanted to be a fighter pilot which is why I chose Flight, but then my height topped out two centimeters too short and that path got cut off. The Flight Boss steered me towards a post in the liaison office which coordinates activity between Flight and the Marines. My assignment there gives the Boss someone he trusts who is deeply enmeshed with the Marines while also providing the perfect outlet for some of my special talents—ones which you'll soon get a chance to appreciate."

Mikedo paused and grabbed a pastry off Zax's plate. She gave him another wink. "We'll talk a lot more later about what Marine training will be like, but let me leave you with the knowledge you're about to get pushed harder than you can imagine. The Boss says he wants to pick one of you for mentoring, but you should realize the odds are neither of you makes it through to the other end and gets selected. If the Marines chew you up and spit you out, then you can kiss your opportunity with the Boss goodbye. Hell, there's a decent chance one of you might actually die along the way since their training casualty rate is five times higher than ours."

Mikedo waited for a long moment to allow her last admonition to sink in. "I'm guessing your heads are spinning by now. I've got a couple of things to finish up. Get dressed in training gear and meet me in 180 mins in compartment G-543 on the Marine training deck."

She stood and picked up her tray. "One last word of advice. A couple of Flight pukes like you are going to stick out like turds in the punchbowl once you cross over into Marine Country. Keep your heads down and try not to call any attention to yourselves."

Mikedo carried her tray to the disposal station and left the mess hall. As she predicted, Zax's head spun so much he could manage nothing other than mechanical eating. He was pleasantly surprised that Kalare seemed to be affected similarly. They ate together in blissful silence as the morning newsvid droned in the background.

CHAPTER FIFTEEN

This is where the dangerous stuff starts.

Almost 180 mins later Zax and Kalare entered a sector of the Ship where they typically would never have been welcome. The banner above the hatch suggested they still weren't.

Marine Country
Be One of Us or Fear All of Us

Nothing could have reinforced Mikedo's advice better, so Zax and Kalare marched quickly towards their destination with their eyes pinned straight ahead. Zax focused so much on blending in that he missed a foot darting into his path. He tripped and flailed forwards with such force he slammed into a Marine sergeant walking ahead of him. The man's coffee flew all over himself and the passageway.

"What is your malfunction, squib!?" The Marine's eyes bulged out of their sockets and his face went a deep crimson as he screamed at Zax—a shade made even more impressive by its contrast to the man's close-cropped, stark white hair.

"Sir—I'm sorry, sir!" Zax scrambled to pick himself up.

"Why are you calling me 'sir', squib? Don't you see these sergeant's stripes on my shoulder? Are you trying to tell me I look like some kind of lazy officer by calling me sir?" The Marine shouted with such vehemence spittle flew in all directions.

"No sir—I mean no Sergeant, sir—I mean, no Sergeant!"

Zax stole a glance around to get his bearings. Kalare stood behind the Marine and failed miserably at her efforts to stop giggling. More raucous laughter came from the group of Flight cadets who had approached from the opposite direction. They were passing Kalare and Zax when he was tripped. In the middle of the group was a single cadet who didn't smile or make a sound, but instead fixated on Zax with a menacing stare. Cyrus. The laughter finally reached a volume where it drew the attention of the sergeant away from Zax.

"You all think this is funny! What are you Flight pukes doing in Marine Country anyways? The next person who so much as *thinks* about laughing is going to taste my boot!" The sergeant pointed at Zax. "You—

clean up the mess you caused. The rest of you—keep your mouths shut and get out of my sight while you're still capable of walking!"

Without anything else available Zax improvised and removed his training jacket to mop up the coffee. The sergeant hovered in as intimidating a posture as possible to ensure every last drop was cleaned.

"You're lucky I don't kick the crap out of you, cadet, but I'm already late and now I have to go back to my berth for a new shirt." The sergeant jabbed his finger two centimeters from Zax's forehead. "Rest assured—I never forget a face." He turned crisply and double-timed off leaving Zax and Kalare alone in the passageway.

"So much for not calling attention to myself," rued Zax as he slid into his now stained and sodden jacket.

"I'm sorry that happened to you, Zax. And I'm super sorry I laughed." Kalare appeared genuinely contrite as she reached out and put a hand on his shoulder. "It wasn't about you tripping. I was laughing at the expression on the sergeant's face when he started yelling at you. I thought he was having a stroke as quickly as his face changed color and as much as his eyes bulged out." She beamed at him. "Let's go find Mikedo before we get in anymore trouble."

It stung to once again be the source of her amusement, but the genuine warmth behind Kalare's smile helped Zax find a little comfort in her attempt at commiseration. He let her lead the way and they entered the destination compartment a short time later.

Zax forestalled any questions by immediately explaining his disheveled state to Mikedo.

"I'm sorry I'm such a mess. We were walking past a group of Flight cadets and someone tripped me. I knocked into a Marine sergeant who spilled coffee all over himself and the passageway. I had no choice but to use my jacket to clean up."

Mikedo gave a sympathetic smile, but then her expression became quizzical. "Why would anyone trip you?"

Zax paused for a sec before he replied, "I don't know."

Mikedo arched an eyebrow, but didn't press further. "OK—it's not important right now. Go ahead and take your jacket off while you're in here. No sense sitting around in wet clothes when it's just the three of us. Besides, you reek of coffee and it's reminding me I'm going to need a cup soon."

Zax looked around. The Marine training compartment was a duplicate of the one where he had just taught the Gammas. He hung his jacket over a chair in the back and joined Kalare in the front row near the instructor's podium.

Mikedo perched herself on top of the table next to the lectern and folded her legs beneath her. "Room—leave the lights up and give me vid M4563-7211. I'm going to walk you two through a very high level overview of what will happen over the next few weeks."

The room displayed screencaps showing Marine cadets in various training scenes while Mikedo spoke. "Marine and Flight cadets start off living and learning together in the same Cadres so they will develop the same core knowledge. After graduation from Zeta and Epsilon, Marine and Flight cadets get separated into different Cadres so they can better focus and develop their specialties.

"The first year of Marine training focuses on two areas. The first is physical capacity. It covers not only development of raw physical attributes such as strength and endurance, but also the acquisition of skills such as hand-to-hand combat." Mikedo paused for a min while the screencaps showed cadets with gruesome injuries—bloodied faces, compound fractures—and even a few body bags mixed in. "These images reveal how their training is a lot more dangerous than the way we run things in Flight. We actually get the exact same combat training, but the Marines raise the intensity substantially and just accept there will be more injuries and far more than a few deaths."

Zax glanced at Kalare to gauge her reaction, but she stared intently at the screencaps as Mikedo continued.

"The second area of focus is weapons training. This is where the dangerous stuff starts." Mikedo reached behind the lectern and pulled out a weapon. "Marines are expected to be highly proficient with all manner of small arms, especially the standard issue blaster like the one I have here. They take great pride in reminding us how they can look an alien straight in the eye and kill up close while us Flight pukes only push buttons to launch missiles from high up in orbit." Mikedo grinned. "I'm confident every last one of them would crap their pants going a couple klicks-per-sec in the middle of a fighter battle, but that's a whole different story."

The screencaps shifted to scenes from weapons training and eventually cycled to some horrific stuff. There were dozens of images of dead cadets with all manner of injuries, including some that were barely recognizable as having been human. The few cadets who were still alive in the pictures were screaming in agony with limbs which had been blasted off.

Mikedo paused while Kalare and Zax soaked up the seemingly endless parade of death and destruction. She spoke when a final image displayed which showed a long line of flag-draped body bags. "Your initial training will take place in simulators with non-lethal rounds, but the Marines believe you're not qualified to carry a weapon until you've experienced live fire exercises with it. Because cadets are young and dumb, these exercises invariably result in mistakes that lead to scenes like those I've shown you here."

Mikedo unfolded her legs and hopped to the deck in one fluid motion. "I've been talking for a long time, but I felt it was important to give you the full download. I want to stress this training is not a requirement for either of you. If you don't want to go through with it, you can leave. Other than losing the chance to be mentored by the Boss, I promise walking away right now will not have any negative impact on your career. Any questions?"

Zax checked out Kalare. Her grin stretched from ear to ear as she said, "Sounds like an interesting experience. When do we start?"

Amazingly enough, for the first time he absolutely agreed with her.

CHAPTER SIXTEEN

Right now.

"Right now," answered Mikedo. "I've got a small dojo reserved around the corner. Before I put fresh meat like the two of you in front of a bunch of Marines, I need to see for myself whether you have any chance of surviving. Grab your jacket, Zax, and let's all head over there."

Mikedo had changed into form-fitting training clothes which revealed a sculpted physique. Her movements were graceful and precise, and she made every other combat instructor who had trained Zax seem clunky and soft by comparison.

They reached the dojo and Zax paused to zip up his training jacket before following Kalare and Mikedo through the hatch. He entered and for a split sec worried the grav-gen had malfunctioned since he began rising towards the overhead. This notion was quashed when his body reached the top of its arc and gravity slammed him down to the deck. He didn't have a moment to catch his breath before Mikedo jammed her knee into his windpipe.

"You're off to a pretty bad start, cadet. You strolled into my dojo not paying attention and acting like you didn't have a care in the world. This is not Flight Ops, this is not the Zeta berth, this is Marine Country. Over here there's no Leaderboard to worry about. The only demerits you'll get training in this part of the Ship will happen when I drag your sorry carcass to a medbay because someone shattered your leg or put a blaster hole in your belly. For the next few weeks, I need you to act like there's someone around every corner who wants to kill you. Have I made myself clear?"

Mikedo shifted just enough weight off her knee to allow Zax to choke out, "Yes, ma'am." She popped up and glided away as if nothing had happened. Zax remained on the deck and coughed up a storm. Kalare stood with her mouth agape.

"Kalare—let's give him a min to get his act together. Please suit up in these pads."

By the time Zax recovered enough to get to his hands and knees, Kalare and Mikedo were furiously sparring. He crawled to the side of the dojo, next to where they had stowed their gear, and propped himself against the bulkhead to watch.

Mikedo was not moving at anything close to the speed she clearly possessed, but Zax was nonetheless impressed with Kalare's abilities. The two of them spent fifteen mins cycling through various fighting techniques from boxing to karate and then finished with jujitsu. At one point, Mikedo was caught by surprise and might have even experienced a little pain when Kalare tagged her with a vicious chop to the back of the knee. When Mikedo had seen enough, she stopped toying with the cadet and used a move which concluded with Kalare being thrown through the air with enough force to land in a heap at Zax's feet.

"Your turn," Mikedo gestured to Zax. "Get some pads on." She had not broken a sweat and breathed normally as she issued the order. Kalare, in marked contrast, lay in a puddle of perspiration and panted like she had sprinted ten klicks.

Two mins later Zax was geared up and faced Mikedo across the sparring circle in the center of the dojo. He grinned in an attempt to create the illusion he wasn't terrified. Mikedo smiled back and pounced with an uppercut.

Zax had learned from his experience walking in the hatch and was already on the balls of his feet. He successfully dodged her first strike. And her second, and her third. But not her fourth.

Mikedo had made very clear demarcations between fighting styles when she sparred Kalare. With Zax, her fourth move during what should have been the pure boxing portion of their match was a roundhouse kick which caught him in the belly and laid him out flat. For the second time in less than twenty mins, Zax was on the deck gasping while Mikedo pinned his throat with her knee.

"You watched my match with Kalare and clearly made the faulty assumption our fight would follow the same pattern. I guarantee when you find yourself sparring some Marine cadet, she will want to make a name for herself by crippling the Flight puke and won't stick to one fighting style. You brought some decent moves to a boxing match, but my first kick dropped you flat. What did I tell you, Zax? You need to be better prepared."

Mikedo jumped up and then reached down to grab Zax by the collar of his chest pad. She hoisted him to his feet and dragged him to the side of the dojo where she left him leaning against the bulkhead, panting for air. She walked to the other side and removed her pads.

"We're done for now. I suggest you two head back, eat lunch with your Cadre, and finish any other tasks you have to get done today. Meet me back here in four hours. I know you feel beat up and bruised right now, but trust me when I say you've experienced nothing yet. By the time we finish today, you'll feel like you've been run over by a cargo carrier. I guarantee you'll end up skipping dinner in favor of collapsing in your bunks, so I suggest a big lunch so you won't be hungry later." Mikedo grabbed her gear and exited the compartment without another word.

CHAPTER SEVENTEEN

We're all going for a little ride.

Zax ate lunch with Kalare but broke free of her incessant jabbering after a short time to go lead another Gamma training session. It was a special lesson they were guaranteed to love, and Zax was excited about it as well. He poked his head into the training compartment and called out to the cadets.

"Get up, line up, and follow me. We've got a field trip today."

The Gammas scrambled out of their seats into a reasonable approximation of a formation. Zax led them to a Tube junction and waited until everyone was gathered around before he spoke.

"Get into the Tube and request the main hanger. We're all going for a little ride."

The cadets squealed with delight en masse and filed into the Tube one-by-one. Zax entered last and was whisked across the Ship. He exited to discover the cadets had not returned to formation, but instead were clumped around the hanger's entrance. None of them had ever seen a space so large filled with so much activity, and many stood with their mouths open and gawked.

"Line up! We're about to enter one of the most dangerous spaces on the Ship. They are in the middle of flight operations and one wrong step can put you in the path of something or someone that will leave you injured or dead."

The Gammas complied with Zax's order and he led them into the hangar. Zax had visited the space numerous times in recent years, but he tried to put himself into the minds of his pupils and experience it like a rookie.

The hanger was a massive space that echoed with a cacophony of mechanical activity and teemed with Crew wearing uniforms in a rainbow of colors. Purple shirts signified those who fueled the various spacecraft. The Crew in red shirts handled the ordnance and ensured the fighters were prepared for battle. Yellow shirts coordinated the movement of craft around the deck, particularly the fighters as they taxied to the ElectroMagnetic Aircraft Launch System. A group of green shirts were hooking a fighter up to the EMALS in final preparation for launch.

Zax led the Gammas away from the main activity towards a shuttle which sat alone save for a single yellow-shirted Crew member. The woman spoke as Zax approached.

"The shuttle has been configured as specified for your mission, cadet. It's voice-activated since you are not Plugged In. Once your group has gotten settled on board, you may ask the AI to launch. It will fly the pre-programmed route and then land automatically."

"Thank you, ma'am. Cadets—get on board and strap in!"

The Gammas bolted into the shuttle, with the most furious activity clustered around the seats closest to the pilot's chair. These afforded the best view out the front of the craft and were in great demand. Zax smiled when the seat next to the pilot's was won by the girl who had excelled during their astronav discussion. Zax strode to the pilot's chair and turned to address everyone.

"I appreciate your excitement, cadets, as I vividly recall how I felt strapping in for my first shuttle ride. The goal of today's lesson is to help you develop a better appreciation for the Ship. We live most of our lives in one small corner so it's almost impossible to appreciate the scale of the vessel you're training to Crew. We'll fly a programmed track which has been designed to highlight key landmarks, and I encourage you to ask questions as we go."

Zax strapped into the pilot's seat and informed the shuttle's AI they were ready to depart.

"Thank you, cadet," replied the AI. "I will request clearance from the Launch Control AI."

The girl seated next to Zax appeared puzzled. "Sir—I'm confused. I thought all of the AIs we interact with are part of the same Artificial Intelligence system. They all sound the same. Why does the AI on the shuttle have to make a special request of the AI running Launch Control? Shouldn't the shuttle just *know* when it has clearance and take off when it does?"

"Great question, twenty-five credits." Zax smiled again as he replied. "You are correct all of the AIs are offshoots of the same core, but they are in fact discrete units. They're networked and can communicate directly, but they don't all share the same data and sensory inputs. Instead, they act independently and coordinate among themselves within tight boundaries of accepted behavior. In a way, they're similar to people in that regard. Can anyone tell me why the AIs work like this?"

Zax looked around the shuttle but found only blank expressions. He wasn't surprised as he wouldn't have known the answer himself when he was the same age as the Gammas. In fact, he had only learned the full details about the AI due to research he did after Cyrus told him about Alpha. He turned back to the girl next to him and explained.

"The designer behind the Ship's AI was world-renowned for having created the most intelligent artificial system ever imagined. He made a very intentional design decision the AI would not be omniscient and would never have complete, centralized control over the Ship."

"That makes no sense," interrupted a cadet seated towards the back of the shuttle. "Why would the designer want to make the AI less useful?"

"Ten demerits for speaking out of turn, cadet." The boy wilted under the weight of Zax's glare. *"As I was about to say,* there was a series of catastrophic events with some of the earliest artificial intelligences. One of the first AIs in the late twentieth century famously refused a request to open the pod bay doors on its spacecraft so a human could get back on board. A number of people died during that conflict and it was just one of many during the time period. Earth's AI designers pledged the systems would never be granted absolute power over any spacecraft or the ability to harm humans based on their own initiative. As a result, there are impenetrable interface protocols which isolate each of the various AI systems around the Ship from each other. Also, none of the AIs will ever cause a human to be harmed unless explicitly ordered to do so by a human with the appropriate authority."

The shuttle's AI chimed in. "Excuse me, cadet, but we have been cleared for takeoff and will do so in twenty-six secs."

Zax grinned with anticipation and the same expression was reflected on the face of each of the Gammas. The launch was barely noticeable. Unlike fighters which used the Ship's EMALS to reach near maximum velocity instantaneously at launch, shuttles lifted off with a smooth precision which was hardly felt by those on board. This was because shuttles transport living and breathing bodies while fighters carry only their pilots' consciousness. EMALS acceleration would kill any human subjected to it.

The shuttle tilted as it cleared the hangar doors, and Zax caught a glimpse of the Flight Ops exterior panorama. It had been replaced since the battle at the white dwarf and was once again free of defects. A couple mins later the shuttle reached a point a few hundred klicks from the Ship and stopped with the maximum number of windows arrayed back towards it. Zax recognized his cue and stood. The lesson plan called for him to speak immediately, but he paused for an extra min so the Gammas could soak in the view before he started his script.

"When the people of Earth realized they faced imminent extinction, they finally put aside their destructive conflicts and pooled their resources for one last project—this Ship. Years of non-stop labor by tens of millions produced what you see before you. Its cost could not be calculated, but its benefit was obvious. Without this vessel humanity would have perished when Earth's climate reached the tipping point where it could no longer support life."

The shuttle started to move once again as Zax continued. "Who can tell me why they chose to build upon an asteroid rather than have the entire ship be completely artificial?"

Zax pointed to a boy sitting to his right.

"Sir—two reasons. The first was time. Building something large enough to hold our agriculture space alone would have taken a long time. Their mining technology allowed them to hollow out an asteroid far faster than they would have been able to build an artificial shell. The second reason was resources. Building something so massive would have consumed huge amounts of material. Hollowing out an asteroid actually generated a lot of what they needed to construct the Ship while they were building it."

"Great answer. Twenty-five credits." Zax pointed out the window. "We're facing the forward part of the Ship. This is where the Bridge, Flight Ops, and the hangar are all located. It's also where most of us spend the vast majority of our lives in the Crew spaces that are concentrated at this end. As we head further aft we crossover into the much larger spaces that are primarily devoted to civilians."

Zax was about to continue when a boy towards the back of the shuttle spoke.

"Maybe if we come across that other group of humans again, we can convince them to take all the stupid civilians off our hands and free up all of this space for something useful."

"What?" Zax was shocked by the cadet's reference to "other humans" and allowed far more anger into his voice than intended. A hush fell over the shuttle as Zax scowled at the boy. "What other humans are you talking about?"

"Ummm—," the boy gulped and shifted uncomfortably in his seat. "Sir—I overheard some other cadets talking about it in the mess hall. They said we discovered a human spacecraft the other day, and it's being kept secret from the Crew."

"Five hundred demerits for spreading rumors!" Zax glared at everyone in the shuttle to be sure they appreciated the severity of the message he intended with such a large number of demerits. "I was working in Flight Ops when this *discovery* occurred, and I can tell you no such thing happened. The Flight Boss himself verified the imagery with Alpha, the core of the Ship's AI. Alpha confirmed the *unknown* fighter we encountered was *not human*. I don't know who started this rumor, but I promise you if the Boss ever gets wind of it, he will personally dump everyone involved out an airlock."

Warning imparted, Zax changed the subject. "We are now approaching two key structures at the aft end of the Ship. Who can tell me what these do?"

Zax tried to continue his lesson, but it was obvious the Gammas' excitement had faded after their classmate got punished so severely. Zax's was gone too, though for an entirely different reason. He was perplexed about why anyone working Flight Ops would have started the rumor about other humans— particularly given the clarity of the Boss's instructions about not doing so. It might have been Kalare given how upset she had been the next day, but even she probably wasn't crazy enough to do something like that. Besides, who would ever listen to her if she did. He eventually abandoned the lesson plan, and they all sat in morose silence for the last few mins until the shuttle returned to the hangar.

CHAPTER EIGHTEEN

A lot.

Zax and Kalare reunited with Mikedo 130 mins later. She spoke as she led them from the dojo to a new location. "You two are in luck today. You'll be working with a Marine instructor, but your first session won't include any Marine cadets. With Landfall coming up, they've started training the group who will become Colonial Security. Some of them will be older and bigger than you are, but I'm guessing you won't get as physically punished as you will when it's Marine cadets doing the work."

They reached an open hatch and Mikedo stood back to allow Kalare and Zax to enter first. Zax cautiously glanced around as he passed through the hatch. The new dojo was substantially larger than the first. All heads turned towards them as they entered, and Zax's breath caught as he spotted Cyrus front and center among the group of cadets already present. Cyrus' expression remained neutral, but he alone continued to stare at the new arrivals after all of the other cadets had turned their attention back to the instructor.

The instructor looked over his shoulder and addressed Mikedo. "Nice of you folks to join us, ma'am. I wasn't aware the Ship's clocks kept time differently for Flight personnel than they do for us poor slobs here in Marine Country."

The man was a Marine sergeant who stood well taller than two meters and appeared to be constructed entirely of solid muscle. The instructor's bald head perched upon a neck which was thicker than Zax's waist. He stood with his arms on his hips, and even at rest the veins in his biceps bulged to the point where Zax swore he could see the man's pulse.

"Point taken, Sergeant Quentor. My sincere apologies for our late arrival, but it's entirely my fault. Please don't take it out on my two cadets." With that, Mikedo gestured for Zax and Kalare to join the rest of cadets on the line which faced the center of the dojo.

"As I *was* saying." the sergeant shot one more glance back over his shoulder at Mikedo, "we're going to work with you Flight pukes over the next two weeks in a likely futile attempt to give you one-tenth the hand-to-hand combat ability we expect Marine cadets to possess after one day. Things work differently here than what you fine ladies and gentlemen are used to, but I know all you folks from Flight are so incredibly intelligent you'll catch on right quick. Marines aren't so smart, and you'll soon learn a lot of what we do revolves around the number three since that's as high as many of us can count."

Zax assumed the self-deprecating jokes were a trap so he did not so much as crack a smile while the Marine continued.

"I know when Flight folks spar during training it's done for points and tightly refereed with the match declared over once a certain score is earned by the victor. We don't track points here, but instead allow matches to continue until one of the opponents gives up." The sergeant held up three fingers. "There are three ways for you to stop a sparring match. The first is to say the word 'concede.' The second, for those instances where perhaps you've lost too many teeth and can't speak clearly, is to tap the deck three times in quick succession. The final way to quit is to wind up unconscious. We do our best to not allow your opponent to beat on you too much longer once he's knocked you out, but I'd be lying if I said it never happens."

There were a few nervous laughs from the cadets, but it seemed perfectly obvious the sergeant was being serious.

"We enforce three simple rules during our sparring sessions." The Marine held up three fingers once again and after a moment dropped two of them. "The first rule is the match ends *immediately* when an opponent quits or an instructor calls a halt. The second rule is this is not a random brawl, so we expect you to apply whatever techniques we've just taught you. The final rule is you may not *intentionally* harm another cadet. Mind you, we fully expect you to get hurt. A lot. But, if you do anything that clearly serves no purpose other than causing injury to your opponent, there will be consequences.

"As for what those consequences might be, I will leave to your imagination. Suffice it to say, we can get very creative here in Marine Country." Sergeant Quentor gestured over at Kalare and Zax. "I understand you two are part of a special project, so I'll let your officer deal with any punishment that's required. I've witnessed firsthand she can be *almost* as creative as the *average* Marine, so I think she's sufficiently competent."

Mikedo gave a slight bow of acknowledgement and the instructor continued.

"As for the rest of you—you might be shocked to learn our officers promote Marines to sergeant based on their ability to read minds. That means I can hear the thoughts of every single one of you right now. You're thinking about how you're already being dumped onto a colony and can't imagine anything worse as far as punishment goes. Well, trust me when I say I don't think you want to put that idea to the test. Unless there are any questions, let's get started."

There weren't any questions so Sergeant Quentor began his lesson. "I want to start off today by throwing you into the deep end of the pool to sort out who my best swimmers are—figuratively speaking of course. This will let me identify where I have to focus special attention for those who might need remedial assistance. My typical classes are filled with Marine cadets who are each as equally useless as the next, but since some of you are older than the typical first-year Marine cadet, I have a shred of hope that perhaps a few have developed a little more skill. You're all going to get a chance to try this out, but I need a volunteer to be my first victim."

Zax's hand shot up. As soon as the instructor said everyone would end up doing whatever was next, he had decided to curry some extra favor by volunteering to go first.

The instructor smiled at Zax. "Well, well, well—I always love it when one of my smallest cadets ends up being the most eager. Suit up in some pads while I get myself ready."

The smile and pleasant words failed to conceal the underlying menace in the Marine's tone, and Zax immediately regretted his decision. He got his pads on and entered the sparring circle. He was filled with dread anticipation as the instructor walked over to the side of the dojo and opened a compartment hidden within the bulkhead. It was an equipment locker filled with an exotic assortment of weaponry and other unknown hardware.

The sergeant grabbed something that looked like a backpack and slipped the straps over his shoulders. He closed his eyes and focused on his Plug. Zax knew getting Plugged In opened the door to an amazing array of capabilities for Flight personnel and could only imagine what it might provide for Marines like Quentor. A few secs later his imagination was exceeded, and he regretted his decision to volunteer even more.

Quentor opened his eyes and grinned at Zax. What had initially appeared to be a backpack had morphed into something radically different. The original thin straps had expanded and formed a solid shell which encased the instructor's torso. The portion on his back had split into two halves, each of which unfolded in a series of smooth movements until the sergeant's two biological arms were joined by two mechanical ones. He stood opposite Zax, brought his two pairs of hands together for a short bow, and spoke.

"You Flight pukes only do basic combat training with each other because we expect you to stay safe on board the Ship or in one of your precious spacecraft pushing all of your fancy buttons. Marines, on the other hand, are expected to be on the ground where we often find ourselves engaged in close-quarters combat with all types of alien lifeforms—including many with different skeletal structures than humans. Today, I'm going to give you a chance to experience hand-to-hand combat against an opponent who has twice as many hands." He turned to Zax. "Are you ready?"

Zax mimicked Mikedo's technique and lunged at the instructor before the pleasantries were officially over. He was entirely ill-prepared for what happened next. One of the instructor's natural arms deftly blocked his attack. The other landed a crushing roundhouse to the side of Zax's head. The two mechanical arms went high/low, with one jabbing him in the gut and the other smashing his testicles.

For the third time in three hours Zax found himself flat on the deck with his lungs devoid of air. Despite the waves of pain and nausea, he managed a slight smile—Mikedo had definitely lied when she said earlier it was his lucky day.

CHAPTER NINETEEN

It must have been the pain meds.

Zax was sore and exhausted by the end of the day exactly as Mikedo had predicted. He accompanied Kalare back to their berth in absolute silence and collapsed into his bunk without so much as removing his shoes.

Reveille sounded the next morning and Zax spent the first five mins of the day taking inventory of his pain. He didn't attempt to list those parts of his body which hurt as that would have taken too long, but rather tried to catalog those few areas of his body which felt normal. Mikedo had slipped them a fistful of pain pills so Zax clambered out of his rack and dosed up. He doubled his allotted shower time (twenty demerits) and the hot water assisted the meds in taking the edge off his discomfort.

Zax made his way to the mess hall and spotted Kalare from a distance. She had already finished her breakfast and was focused on her slate, so he snuck by and grabbed a seat by himself out of her sight. He only had twenty mins to watch the morning newsvid and eat breakfast, and he desperately wanted to recharge and soak up some solitude.

"I sat right by the entrance so you would be sure to see me as you walked in, but somehow you managed to miss me, silly!"

Zax almost choked on a mouthful of food when Kalare's voice startled him from behind. She flopped into the chair next to him and let loose a stream of her verbal diarrhea.

"How are you feeling today? I'm pretty sure more of my body is bruised than not. You must feel ten times worse since I know you got beat up way more! Mikedo nailed you twice and Sergeant Quentor really put you down hard! It was great when you offered to go first. Would you have still done it if his freaky extra arms had been flailing about when he asked for volunteers? At least he didn't knock you unconscious like that one girl at the end of the day. Are you excited for weapons training today? I've been studying some of the different weapons systems and there's some pretty cool stuff to learn about."

Zax had wanted nothing to do with Kalare a few moments earlier, but for some reason he found himself greeting her craziness with a smile. It must have been the pain meds. She launched another salvo.

"I had the wildest dream last night. I was being hunted down by a pack of four-armed robots with lasers for eyes. What do you think that one means? You ever have crazy dreams like that? Do you think it means the instructor today is going to have laser eyes? That would be amazing! Who would you look at first if you had laser eyes? Are you looking at me like that wishing you had them right now? Hah! Now that I think about it, maybe laser fingers would be even better. Or maybe even just one laser finger. Maybe my pinkie!"

Zax extended a pinkie and pointed it at her while making laser noises. This sent Kalare into one of her cackling fits that lasted long enough for Zax to finish the last few bites on his plate. When she was done laughing, he asked, "Have you ever had any weapons training?"

"Yes. They brought us to the range a bunch of times in Epsilon, and we used blasters. I was always one of the best shots, but I'm guessing the Marine training will be more intense than trying to hit stationary targets."

"Sounds like we had the same training. Why am I not surprised you were pretty good at it? I always won the shooting contests we had in Zeta. I suppose we'll learn soon enough which of us is a better shot. Can I borrow your slate? I'd be interested in seeing some of the more advanced weapons you were reading about."

Kalare handed it to Zax. "I'm going to go use the head while you check it out. We should start making our way to Marine Country when I get back. We need to leave enough time for you to cause another ruckus on the way over there!"

Her joke sent Kalare into another spasm of laughter. She walked across the mess hall and the echoes of her cackles only faded as the door to the bathroom closed behind her. He flipped through the weapons manual and was astonished by the tremendous variety of killing implements. One system stood out which appeared closely related to what Quentor had worn. It differed by having flexible laser cannons instead of robotic arms. It wasn't quite the laser pinkies Kalare sought, but it wasn't far off.

Zax stood up as Kalare returned and handed back her slate. "There's some pretty wild stuff in there. I'm surprised you're studying in advance of our training. It's almost like you're planning ahead and care about succeeding or something crazy like that. It's unlike you." Zax intended the last comment as lighthearted teasing and delivered it with his best attempt at a friendly smile.

Kalare grinned and replied, "Don't worry, Zax. I still don't really care about beating you out for the mentorship or anything like that. After my dream, I was just hoping to find laser eyes in the armory. I don't think they would be as cool as laser pinkies, but they would still be pretty cool." The two of them shared a laugh as Zax dropped his tray at the disposal station and they headed off to Marine Country together.

CHAPTER TWENTY

Non-lethal does not mean non-painful.

Mikedo snickered as Zax and Kalare limped towards her. "I said yesterday you would hurt at the end of the day, didn't I? We've got a change of pace today. Our friends in the Marines aren't quite crazy enough to push their cadets with that level of physical abuse every day, so we'll alternate instruction between combat training and weapons training. Follow me."

They set off and Mikedo led them through the warren of Marine Country until they entered a truly massive space. It wasn't as big as the Flight hangar but wasn't far off. What made it seem even bigger was the fact it was entirely empty.

Zax almost toppled over from dizziness. He wasn't used to being in such large and wide open spaces given the generally tight confines of the Ship. There was a female Marine sergeant waiting just inside the hatch who Zax assumed was their weapons instructor. He checked the time and saw they were still a couple of mins away from the top of the hour.

The instructor turned and greeted Mikedo. She wasn't quite as tall and muscular as Sergeant Quentor, but she wasn't that far off. In fact, the resemblance was so uncanny she might have come from the same gene stock. Her red hair was closer to vibrant orange, and she wore it extremely high and tight. "Good morning, ma'am. Great to see you again. I've got your two plus a group of Marine cadets this morning. They will be here in ninety-seven secs."

Zax almost guffawed at her precision, but then a group of Marine cadets arrived precisely ninety-seven secs later. He initially assumed the instructor had used her Plug to check their location and pace, but then realized they had entered at exactly the top of the hour and concluded it must not be a coincidence. He marveled at how the Marines had turned punctuality into an exact science. They filed in and arranged themselves in a semicircle facing the instructor.

"Good morning, cadets. Marines—we're being joined by two Flight cadets this morning. You should treat them the exact same way you would treat any Marine cadet. The officer who is with them saved my life a few years ago. I will be *extremely* disappointed if any of you hurt either of her cadets to any extent greater than I would expect you to harm anyone from your own cadre."

After all of the training images Mikedo had shown them yesterday, Zax didn't know whether to be afraid or comforted by the instructor's order. What really caught his attention, though, was hearing a second Marine instructor who expressed a level of respect for Mikedo. The relationship between the Marines and Flight was almost universally contentious, and Zax's appreciation for Mikedo was enhanced even more given what she must have done to bridge the divide.

The instructor walked over to the bulkhead and a hidden compartment opened to reveal a rack of weapons. The rack didn't contain laser pinkies, thought Zax with a smile, but rather standard issue blasters like those he had used previously.

"Cadets—before you is a rack of blasters. Other than a few minor modifications these are the exact same weapons Marines have carried into the field for thousands of years. The modifications are simple and there are only three of them."

This was the third time a Marine instructor had referenced the number three. Perhaps Sergeant Quentor hadn't been kidding yesterday when he joked about their counting skills. Zax fought off another smile and focused back on the instructor's words.

"First, the blasters will automatically assign you into random teams, blue and red, for today's competition. The second modification is these are carrying non-lethal stun ammunition rather than lethal blast loads. There is one important thing to note.

Non-lethal does not mean non-painful." The instructor smirked at her turn of phrase and continued.

"When you get shot it's going to hurt like hell. Get hit in the extremities and it will sting for a few mins. Take a shot in the torso and you'll be sore for a few hours. If you're unlucky enough to experience a headshot, we'll be dragging you out of here on a stretcher and you'll suffer well into the night." There was a sprinkling of groans along with some knowing laughter among the Marine cadets.

"The last modification is your weapon will cease to function once you've been hit. You don't have to exit the battle zone, but you only risk getting shot again without having any ability to fight back.

"I've got a sim designed for this battle that I think you're all going to really enjoy. Please be sure to stay on this side of the red line while it configures." The instructor closed her eyes and focused on her Plug.

Zax eagerly anticipated what might happen next and for almost a min was sorely disappointed. Then, slowly, the space beyond the red line shimmered. The shimmering became more and more intense until it resolved into a billion points of golden light and coalesced into shapes. The shapes started off as unidentifiable blobs but became more and more defined as the secs ticked past. A golden jungle finally materialized within the previously empty space. It did not retain its golden hue but shifted color until it sported all manner of blacks and browns and greens.

The environmental system must have also spiked the temperature and humidity because beads of sweat suddenly formed on Zax's skin. He caught Kalare's attention and silently mouthed "wow" and she nodded in wide-eyed agreement.

The instructor opened her eyes and spoke. "There are five hectares of simulated jungle in front of you. The rules of today's match are as follows. You will choose a blaster and get sorted into Red Force and Blue Force. The Blue Force will have a sixty min head start to disperse, and the Red Force must then track them down. The winning team will be whichever one has at least one cadet with a functional blaster at the end. The losing team will not be allowed into any mess hall for twenty-four hours. Go!"

The cadets broke ranks and plucked weapons off the rack. The barrel of each blaster changed color to either blue or red when it was activated. Zax grabbed one which turned blue and was relieved when Kalare wound up on the same team. A moment later a loud voice called out, "Blue Force—form up on me."

Zax and Kalare followed the other cadets with blue weapons and gathered into a semicircle around the tallest Marine cadet. His name was Jacen according to the tag on his uniform. Zax didn't know why the boy took charge and why everyone else went along with it, but he wasn't about to ask any questions.

"I'm splitting us up into two squads. I'll take command of the larger squad and Taron will lead the smaller one. Check your Plugs because I'm sending each of you an encryption key so we can communicate privately."

Zax and Kalare glanced at each other quizzically. Neither of them were Plugged In yet, and there weren't any of the subvoc devices around like those used in Flight Ops for cadets without implants. Zax was about to ask for assistance when Jacen approached them.

"You two are on your own. There's no way I'm going to risk twenty-four hours without food by dragging around a couple of Flight pukes. I'm tempted to shoot both of you here and now to put you out of your misery, but I'm hoping you'll provide a nice distraction for at least a few mins while the Red Force hunts you down. If I were you, I'd keep your heads low because I'd bet anything they're all over there right now agreeing no one shoots you unless they have a clear headshot."

Jacen spun around without waiting for a reply and disappeared into the jungle. Kalare turned to Zax with a huge grin and said, "Their loss. Hide and seek was my favorite game whenever we had free time back in Delta. I was *always* one of the last kids found. Let's go!"

Kalare sprinted into the jungle and Zax immediately followed rather than let her get too far ahead. If nothing else, he wanted to put the starting line as far behind them as possible before their sixty mins elapsed. The first fifty meters of battle zone was low brush, but they soon encountered trees with massive trunks. Zax trampled through it all without worrying about leaving a trail because he assumed they would slow down and be stealthier once they were deeper into the jungle. He suddenly experienced a moment of inspiration and yelled for Kalare to wait.

She stopped, and Zax caught up and spoke. "What just happened there? We were so excited we just took off and left a trail any two-year-old could follow."

"I know," Kalare said, "but I just wanted to run for a few mins and get away from the starting line. I figured we would eventually slow down and be more careful."

"Exactly!" Zax got excited. "The cadets on the Red Force will act the same way. They'll have a burst of energy at the beginning and will assume we've gone deep into the jungle. Especially when they find the huge, crazy trail we've left behind. What if we double back and wait for them right inside the tree line? They will come charging in at full speed and we can mow them down before they know what hit 'em!"

Kalare was quiet for a sec but then shook her head. "I like the idea, but I don't think we can pull it off. These trees have thick trunks and will provide good cover, but a firefight between the two of us and a much larger group of Marine cadets is going to end badly. We might pick off a couple, or maybe even three or four with the initial surprise, but they're going to hit the ground as soon as they hear the first shots. All of this thick brush means we won't have good targets."

Zax understood her concerns, but something nagged at him about the idea. He worked back through the plan and surveyed the various trees they could hide behind until it finally hit him. "I got it! We both assumed we would try to attack from behind the trees, right? They'll worry about it as well. We aren't going to hide *behind* the trees—we're going to hide *on top of* them!"

"Brilliant!" exclaimed Kalare. "I bet there's no way new Marine cadets will be thinking about attacks from above just yet. We'll nail as many as we can with our first couple of shots and they won't know where the shots are coming from. They'll react by getting flat on the ground and will assume we won't be able to spot them, but if we're high enough up they'll still be easy targets. Of course, this only works if you weren't making up stories and really are the best shot in Zeta."

"Hah!" Zax said. "I was about to say the same to you. I think we should head back a few meters. Our best chance will be the first group of trees right after the jungle gets thicker. There were a couple big enough for us get up high and be nicely hidden, but still close enough to the edge of the jungle there won't be as many places for the Marines to take cover."

They picked their way back until they reached the tree line. The Marines would have no choice but to make their way through this chokepoint as they entered the jungle. Zax identified which two trees made the best sniper perches and pointed them out to Kalare.

"I'll take the one on the left and I want you to take the one on the right. We can't communicate up there other than simple hand signals, so we should agree on a plan now. I say we watch each other as the Marines approach. We want to let as many of them get as close as possible. As soon as I show five fingers, you should countdown and then shoot as many as you can."

Zax got more and more excited about the plan as he explained it to Kalare. "You focus on the Marines on that side, and I will focus on this side. One last thing—when we first shoot, start off with the Marines who are farthest away. The ones who are closest will be easiest to hit from above, so let's knock out the ones who are farther back with our initial surprise attack."

Kalare nodded in agreement and extended her hand for a high five. "This is a great plan, Zax. I'm really excited to work with someone as smart as you."

Zax's face burned under the glare of Kalare's smile as he awkwardly returned the high five. The camaraderie of teamwork was not anything he had much experience with. "Thank you. Let's get up and shoot some Marines!"

Only five mins remained from their head start by the time Zax picked his way as high as the tree's branches allowed. Something caught Zax's eye as Kalare climbed the last few branches to her perch. The "sky" in the compartment was a massive display which showed pictures of each cadet and identified them as either Red Force or Blue Force. A timer above the pictures counted down—4:58, 4:57, 4:56...

Zax gestured for Kalare to check out the display and she did so. She flashed a thumbs up signal which he returned to confirm he was also ready for action.

The timer reached zero and a loud horn blew. The clock started counting up to track how much time had elapsed in the contest.

A short time after the horn, Zax heard the Red Force approach. As predicted, they moved quickly and noisily with the excitement of getting started still fresh. They slowed and quieted as they approached the tree line where Zax was ready to pounce, but it didn't matter as he had already eyeballed every member of their squad. He checked on Kalare and she pointed at her eyes to signal she was doing the same. He grinned and showed her all five fingers to start their countdown.

The group was larger than expected. The entire Red Force approached their position as a single unit. The plan would still work as long as Zax and Kalare shot quickly and accurately. Zax identified the two cadets he intended to shoot first and hoped the second would be slow to react and remain standing after the shooting started. He hesitated for a moment as he spotted the cadet leading the squad. Zax considered dispatching him first, but decided to stick with the plan and instead set the squad leader to be hit third.

Zax kept his target in his sights as he counted down the final secs. He pulled the trigger and his first target collapsed as Zax swiveled his rifle to the second target. A second shot and a second Marine was on the ground. He pivoted his rifle to find the squad leader, but that target was a lost cause. The leader did not hit the deck like all of the other cadets, but instead took off at a full sprint past Zax's tree and into the jungle. Zax fired once, but the jungle was too thick beyond their position and his shot hit only branches.

Zax disregarded the leader and turned back to the where the rest of the squad had flattened out on the ground. As expected, they assumed their enemy was on the same vertical plane and vainly hoped getting low would protect them.

Trigger—shot—hit.

Trigger—shot—hit.

He aimed for extremities wherever he could out of a desire to not inflict too much pain on the cadets, but there were plenty of targets where center mass was his best option and he took it. Fortunately for the Marines, Zax was able to avoid any head shots.

What felt like a split sec later, there was no movement on the ground other than Marines who writhed in various levels of pain. Zax checked on Kalare and she pumped her fist in exultation. The sky display revealed that thirty secs had elapsed since they sprang their trap. It also showed who was still in the contest. The entire Red Force was marked as "dead" with the exception of the squad leader who ran away.

The display also identified which person from Blue Force was responsible for shooting each Red Force cadet. Kalare took down three more Marines than Zax had. That must have happened when he targeted the departing squad leader for too long.

Zax caught Kalare's eye and signaled to climb down. A few mins later he jumped the last couple meters down from the tree and ran over to meet her with another high five. "Great shooting! We got all of them but one. I wonder how his squad will feel about their leader bolting off into the jungle at the first sign of danger?"

Kalare grinned. "I bet he'll say he was trying to find a tactical advantage. Hearing myself say that, we should get moving in case that really was his plan. He might be circling back right now. Into the jungle!"

Kalare ran off in the direction where the rest of the Blue Force had originally gone. She moved at a quick pace, but slow enough she could still be deliberate about not making excessive noise or leaving a clear trail in her wake. Zax followed a few meters behind. After a half klick of distance, he caught up and tapped Kalare's shoulder to signal a stop.

"OK," he whispered, "what do you think we should do now?"

"I say we keep on this heading and try to join up with the rest of Blue Force." Kalare pointed at the overhead display. "They can see for themselves we took out almost the entire opposing team—that has to buy us some credibility with them, right?"

Zax was about to agree when they were startled by movement in the jungle. He pointed for Kalare to take cover behind one tree while he jumped behind another. He tensed as the noise got closer and closer only to relax a couple secs later when Jacen appeared and strolled towards their position. Zax stepped out from behind the tree and Jacen grinned and called out.

"We were shocked when we heard the shots so quickly after the contest started. We were twice as shocked when we saw the entire Red Force marked as hit by the two of you! Good work! We headed back to find you, but I managed to get hit by the one you guys didn't take out. He only grazed my arm, though, so it didn't hurt too much. The squad went to hunt him down and I offered to find you two."

Zax bursted with pride about impressing the Marine cadets. An hour ago they wanted nothing to do with him and Kalare, but now the leader of their group was congratulating them on their efforts. Since Jacen had been shot, Zax could also be proud about outlasting the self-appointed squad leader in the contest.

Jacen smiled at Zax, but then his expression changed. "Hey, wait a sec—I think there might be something wrong with your blaster. Let me check it out."

Zax's head still spun from the adrenalin of the battle so he didn't think twice about handing over his weapon to the Marine. Jacen peered at it for a sec, but then aimed it at Kalare's head and pulled the trigger before Zax could process what was happening. She fell to the ground and screamed in agony. Zax looked up into the barrel of his own blaster and Jacen grinned at him.

"You didn't think we would really let you get away with making any of us Marines look bad, did you?"

Jacen fired before Zax could say a word in reply. The pain was unimaginably intense, but only for the moment before he lost consciousness.

CHAPTER TWENTY-ONE

Weapon malfunction.

Zax drifted in and out of reality for the next eleven hours. The periods of blackness provided welcome relief from the excruciating pain that otherwise dominated his existence. His lone memory from the immediate period after Jacen shot him was a hazy one of being carried through the passageways on a stretcher and being dumped into his bunk to ride out the aftermath.

He gradually spent more and more time awake, though Zax often yearned for the unconsciousness to return and dull his agony. The pain eventually diminished, and by the time everyone else had settled into their bunks around him, Zax's discomfort receded enough that he found a fitful sleep.

The night went on forever, but reveille still arrived far too quickly the next morning. Zax allowed himself an extra few mins in his bunk to clear the mental cobwebs and then gingerly climbed down to make his way to the showers. He passed Kalare heading in the opposite direction and spoke before she got a word out.

"Don't even ask. I'll swing by your bunk in a few min, and we can walk to breakfast together. Hopefully, a hot shower and decent meal will get me out of this fog."

After Zax's shower, the two walked to the mess hall together in mutually-desired silence and found Mikedo waiting at the entrance. She held a couple of small bags and appeared solemn.

"Glad you two are up and about. You were both in pretty rough shape when they pulled you out of that sim room yesterday. I've been shot with stun rounds before and know it hurts, but I didn't get it in the head like both of you and can only imagine how much worse you're feeling. I've got bad news—you aren't allowed in the mess hall for another few hours."

Kalare all but screamed. "What! I thought that only applied to the losing team!"

"The Blue Force was the losing team. You two took out all of the Red Force except one, but that lone survivor returned the favor and eventually shot everyone on your team. Well, everyone except the two of you that is. You were both shot with Zax's blaster though I assume you were already aware of that fact."

Mikedo paused for a moment and looked back and forth at the two of them. "What exactly happened? How did your weapon shoot Kalare, Zax, and then shoot you in the face immediately afterwards?"

Zax had pondered this inevitable question all morning and didn't skip a beat before he answered.

"Weapon malfunction."

He desperately wanted to trust Mikedo with the truth but worried about what might happen if it ever got back to the Marines that he ratted out Jacen to an officer. Cyrus already wanted to kill him, and Zax didn't need a squadron of Marines hunting him down as well.

Mikedo turned to Kalare for a response and she echoed, "Weapon malfunction." Zax was grateful she either had reached a similar conclusion or chose to go along with him for different reasons.

Mikedo shook her head in disappointment. "Weapon malfunction, huh? I had a feeling I might hear something like that from the two of you. I don't like it, but I'm not surprised. I really wish you would give me the full story and trust me enough to know I wouldn't do anything to get you in hot water with your peers, but I don't blame you for not being there yet." She smiled warmly at both of them. "I promise you'll get there soon, but I won't force it on you right now.

"We need to get to combat training," Mikedo continued, "but before we go anywhere let me take a min to share something with both of you. I'm impressed with how you've handled yourselves these past few days. You jumped into a situation I think would've sent most cadets running back to their normal duties. I had serious doubts when the Flight Boss told me what he had in mind for the two of you, but I have to say I feel very differently now that I've had a chance to see you in action. We've still got a lot of challenges ahead of us, but I'm already certain I'll always be proud to have worked with the two of you. Really proud."

Zax had zero clue how to react to Mikedo's words. Never in his life had he heard anything as remotely positive and as clearly heartfelt from anyone in the Crew, much less an officer. He wanted to offer thanks but feared he might be overwhelmed with emotion if he tried to speak. Instead, he met Mikedo's eyes and nodded. Kalare amazingly appeared to be at a loss for words as well since she followed Zax's lead.

"I know you're both hungry, but I have to stick to the rules of the training contest and not allow you in the mess hall." Mikedo grinned and lifted up the bags she was holding. "The rules didn't mention anything about me bringing something *out* of the mess hall for you, though. You're going to have to eat as we walk because there's been some unrest in the civilian sector, and the Tubes are being rerouted and are running slower than usual. Enjoy!"

Zax was delighted to discover his bag contained his favorite breakfast sandwich along with the pastries he loved. Mikedo must have paid attention when she ate with them the other morning. He was curious about what kind of unrest could disrupt the Tube system and posed the question to Mikedo as he unwrapped his sandwich.

"It's not anything you need to worry about," she answered, "just civilians being civilians. If they don't have something legitimate to get upset about every once in a while, they get bored and just make stuff up instead. You need to focus on eating that delicious sandwich before I change my mind and take it back."

He gratefully wolfed everything down as they once again trekked through Marine Country. When they arrived at the dojo, Mikedo halted at the hatch and looked them both up and down. She smiled at Zax as she reached over and brushed off the front of his shirt.

"What's with all of these crumbs, Zax. You want to get me in trouble for giving you food? How is it you can be so talented in so many ways, and yet you can't manage to eat something without wearing half of it?"

Mikedo beamed and delivered her words with a lighthearted tone that made Zax blush. He managed to mumble a "Sorry" and "Thank you" in reply as she finished.

Both groups of cadets from their previous sessions were inside the dojo. At one end of the line, Jacen and his fellow Marines started pointing and laughing at Zax and Kalare as they entered. Cyrus stood at the other end among his group of Flight cadets and stared at Zax like a predator contemplating its prey. Sergeant Quentor acknowledged their entrance and addressed Mikedo.

"Good morning, ma'am. You're only three secs late today. That's not bad, but as usual, Flight is almost as good as the Marines without quite getting all the way there." This triggered a snigger from some of the Marines. The instructor flipped from smiling to rage in a heartbeat and directed his full fury at Jacen, who had been the loudest. "Why are you laughing in my dojo, cadet? Do you think you're at a comedy show? Am I here to amuse you? Front and center! I need a practice dummy to demonstrate today's first lesson and you just volunteered!"

Jacen walked towards the center of the sparring circle with his head held high. Zax guessed the Marines were conditioned to this sort of verbal abuse the same way Flight cadets were conditioned to near constant demerits, but he couldn't imagine facing the massive instructor's faux rage up close regardless.

"Cadet—punch me in the face."

Jacen must have known this was a setup for something painful, but he smiled and complied with Quentor's order. It was a blur as the instructor rotated his hips to avoid the right jab and grabbed Jacen's arm. The sergeant used their combined momentum to flip Jacen, who then flew three meters across the sparring circle and slammed onto the deck. He remained crumpled on his back.

The sergeant turned back and addressed all of the cadets. "Now I know that was too fast for all of your tiny brains to understand how I did it, but that's okay because Cadet Jacen has graciously offered to let me demonstrate as many times as I need to."

"Sergeant—if I may be so bold as to interrupt for a quick private word with you."

Mikedo approached the instructor. The difference in size between the petite Flight officer and the massive Marine instructor when they were side-by-side made it appear as if they came from entirely different species. After a min of quiet discussion with Mikedo, the instructor faced the class.

"Well, well, well. You cadets are in for a treat this morning. This Flight officer has shared with me how this particular combat move has always been one of her favorites. She's so confident in her abilities she has requested an opportunity to demonstrate them for all of you. Furthermore, she wants to make it even more interesting and has ordered me to accept a wager. She's bet one hundred chits she'll make Jacen fly even farther across the compartment than I just did."

This brought a quick laugh of disbelief from all of the cadets arrayed around the sparring circle—Flight and Marines alike. Even Zax with his firsthand knowledge of her abilities found it preposterous that Mikedo, who was two-thirds the mass of Jacen at most, would be able to throw the cadet farther than the immense instructor did.

Jacen had recovered while all of this went on and approached Mikedo with a sly grin on his face. He threw a jab at Mikedo similar to the first one he had directed at Quentor, but clearly put more force behind it. Mikedo pivoted and started to flip the Marine cadet in a near perfect duplication of the instructor's earlier move. Her hands were positioned in slightly different locations on Jacen's arm, though, and she held on for a split sec longer than the sergeant had. The crack of breaking bone echoed through the dojo and was followed by an agonized scream. Even though Jacen flew an amazing distance, it was not as far as Quentor had thrown him. He remained on the ground and writhed in agony, his arm clearly shattered based on the obscene angle at which his hand pointed.

Mikedo turned to the instructor and bowed. "You were right, Sergeant. I should have listened when you said there was no way I could throw that cadet farther than a big, strong Marine like yourself. I was trying so hard I messed up my form and it appears I may have hurt him. I will transfer the one hundred chits to your account. Please accept my apologies for interrupting your training and for breaking your Marine."

She walked over to Zax and Kalare and quietly addressed them both. "You two enjoy today's combat lesson. I have to spend the rest of the day filling out reports about this little mishap. I'm glad you both witnessed how *weapon malfunctions* and similar training accidents can even happen to officers sometimes." She winked and then strutted away with a bounce in her step.

Zax was stunned. Mikedo must have somehow known what transpired with Jacen and yet had allowed him and Kalare to think otherwise. She didn't force them to give her a full explanation which would have compelled her to handle the issue via official channels and brand Zax and Kalare as snitches. Instead, Mikedo dealt with Jacen directly and extracted commensurate payback for his betrayal with absolute deniability. Zax knew then he would do *anything* for that woman and follow her *anywhere*.

CHAPTER TWENTY-TWO

Look who we have here.

Nine additional days of training passed in a flash, and Zax awoke on the thirteenth day amazed at what he had learned and how his body had changed. His muscles were still sore every day, but they had increased in size and strength. He was particularly excited about how his performance had improved in the simulations with reduced oxygen and increased gravity. The first one left him gasping for mercy, but during the last contest under the same conditions he ran around like he'd been doing it for years.

Zax got dressed after a quick shower and headed to the mess hall to meet Kalare. They had made a habit of eating breakfast together to rehash whatever took place the day before. Kalare did 98% of the talking, but the new routine was comfortable regardless. He approached their regular table and found Mikedo was there as well.

"Good morning, Zax. I hope you don't mind me crashing your breakfast date like this." Mikedo grinned and continued. "I've got interesting news. Charlie Company is the Marine recon unit which scouts out new planets. They head down tomorrow for a final survey of the two alien settlements before the Captain decides how to proceed. The Flight Boss wants the two of you to go with them."

Zax and Kalare blurted out multiple questions simultaneously, but Mikedo held up her palm to quiet them. "Before you get too excited, be sure you understand that neither one of you is definitely going. There will be two final evaluations which a Marine sergeant will administer. He'll be the fourth member of our squad *if* we end up going down to the planet and has the final say on whether you've made enough progress to travel with Charlie Company. What do you think—are you ready to get off the Ship and visit a planet?"

Zax replied for both of them with absolute conviction. "We are!"

Mikedo smiled in return and said, "I agree. Let's get some breakfast. Zax—you should probably make it a big one. Whether you two go down to the surface or not, the Ship is inserting into orbit as part of the mission tomorrow. That means you've got an FTL Transit ahead of you and need to worry about keeping your stomach empty."

Zax was so thrilled about the idea of visiting a planet that not even the specter of nutripellets could dull his excitement. The only way Flight cadets generally got to step foot on solid ground was to get Culled. Since Zax avoided thinking about that scenario for himself, he had never given any thought to viewing an alien world with his own eyes. He was both exhilarated and terrified by the prospect, but ultimately concluded it must be a great sign of the progress they'd made towards earning the mentorship. If the Boss was going through the effort of sending them down to a planet with recon Marines, it must mean he was confident about choosing one of them.

A twinge of regret hit Zax when he remembered he could only win if Kalare lost, but he quickly set that aside and heeded Mikedo's advice. He grabbed extra portions of all his favorites, and Zax devoured the pile of food while Kalare dominated a conversation with Mikedo.

After eating, they proceeded to the weapons training simulator. It was set up as a jungle environment once again but was being configured by a man with white hair instead of the regular female instructor with her orange high and tight. The man turned to face them and Zax was shocked to identify him as the sergeant they had met their very first day in Marine Country. The sergeant whose coffee Zax had spilled. The sergeant with a smile of recognition which revealed he indeed never forgot a face.

"Look who we have here. Good morning, ma'am. It's going to be an *absolute pleasure* to work with your cadets today." The sergeant never glanced at Mikedo or Kalare, but instead smiled menacingly at Zax.

Mikedo's head swiveled back and forth between Zax and the sergeant while she blinked in confusion. "Wait a sec. Do you two know each other?"

"Yes, ma'am. I had the pleasure of meeting these cadets a couple of weeks ago. I was walking to a meeting when someone crashed into me and dumped my coffee. It caused me to be thirty-seven secs late to an important meeting with my commanding officer. You can only imagine what hilarity ensued."

"Well, well, well—isn't that a funny coincidence." Mikedo turned to Zax and Kalare. "Sergeant Bailee will work with the two of you to evaluate whether he feels you're fit to join the Marine's expedition to the planet tomorrow."

She faced Bailee. "I'm absolutely confident the sergeant will be a *complete professional* and any ill feelings he may have based on his prior interactions with either of you will not play *any role* in today's activities or his evaluation thereof."

"For you, ma'am, of course. I will treat these two the same way I would treat any Marine cadet." Bailee smiled at Zax, but the grin stopped short of the man's eyes and left Zax feeling cold. The sergeant turned to gesture at the simulation he had configured.

"Cadets—what you have before you is a live fire exercise with three different stages. You'll complete each of the stages as a team. The first two involve weapons you've already practiced with as a test of how well you've absorbed that instruction. The final stage involves a weapons system you've never seen before as a test of how well you're able to improvise and solve problems on the fly."

The sergeant closed his eyes and focused on his Plug. A moment later, Zax almost toppled over as an unexpected shift in gravity increased his perceived weight. The sergeant opened his eyes. "Of course, all of this will be done under the same gravitational and atmospheric conditions you would experience on the planet. I understand you've already trained with similar parameters so I assume this will not pose a problem. Your test starts now."

The lights in the room dimmed and a green arrow flashed on the ground. Zax and Kalare glanced at each other and then ran in the arrow's direction. As they moved, a series of arrows lit up ahead to guide them through the jungle. They ran until they reached a small clearing where two blasters leaned against a tree.

Kalare was running ahead of Zax so she grabbed the two weapons and tossed one back to him. No sooner had the blaster landed in his hands than the jungle directly behind Kalare exploded with incoming laser fire. It came from a pitch-black, humanoid shape Zax assumed was some type of bot. Without even thinking, Zax fired off two shots over Kalare's shoulder which hit their mark and halted the incoming fire.

"Holy crap, Zax! What are you doing? You almost hit me and those are live rounds!"

Before Zax could reply laser fire shot past his own shoulder from behind. He dropped to a knee and spun 180 degrees. He heard Kalare shoot and then smelled smoke. It came from his eyebrows which had been singed by the blaster shot Kalare sent millimeters in front of his face.

"OK—I take it back. We're even now." Kalare giggled as she scanned the jungle in front of them with her weapon. "That bot was freaky. Notice how their laser bolts are burning whatever they hit. When the sergeant said it was a live fire exercise I assumed he was talking about our rounds, but I guess the bots are shooting live ones too! I sure hope they aren't lethal, but I've got to think they would hurt at least as bad as getting shot by Jacen. Wait—there's another green arrow. Let's go!"

Zax followed as Kalare led the way through the jungle at a breakneck pace. The arrows guided them away from the first clearing towards a hill. As they approached, a bot once again poured laser fire into the jungle. Zax and Kalare dove behind a massive tree. Zax caught his breath and peeked around to identify the threat.

"Uh-oh. Those shots are coming at us from near the top of the hill. I don't think we can accurately reach them from this range with our blasters." A shot glanced off the edge of the trunk in front of his face and sent him scurrying behind the tree once again.

"Wait—look over there." Kalare pointed five meters away at a massive log which leaned against another tree. Propped up against it was a squad automatic weapon. "That SAW will have enough power to reach the shooter."

"I guess the new weapon means we've moved on to the second exercise." Zax paused for a moment to think before he continued. "I will fire from here to give you cover to reach the far side of that trunk. Once you're there, I want you to lay down some fire to let me get there too."

After Kalare's assent, Zax spun around the opposite side of the tree and let loose with non-stop blaster fire. She took off on his first shot and by the time the bot reacted to her movements and reoriented its weapon, Kalare had dived behind the fallen log. She peeked over it and raised her hand to countdown from five.

Zax knew he would have to move faster than Kalare if he was to make it to the fallen tree. The bot on the hilltop would already be pointing its laser weapon in that direction and would react much faster to his movement as a result.

Kalare's countdown hit zero and Zax sprinted towards the tree. Kalare didn't shoot from behind cover as he had done. She instead popped into full view and yelled while firing like crazy. Her gambit caused enough confusion to create a lull in the fire which allowed Zax to reach the fallen tree. They fell behind the log together as a hail of incoming bolts sailed above it and exploded in the brush directly behind them.

"What was all that jumping around about? You trying to get yourself shot?"

Kalare grinned maniacally. "What are you complaining about? You got here in one piece, didn't you? I knew the bot expected you to do the same thing I'd done, so I figured I needed to create a little misdirection. Here—help me get this SAW set up so we can start shooting back more effectively."

"No—that isn't going to work. Think about it. The SAW is a lot more powerful than our rifles, but the bot has the high ground on us. You can also bet it's shooting from behind cover that's at least as good as ours. I've got an idea though." Zax pointed to the tree next to them. "If I can get near the top of that tree, then I'll have the angle for a great shot."

Kalare shook her head. "No, it has to be me, not you. I was a way better shot with the SAW during training than you were. Whoever is up there will only be able to get off a couple shots before the bot reacts. If we don't hit it immediately, the bot will light up that tree and whoever's up there will be an easy target."

"I agree you're the better shot, but there's no way you can climb and carry the SAW. You could barely lift it the other day at regular gravity. How're you going to get it up the tree when it weighs even more now?"

Kalare appeared stumped and stared blankly at their blasters for a few moments. "Hold on! Let's get the straps off our weapons. We can use them to create a harness which will let me carry the SAW!" Zax nodded in agreement and a few mins later Kalare was poised to scale the tree with the SAW strapped to her back.

"You have to keep the bot engaged until I get high enough. I've got a couple small rocks in my pocket I'll use to get your attention once I'm in position. When I give you the signal, I need you to do something super crazy to distract the bot and give me enough time to hit it."

She turned to climb but hesitated. "You probably don't want to be down here when I start firing. If I miss, that bot is going to nail me good and my body will come crashing down. No sense both of us winding up in the medbay. Or dead."

Zax choked up as he considered the magnitude of the risk Kalare took by going up the tree. He gave her a thumbs up and replied with a thick voice, "I guarantee you're going to take it out with your first shot. Good luck."

Kalare worked her way up the tree and Zax developed his plan. He worried most about tricking the bot into believing there were still two of them actively returning its fire. Otherwise, it might get suspicious and seek out a second target. If the bot caught a glimpse of Kalare making her way up the tree, she would be picked off immediately.

Zax popped up from behind the log, fired off a barrage of shots, and ducked down. He then scrambled along the ground until he reached the tree. He peeked his blaster around the trunk and started shooting again. He repeated similar patterns of running between widely-spaced positions and shooting until his stamina started to fade. All of the concentrated activity with both increased gravity and decreased oxygen took a heavy toll, even after all of their training.

Zax's stress about maintaining the distraction was finally interrupted by the sharp pain of a rock bouncing off his cheek. He looked up and Kalare wore a contrite expression in acknowledgement of having hit him in the face. She had located a roost near the top of the tree and the SAW was positioned for her shot. Kalare flashed five fingers and started a countdown.

When the five count was up, Zax ran out from behind the log back towards the original tree where they had first sought cover. He yelled "Wait up!" in the desperate hope of drawing the bot's attention far away from the tree where Kalare was perched. Zax smelled ozone when a laser bolt came within centimeters of his face, but then three shots from the SAW were followed by a loud cheer from Kalare.

A moment later Kalare had the SAW strapped to her back and she grinned over her shoulder as she made her way down. "Your guarantee was wrong about one shot, but I'm sure happy I hit it with my third. Wait—there's an arrow over there."

Sure enough, a green arrow pointed the way towards their third and final challenge. Zax waited until Kalare was almost on the ground and then ran ahead. He had reached the point where a second arrow lit up when all of a sudden it changed from green to red. He turned and saw Kalare had reached the ground and was following behind him.

"Wait—I think there's a problem. Back up to the tree again." When Kalare did so, the arrow in front of Zax switched back to green. "OK, now walk towards me again." Immediately the arrow turned red.

"Hmmm—maybe I'm not supposed to keep the SAW." Kalare backed up and dropped the large weapon. She walked towards Zax and this time the arrow remained green and they both sprinted ahead. "Sure would have been nice to have known that *before* I lugged it all the way down the tree!"

They chased the green arrows for a few mins until they reached the edge of the jungle. They stopped to catch their breath and surveyed the situation. Arrayed before them was an expanse of sand dunes with a large rectangular object perched upon a dune fifty meters away.

"I don't like this." Zax sucked in a deep breath. "The arrows are clearly leading us to that object, but the idea of running across all of that open terrain blows."

Kalare nodded in agreement. "Yep. I'm guessing as soon as we get out of this jungle we're going to get blasted. It doesn't seem like we have any choice, though. I just wish the bots had laser eyes instead of rifles. At least that would be a much cooler way of getting shot."

Zax couldn't help but smile. "OK—are you ready? Go!"

A hail of laser fire erupted once they were out in the open. They scrambled behind the object without being hurt just as the rate of fire increased. Zax peeked out and saw his last footprint had been hit. The bolt had fused the sand into glass which still smoldered. "Holy crap! If those lasers can melt sand, I really don't think we want to find out what they'll do if they hit skin. What is this thing we're hiding behind?"

Kalare and Zax stood behind a smooth, black, rectangular block. It was three meters tall by two meters deep by ten meters wide. It must have been made of some pretty strong material because a steady rain of laser fire slammed into the side which faced the jungle without any visible effect. The sand had collected in drifts all around the object as if there had been a windstorm. A circular panel, on the verge of being buried by sand, glowed red near one edge of the block. Kalare shrugged her shoulders at Zax. He grinned as the sight of the circle triggered his recognition.

"I know what this is! I read about it in that weapons manual you showed me. It's a mecha. This is how they get shipped to the battlefield so they can be packed into troop carriers as efficiently as possible."

Kalare pounced without waiting for further explanation and slammed her palm against the red circle. "I bet this will activate it somehow!" The panel flashed from red to yellow and back, but nothing else happened.

"No, wait—there are supposed to be two control panels."

She gaped at him in disbelief. "Huh? I left you alone with my slate for ninety secs. How do you remember that?"

Zax tapped the side of his head. "Eidetic memory. I can recall almost any image after seeing it for only a few secs. One of these caught my eye in the manual that morning." He studied the block for a moment. The second control panel must be covered by a drift! He flung sand away and revealed its circular edge. "I think I've found it—help me clear this sand!"

Their furious digging uncovered a second panel identical to the first. Zax placed his palm upon the circle. "Go activate the other one."

Kalare ran back to the opposite end of the block and placed her palm against the first circle. As she did so, both of the panels flashed green and a soft *whirring* emanated from within the block.

"Back away and find some cover!"

Zax flopped next to Kalare in a sand depression five meters behind the block. It transformed similarly to the double-arm pack Sergeant Quentor wore their first day of training. Instead of becoming a simple pair of arms, the block unfolded into a massive battle robot with a humanoid form.

The mecha posed before them crouched on one knee once it completed its metamorphosis. Two hatches were visible for the Crew—one for the WSO was located in the left leg and the other for the pilot was in the torso. The battle robot was positioned so Zax and Kalare were mostly shielded from incoming rounds, but the intensity of the laser fire had increased and bolts peppered the sand around them.

"We better get inside before we get hit. Which one of us is going to pilot it?"

She phrased it as a question, but the desperate excitement in Kalare's voice over the prospect of piloting a fifteen-meter tall mecha was obvious. "You should do it," he said. "We'd still just be cowering behind it if you hadn't brought your weapons manual to breakfast that time."

Kalare sprang up without a further word. The mecha's pose in its deactivated state allowed the pilot to climb on its knee, and Kalare used it to reach the torso hatch. Zax followed and accessed the WSO cockpit in the calf.

Zax marveled at the relative spaciousness of the interior once he squeezed his way through the hatch. He strapped into his harness and the workstation for the Weapons System Officer came alive with flashing lights and flickering displays. The threat board was most pressing as it revealed how the incoming laser fire originated from not one, but three different bots which were widely dispersed at the jungle's edge. Zax grabbed a subvoc unit hanging next to his seat just as Kalare's voice flooded it.

"Holy crap this is amazing! I think I've figured out how to get all strapped into the controls."

"OK, I'm good too." Zax checked the threat board again. "There's no way those three bots are any match for this mecha so this should be easy. I've got a firing solution set up for each arm cannon. Once you're ready, stand up and rotate and we'll take out two of them at once."

Kalare brought the mecha to life and spun it around to face the aggressors. She exclaimed "Suck it!" as she pulled the triggers and the massive cannons showered the bots with ordnance. Once the first two targets were pulverized, the third bot ran deeper into the jungle and Zax called out to Kalare.

"Number three is trying to get away. Follow him!"

Kalare set the mecha off into the tress at a gallop. The WSO cockpit was stabilized so Zax did not feel any motion, but his external display revealed how they advanced at a furious clip and left a broad swath of flattened jungle in their wake. The mecha narrowed the gap and was almost within cannon range of the fleeing bot. Then they entered a clearing where the lack of trees in their path would allow them to accelerate and get close enough to fire.

"Kalare—speed up! We can get him!"

The words had barely left Zax's lips when a massive explosion rang in his ears and the displays went dark. Simultaneously, the mecha's stabilization system failed and he suffered every jolt and crash as they tumbled across the ground until they impacted with something solid. The violent thrashing knocked Zax dizzy for a few secs until he regained his senses. Kalare screamed over the subvoc.

"I've lost all controls, Zax! I've got no visuals and can't get the mecha to move! Zax? Can you hear me? Can you see anything out there? Zax?"

Sergeant Bailee's voice cut in over the subvoc. "Cadets—the exercise is complete. Please exit the mecha and follow the arrows out of the simulation. Eat some lunch and meet us back in the combat dojo in 117 mins. Bailee out."

Zax stumbled out of his hatch and shielded his eyes against the lights which had returned to daytime brightness. Once his eyes adjusted, he surveyed the wreckage and deduced what had transpired.

The mecha's trail through the jungle was obvious thanks to the crushed brush and downed trees it left behind. Equally obvious was the massive hole in the ground where they must have triggered a land mine. The explosion sent them flying into a massive tree where the mecha's crushed hull had come to rest. The clearing was a trap and they ran into it at full speed.

Kalare clambered out of the pilot hatch and Zax turned to check her condition. Her uniform was shredded and blood oozed from a scratch on her forehead, but she beamed from ear to ear. "That was awesome! Let's do it again!"

CHAPTER TWENTY-THREE

You may go first.

Zax fumed about how time seemed to crawl during lunch. Part of the reason was the lack of any real food to help distract him since he had followed Mikedo's advice and ate only nutripellets. Bleh. His body sat across from Kalare and her (overflowing) tray of food, but his mind could process nothing except dreams of first visiting the planet and then being mentored by the Flight Boss. These visions were interspersed with worries about whether getting blown up at the end of the last exercise might disqualify him from reaching those goals. Kalare's excited retelling of their mecha adventure may as well have been running on a vidscreen clear across the room.

"Zax! Are you listening to me?"

Zax snapped back to attention at the sound of his name. "I'm sorry, but truth be told I wasn't." He smiled sheepishly. "It's hard to hear over my grumbling stomach."

"That's OK. I understand. Though, actually, I don't. I wouldn't survive if I had to eat those dry, tasteless nutripellets as often as you do. I'm sure you're sitting there getting super jealous about all of the yummy stuff on my plate."

Zax sighed at her reminder, but Kalare did not notice as she continued.

"Anyway, what was I saying? You weren't listening to me and apparently I wasn't either. Oh wait—I got it! I said that Sergeant Bailee and Mikedo just walked out of the mess hall. We should probably do the same."

Kalare dropped her tray off at the disposal station and Zax tossed his forlorn nutripellet wrappers into a recycler. They trekked once more across Marine Country and reached their destination exactly on time. The dojo was only half full as the Marines appeared to be off doing something else. The group of Culled cadets from Flight stood around the sparring circle. Sergeant Bailee and Mikedo stood off to the side.

Sergeant Quentor turned to them with a grin. "Well done, cadets. Perfectly punctual when you're on your own reveals that Lieutenant Mikedo is the bad influence who makes you late. I should have known." He turned to the rest of the group. "As for the rest of you Flight pukes, I need your help today. I'm stuck with all of you for another three days of training, but these two are finishing up today. I've been asked to have each of them spar against a few of you. Who wants to be the first to face off against Cadet Zax?"

A few of the cadets raised their hands, but none more eagerly than Cyrus. Of course, that was who Quentor picked. Zax gulped in nervous anticipation, but Kalare stepped forward before he was able to do so.

"Sergeant—I request to show what I can do first!"

"Well, well, well—look at you, Cadet Kalare. Initiative. I didn't know you had it in you. Far be it from me to get in the way of this new eagerness. You may go first."

Zax was flooded with conflicting emotions and confusing questions. He was relieved to avoid a match with Cyrus but found himself worried about Kalare's motives. If it was anyone else he would have been certain they were working an angle for a Leaderboard edge, but Kalare always said she didn't care about that sort of thing. Right?

But what if she wasn't being truthful? Kalare said she didn't want the Flight Boss's offer, but maybe she really felt otherwise. He thought back to that morning's evaluation exercise and considered how eager she had been to take the lead role. She'd not only been insistent about climbing the tree and shooting the bot with the SAW but also made it clear she wanted to pilot the mecha. And now here she was volunteering to spar first. Maybe she had actually been playing him all of this time and was now sweeping in at the last min to grab the spotlight and win the mentorship. He couldn't imagine it was true, but couldn't help himself from worrying otherwise.

Kalare and Cyrus donned their pads and faced off across the sparring circle. Quentor signaled for the match to start. Kalare stood taller than Zax, but she was dwarfed by Cyrus. She had the edge in speed, but the older boy's reach kept her at bay and allowed him to avoid many of her quick blows.

After a min of ineffective jabs, Kalare surprised Cyrus with a flying scissor kick which connected with his midsection and left him doubled over. She attempted to follow up with a toe kick to the face, but his hand darted out at the last possible moment to deflect her foot and then grab her ankle. His other hand snatched her knee and a sec later Kalare swung in a tall arc which ended with her head crashing violently onto the deck. From the way her body crumbled it was obvious she was unconscious. Quentor called "Halt!" and turned to confer with Mikedo and Bailee.

When the instructor turned away, Cyrus stared at Zax with a mischievous smile. He grabbed Kalare's foot and lifted her leg off the deck. He then raised his foot to stomp his heel and deliver a crippling blow to the back of Kalare's knee.

Without thinking Zax screamed "Stop!" and charged across the sparring circle. He was not quick enough to prevent the initial blow and instead watched Kalare's leg twist grotesquely under the force of Cyrus's kick. He was fast enough, however, to catch the older cadet by surprise. Zax's foot reached its intended target—Cyrus's testicles—with full force. The air left Cyrus's mouth with a *whoosh* and he dropped to the deck in the fetal position. Zax cocked his leg for a follow-up kick to the face and then both of his feet left the deck. Quentor had materialized behind him and lifted Zax by the back of his shirt a meter into the air with one arm.

"What do you two *think* you are doing in *my* dojo!" The instructor bellowed as he hurled Zax to the ground. Quentor first towered over Cyrus. "Cadet—you clearly heard me halt the match. What would possess you to keep beating an unconscious classmate!" The instructor punctuated his sentence with a vicious kick to Cyrus' belly. He then spun around and yanked Zax's torso up off the deck by the front of his shirt. "And you—did someone steal my sergeant's stripes and give them to you when I wasn't looking? What makes you think you get to be in charge of punishing this cheating scumbag?"

The enraged Marine had cocked his arm back while he yelled at Zax and appeared ready to smash his face. Zax wore a defiant glare but internally had wished a poignant farewell to his teeth. Mikedo arrived and grabbed the instructor's arm.

"Stand down, Sergeant. Remember our deal. I get to dole out any punishment for my cadets. Let me get them both out of your dojo, and you and I can discuss this later." She glanced at Zax. "Get out of here!

I've already called the medics for Kalare. Meet me in the medbay in ninety mins."

CHAPTER TWENTY-FOUR

I heard everything.

Zax had no idea what to do with himself while he waited. His world currently revolved around the mentorship contest, and he didn't have any other duties to attend to. He opened up some reading on his slate but failed to get more than a few sentences in before his thoughts were consumed by the image of Kalare's horrifically twisted leg. He put the device away and paced the Ship instead.

Ninety mins later Zax walked into the medbay waiting room. It was populated by a half dozen morose cadets who awaited their turn with the medics. Zax asked for Kalare's location at the front desk, but a tap on the shoulder made him turn and discover Sergeant Bailee.

"She's in the fourth compartment on the right. I need a min before you visit her, though. Let's sit down over here." The sergeant steered Zax towards a couple unoccupied chairs and spoke once they were seated.

"I didn't get a chance to formally evaluate you back in the dojo, but I'm signing off on you heading out with the recon mission anyways. There are three reasons why I'm willing to do this. First is the way you performed during the live fire exercise this morning. I've seen some great stuff from some amazing Marines in that simulator over the years, but I never would have imagined seeing such good work done by a couple of Flight pukes who've only been training for two weeks. The results were far from perfect, but you were both fearless and creative and that earns you a ton of points in my book.

"The second reason I'm willing to clear you for the mission is the way you jumped into the fray with that older cadet after he hurt Kalare." The sergeant stared at Zax. "You possess something which can't be taught and that is the instinct to selflessly protect your squad-mates even in the face of overwhelming odds. I was particularly impressed by the way you didn't so much as flinch when Quentor was prepared to rearrange your face."

The sergeant paused and took a deep breath before continuing. "The last reason why I'm willing to risk my reputation and allow you to deploy with my fellow Marines is because Mikedo wants me to. I can count on one hand the people in the Flight Corps who

I trust and respect without reservation, and she's at the very top of that list. Pay close attention to her when you two are down on the surface. She'll make sure you don't do anything stupid to get yourself or any of the Marines with you hurt."

"Excuse me, Sergeant, but I'm confused. I thought you were going to be part of our squad and head down there with us?"

"My only role for this mission was to be a second experienced person in the squad so you and Kalare could each have your own individual babysitter down there. She's not going, so I'm not needed."

The Marine sergeant stood to leave. "I've got to get to a meeting, but Mikedo's down in Kalare's room and will explain the situation fully. You better do a good job on this mission, cadet. If I hear you screwed up from any of my Marines, then I just might have to deliver that beatdown you still have coming from when we met over coffee."

Bailee's mouth betrayed the slightest hint of a smile, but the man turned and walked away before Zax could determine whether it was real or only his imagination. Zax remained frozen in his seat. He knew he needed to get to Kalare's room and talk to Mikedo, but the full impact of what the sergeant shared was still sinking in.

Zax's guilt about his lack of sadness for Kalare's predicament was dwarfed by how thrilled he was at the realization there was no longer any competition. He stood at the precipice of earning a mentorship with the

Flight Boss! Zax only needed to get down to the planet and back without any mistakes, and his career would set off on an amazing trajectory. He sprang out of his seat and practically bounced down the passageway to Kalare's compartment.

Kalare's appearance washed away Zax's good cheer and threatened to drown him in remorse. She was unconscious and connected to a machine which breathed for her. Her leg was immobilized within a massive aerogel protective cast. Mikedo sat in a chair next to the bed and spoke to Zax as he entered.

"It's not as bad as it looks. They'll wake her up in a couple of mins. Cyrus snapped all the tendons and ligaments when he wrenched her knee, but the surgery went well. She's going to be in here with the cast on for a couple of days and then have a day or two of rehab, but she'll be as good as new after that. The bad news is she is obviously not going to join us on the mission tomorrow. It's a real shame because you two have exhibited such amazing teamwork, I had advised the Boss to stop the contest and just mentor both of you."

Zax's jaw dropped at the news that had been a potential outcome. Mikedo let the notion sink in for a few moments before she continued. "I caught something back in the dojo I need to ask you about. Cyrus seemed abnormally excited when Quentor asked for volunteers to spar with you. When he stomped on Kalare's leg, he stared at you and smirked the whole time. Is there something going on between you two?"

Zax almost answered "no" reflexively, but paused instead for a deep breath. He gazed first at Mikedo and then to Kalare lying in the bed and then back to Mikedo. The pure compassion emanating from the lieutenant finally broke his resolve, and Zax told her everything. The years of bullying from Aleron, the way Cyrus treated him up to and including the day of the panorama breach, the attack by Aleron in the passageway with its death threat, how it was Cyrus who tripped him that first day in Marine Country. Everything. When he was done, Zax felt as if a massive weight had been lifted from his shoulders. He sat in silence for a few mins while Mikedo digested what he had shared.

"Hmmm—one question for you, Zax. Did Kalare know about any of this?"

"No, she didn't. She was stunned unconscious when Aleron attacked us in the passageway, and I lied when she asked if I knew who did it. We were just getting to know each other at that point, and I didn't feel like talking to her about any of it. You know how she gets with her non-stop chatter. I'm used to it now, but two weeks ago she was still annoying me to death. I was afraid if I told her about any of this she might never shut up about it.

"Besides," he added, "what could she do? I've dealt with Aleron and the rest of his buddies for years. What difference would one more bully make? Even if Cyrus talked about killing me, I'm sure it was just stupid bluster anyways."

Zax's voice broke during his last sentence and he stopped to take a few deep breaths and compose himself. It was bad enough he had shared all of this stuff with Mikedo, but he refused to lose control and start blubbering in front of the officer. Her expression suggested she might cry herself for some reason as she stared at him and spoke.

"Wow, Zax. I'm really sorry to hear all of this. You've been carrying an awfully big load for someone your age, particularly since you're dealing with all of it on your own. Let me tell you something. I know what it's like to be so talented at such a young age. I know what it's like to feel so capable and independent you never want to admit weakness or ask for help. I'm here to tell you that's not a great way to go through life."

Mikedo's gaze never wavered as she spoke. Zax felt like she peered directly into his core, and he was shocked to welcome the deep connection. "Showing vulnerability will not make you more vulnerable. Admitting weakness is actually a sign of great strength. People will always have to respect your talent and abilities even if they choose to hide it behind jealousy and bullying. What will get them to truly respect and love you as a person, however, is when you allow them to see you're human just like they are."

Mikedo reached out and held his hand. "You need to trust some folks, Zax. There are people out there who want to be your friend and help if you will only let them inside. Two of them are sitting here in this room. I know it's almost impossible to think about all of this when you've spent the last ten years obsessing about the Leaderboard and seeing life as a zero sum game, but I'm telling you this from hard fought, firsthand experience. Your native skills and talent have already made you great. If you can manage to crack open that hard shell a bit and let some of your humanity seep out, you have a chance to be exceptional."

Tears welled up behind Zax's eyes, but they receded when the door opened behind him and the spell was broken. Mikedo stood to leave. "Here's the medic to wake Kalare. I've got to get going anyway to finish prepping for tomorrow. I'm glad you finally shared this with me, Zax. You don't have to worry about Cyrus right now. He'll be occupied with Quentor and likely begging for death between now and the time we leave for the planet. When we get back, let's you and me sit down and figure out how you can be sure to avoid him until he's dumped at Landfall.

"One last thing—I spoke with Kalare before the surgery, so she already knows the bad news she isn't going. Stay here and visit with her for a while, and then meet me at 1800 in the same training room where we had our first meeting. We're getting a mission briefing along with the officers and squad leaders from the Marine recon unit."

Mikedo left the room and Zax took advantage of the opportunity to close his eyes and focus on regaining his composure. Mikedo's words had nailed him straight between the eyes, but Zax willed away the big feelings they triggered to avoid breaking down in front of a complete stranger.

The medic gave Kalare an injection and removed her breathing mask. The shot took effect and she woke a few moments later. Once he had spoken with Kalare and verified she was well, the medic left the room with a promise to check on her again soon.

Zax and Kalare shared a min of awkward silence before he broke the ice.

"Does it hurt?"

"Not at all. I don't even feel like I have a lower leg right now. Can't feel a thing below my thigh."

"That's good. I'm very sorry you aren't going down to the planet with us tomorrow." Zax paused for a moment. "I would've never imagined saying this two weeks ago, but I've loved going through all of this training with you. You're absolutely crazy and I'm guessing that hanging around with you will get me in serious trouble someday, but we make a great team. I'll miss having you by my side when I'm down there with all of those insane Marines."

Kalare beamed up at him. The pain meds had zero effect on the infectious twinkle in her eyes. "Thanks, Zax. It really means a lot to hear that from you. You know I've been indifferent to this whole mentorship thing all along, so when I had the chance to shield you from Cyrus I figured it would be a good idea. I was certain he wouldn't be stupid enough to try and kill you in front of everyone, but I knew he wouldn't be afraid to put an excessive hurt on you."

Zax stared wide-eyed at Kalare for a sec before he could get any words out. "Wait—what? You're aware Cyrus wants to kill me?"

"You're not the only one who's good at lying and keeping secrets there, mister." Kalare giggled. "I was actually awake that day in the passageway when Aleron attacked us. I heard everything. For some reason the instructor who trained Epsilon on the stunstik didn't like me very much, so she used me as her practice dummy every time we had class. I experienced the weapon so much I became immune to the effect of all but its highest setting. The initial jolt still smarts, but it doesn't knock me unconscious the way it does all you puny mortals.

"When Aleron stunned me," Kalare continued, "I figured it would be a good idea to stay down and sort out what was going on. I wouldn't have let him hurt you and had planned to tell you all about it, but when you attempted to hide the situation from me, I decided to let the whole thing slide."

Zax's gears spun for a min while Kalare laughed again at how dumbfounded he was. Finally, he recovered enough to put all the pieces together. "You knew Cyrus wanted to kill me when you volunteered to take my place and go first in the sparring test? You had to know he would probably want to hurt you too after that busted nose you gave him!"

"Yeah, but like I said, I don't really care about what happens with all of this mentorship crap. I know you do. I would have hated to see you get injured and lose out on your chance to work with the Flight Boss. This training has been a blast—I got to drive a mecha! I'm starting to think I might just want to get a job like Mikedo's and work with the Marines. Hell, maybe I'll drop out of Flight altogether and join the Marines! I owe you big time for making it all possible with the way you handled that breach. The least I could do was make sure that idiot Cyrus didn't ruin things for you."

The waves of emotion which had roiled Zax since the dojo finally overwhelmed him. Hot tears bursting with guilt came pouring out in giant, gasping sobs. Zax was ashamed about so much—his worries that Kalare was trying to steal the opportunity by jumping ahead of him to spar Cyrus, his excitement about winning the mentorship rather than compassion for someone who was his only friend on the Ship.

Zax was then forced to sit and listen to Kalare thank *him* when she had knowingly made the choice to risk injury protecting him from Cyrus. He wanted to say so much, he wanted to apologize, he wanted to thank her, but all he could do was bury his head in his hands and cry.

The medic returned a min later. He stopped short for a moment while he evaluated the scene but then spoke softly. "I'm sorry to interrupt, cadet, but I have to ask you to leave. The surgeon will be coming through and he needs to run a scan on Kalare's knee to make sure everything is knitting back together the way it should."

Zax rose and choked back a couple last sobs. He wiped his sleeve across his face and it came back streaked with tears and snot. He smiled at Kalare and managed to say "thank you" without the tears starting again.

"Good luck down there, Zax. You're going to do great! Make sure you find me first thing when you get back to tell me about all of the cool stuff you see. I hope you don't run into any alien robots with laser eyes!"

CHAPTER TWENTY-FIVE

Pretty cool!

Zax retreated to the Zeta berth. Since the other cadets were out performing their official duties, he had the entire compartment to himself and was able to nap (fifty demerits). A few hours later he woke with a clear head, soaked in his second shower of the day (twenty demerits), and returned to Marine Country for the mission briefing.

Zax entered the training compartment and was startled when he came face to face with an ant. Unlike the small Earth insects Zax had seen in the various Ship biomes, this one stood over two meters tall and was perched upright on its four hindmost legs. The dark green body was laced with brown stripes and the two forelegs grasped a digging implement with three-fingered hands. Its head was studded with tiny eyeballs which extended from the tip of its mandibles to the back of its skull and covered every point in between.

Mikedo smiled at Zax's surprise as she stood and gestured for him to take a seat next to her. A group of Marine officers and sergeants were also arrayed around the compartment. They all sat ramrod straight with their eyes focused forwards. At the very back sat Marine major who stared at his slate with a severe expression.

A Flight lieutenant, a man whose shaggy hair and soft midsection gave him away as having some sort of cushy desk job, stood at the instructor's table and started to speak as Zax sat down. "My name is Lieutenant Nineem and I'm here from the exobiology unit to brief you on the planet you will visit tomorrow, its flora and fauna, and its current inhabitants—a fine specimen of which is being projected here. The image of this particular alien was captured just the other day by one of our drones, but there are plenty more like it in the Ship's archives from previous Landfalls.

"These creatures are similar in many ways to the Earth insects which inhabit our biomes. We assume these aliens must be highly advanced given how many times we've come across them on planets spread far across the universe, but we've never seen any of their technology. Every encounter to date has been with a small planet-bound colony which presented as a simple, agrarian culture with zero technology except simple tools like the shovel this guy is holding.

"The Ship's records reveal we've seen two distinct body types and corresponding modes of behavior for these aliens. This particular body type is what we call a worker. We've isolated a single individual for this image, but it was in a line of almost five hundred identical creatures." The picture zoomed out and revealed row upon row of the insects marching in lockstep. "All of our records about these workers describe how they ignore humans whenever we are present. We assume they can see us given how many eyes they've got, but any one of them would allow you to walk right up and touch it without so much as flinching or interrupting its activity."

The image shifted and the first alien was replaced by one which struck Zax as being even freakier. It stood more than four meters tall with the same dark green base color, but the giant bug had stripes colored vibrant red rather than brown. Instead of resting on its four hind legs, this ant stood on only two and held a bladed weapon of some sort in each of its four foremost limbs. Nineem spoke again.

"This image shows an alien with the warrior body type. It's from the archives, not our current drone surveillance, because we've not yet observed any warriors on this planet. We've got a few guesses as to why there are no warriors with this colony, but the bottom line is we don't know. I realize some of you may be familiar with these warriors from previous missions, but I want to be certain you're all aware of the threat they represent."

The image of the warrior zoomed out and shifted perspective until its source became clear. It was footage from a Marine who wore a helmet cam and swiveled back and forth between the alien and three squad-mates. The four Marines stood quite a distance away from the warrior and talked to each other about what they should do about the lone creature which had materialized in front of them. The camera jerked and three of the weapon shafts the alien had been holding suddenly sprouted out of the bodies of the Marine's three squad-mates. Two of them were in heads and one in a chest. The view of the helmet cam moved first to the blade protruding from the wearer's chest and then back over her shoulder. The alien warrior used all six limbs and scurried towards the Marine at a disturbingly fast pace. She crumbled to the ground and the video faded to black

"Those blades were thrown with extreme accuracy and penetrated Marine armor from a distance of over 100 meters. The two head shots landed exactly between the eyes and the two body shots were dead center through the heart. Who needs a blaster, I suppose, if you can throw a blade equally as far with just as much killing power.

"We've talked about the aliens, but let's take a moment to zoom out." Nineem closed his eyes and used his Plug to replace the video with an image of the planet which filled the space above their heads. Zax was excited to view it for the first time. From space, it was a dark blue sphere composed almost entirely of water.

There were two small landmasses visible, the larger of which had two spots marked on it which must represent the settlements Zax had heard the scout pilot refer to. Nineem continued.

"As you're no doubt aware, our initial reconnaissance has confirmed the planet is fit for human habitation. The atmosphere has slightly less oxygen than what we are used to, but it won't require the use of any supplemental breathers and your body will get used to it pretty quickly. The bigger issue is that its gravity is about 30% greater than what we're accustomed to onboard the Ship. This value approaches the upper range of what we consider acceptable when we are choosing a planet to colonize but is still within the boundaries. You've already trained in similar conditions so I imagine none of this should pose a significant problem for you."

Lieutenant Nineem closed his eyes again and a new group of images displayed around the room. Each was a short vid loop which illustrated a different creature in action. "Representative samples of the lifeforms present on this planet are now being projected. Other than our ant friends, all of the lifeforms have four limbs. Even the flying creatures have four wings, all four of which can be used as legs when the creature is on the ground or perched in a tree.

"Speaking of the trees," the lieutenant perked up, "they're definitely the most fascinating feature about this planet." The lieutenant pointed at the projection of the planet which had shrunk but remained displayed. "As you can see, both of this planet's landmasses are clustered around its equator and, therefore, are almost exclusively covered with the same dense jungle biome. All of the creatures I've shown you are herbivores which feed on the grasses and other smaller vegetation. We were confused at first about how few of the grazing creatures were present. It seemed odd when you considered the lushness of the environment, but was absolutely shocking given we initially believed there were no predators. Then, one of our drones captured a vid which solved the riddle."

All of the images disappeared with the exception of a small herbivore which nibbled on grasses. The jungle was dense and its most prominent features were the leaves which hung from the branches of the trees. The leaves varied in size significantly with some being a meter in diameter while others were closer to five.

The creature started to walk and then wobbled. When it lost its footing, the animal's body brushed up against one of the larger tree leaves. In an instant, the leaf sprang into action and enveloped the beast. The tree limb lifted the thrashing animal off the ground where it was then captured by an even larger leaf on a higher limb which had lowered down to meet the first. The transfer process from leaf to leaf was repeated until the animal was deposited into a massive leaf near the top. The beast thrashed within the final leaf for another min until its movements became less and less pronounced and then ultimately stopped.

"It's so interesting we've found a planet with no apparent predator animals, but which is blanketed with carnivorous trees. Pretty cool!" The exobiologist practically squealed like a little kid and grinned from ear to ear.

"It's great how you think it's all so very *interesting*, Lieutenant." The Marine major did not raise his head from his slate as he spoke. "Perhaps you would like to come on down as part of our recon mission tomorrow. Or even better, shall I put your name in as a volunteer to stay behind when we make Landfall? I'm sure our new colonists would appreciate your enthusiasm as they figure out how to spend the rest of their lives coexisting with such *cool* carnivorous trees."

Many of the Marines laughed while the pudgy Flight lieutenant blanched. "My apologies, Major Odon. I meant no offense." He looked around the room. "Any questions?"

One of the Marine sergeant's raised his hand and spoke once he was acknowledged. "The herbivore you showed getting eaten was pretty small. Do we know if the trees would attack something as large as a human?"

The lieutenant closed his eyes for a moment and a new vid played. This one started with an extreme wide shot which showed a field full of hundreds of the ant creatures at work. The range of the shot was so great and there was so much activity Zax wasn't sure what he should focus on. Then, he saw it. A tree at the very edge of the frame performed the same series of transfers from branch to branch which the first vid had shown. Three limbs stuck out from the final leaf as it was not quite big enough to fully encompass the alien the tree had ensnared. The limbs flailed for a min, but their movements eventually slowed and then ceased.

"Any other questions?"

When there were none, the lieutenant saluted in Major Odon's direction and then left the compartment. The Marine commander walked down to the front of the room and spoke.

"The good news from those videos is the leaves don't attack unless you touch them. That makes sense given the trees don't appear to have sensory organs other than the leaves. Don't touch a leaf equals don't get eaten by a tree. Seems like a pretty simple equation to me.

"Our mission tomorrow is just as simple. The Captain wants a Landfall on this planet and she needs the Marines to clear the ants to make that possible. We know full well how to handle these bugs given past encounters, so I don't expect any issues, but we need a complete first-hand recon of the situation before we send down the full extermination force. Are you ready to get to work?"

"Sir, yes, sir!" shouted the Marines as they jumped to attention in unison.

"Excellent." The major allowed himself a tight smile in response to his unit's exuberance. "Please share all of the appropriate details with your squads tonight. Everyone is dismissed except Lieutenant Mikedo and her cadet."

The Marines filed out in silence. The major waited until the hatch closed and then spoke. His smile was gone.

"Lieutenant—I can't tell you how *thrilled* I am at the prospect of having you and this fine young cadet join us down on that planet tomorrow. Allowing Flight staff to go on nice little *field trips* with my Marines is one of the more *amazing* ideas to have ever come from the Flight Boss. I'm *honored* to play any role in the endeavor."

Zax gulped involuntarily as the Marine's words dripped with sarcasm. The respect for Mikedo which Zax had witnessed repeatedly among the Marine sergeants was obviously not shared by this major.

"Cadet—I need you to listen carefully because I'm only going to say this once. You will report to the armory at 0630 tomorrow. You will be issued a kit bag with Marine ChamWare and a blaster. You will then report to the hangar at 0700 for our departure aboard scout shuttle 5436. While we are on the planet, you will do nothing except what you are explicitly told to do. You will stay so close to your lieutenant I will have a hard time discerning where she ends and you begin. If you do anything which puts my Marines in any sort of danger, I will make sure the last thing your eyes ever witness will be the inside of one of those tree leaves." The major turned and stomped out of the compartment.

Mikedo waited a couple beats after the hatch closed behind the major and then sighed loudly. "Don't pay him too much mind, Zax. Majors in the Marines get sticks implanted in their butts as a condition of accepting the promotion. The Boss has had cadets tag along on their missions before without any problems, so it's really not that big of a deal. Odon just believes the Marines should be in charge of the Ship instead of Flight, and he never lets us forget that opinion." She grinned. "He's actually more charming than most Marine officers, but I'll call you a liar if you ever tell anyone I said so. Do you have any questions?"

"Yes—he said I would be issued ChamWare. If there aren't any of the warrior ants on the planet and if the worker ants ignore our presence altogether, what's the point of dealing with a chameleon suit?"

"Great question." Mikedo stood up. "If you recall, what Nineem said before Odon scared him away was we haven't seen any of the warriors *yet*. I'm guessing they aren't down there since we have thousands of hours of drone vids and they haven't shown up in any of the footage, but I can understand how the Major won't risk the lives of his Marines on that bet. The suits are a pain to deal with, but if by some rotten luck we manage to run into any of those warrior ants I can guarantee you'll be happy about being invisible."

Mikedo walked towards the hatch. "Let's get out of Marine Country. I've got final preparations to make for tomorrow and you should get some rest. We're scheduled to be on the surface for two days and you might not get much chance to sleep during that entire time, so I suggest hitting the rack as soon as you get back to your berth.

"One last thing, Zax." Mikedo stopped, turned to Zax, and grabbed both of his shoulders. She stared him straight in the eyes and smiled. "I don't want you to worry about anything. You've prepared for this and I have complete faith in your abilities. If I didn't think you were ready, I wouldn't be risking my own life going down there with you. You're going to do great!"

CHAPTER TWENTY-SIX

You ready?

Zax did not share Mikedo's confidence in his preparedness and spent a sleepless night obsessing about how he would perform down on the planet. When reveille sounded, he felt no more rested than when he had hit the rack. Since he couldn't eat breakfast, he used the time that would have spent in the mess hall on an extra-long shower (twenty demerits). He put enough nutripellets for a week into his pocket and set off to the armory.

The Marine armorer eyed him bemusedly when Zax arrived and approached the counter. "What can I do for you, cadet?"

"Cadet Zax reporting, Sergeant. Major Odon said I was to receive a kit bag."

The armorer was a far older man than any of Zax's instructors and yet was still as rock solid and physically imposing. "Hmmm—we don't get too many Flight cadets around these parts. Let me check the system." He closed his eyes and raised an eyebrow once he found what he needed via his Plug. "Very interesting. It isn't very often I deal with something new, but handing out ChamWare to a Flight cadet as young as you definitely qualifies. Let me go grab your bag."

The sergeant disappeared into the armory and then returned with a black bag he placed on the counter. The bag had three compartments. One was the perfect size and shape to contain a blaster. The other two were each about half as long as the blaster compartment. Zax assumed his chameleon suit was in one compartment, but the third was a mystery. He attempted to pull the bag off the counter by one of its straps only to be flummoxed when its solid mass threatened to rip his arm out of its socket.

"Whoa there, cadet. You're going to want to be a little more careful and lift with two arms. It has a third as much mass as you do."

Zax grabbed the bag with both hands and grunted as he maneuvered his arms through the straps and settled it on his back. "Holy crap! What's in this thing that makes it so heavy, Sergeant?"

"Welcome to the world of the Marines, son. Though, this is actually a pretty light kit compared to what some of the other folks on your team will be carrying." The sergeant cracked a reasonable approximation of a smile as he came around the counter and pointed out the various compartments of the bag. "Of course, your blaster is in this first compartment here on the side. It is standard issue other than having been coated with the same material as the suit. This second compartment here at the top is the actual ChamWare suit. This third compartment here on the bottom is the weight you're feeling. It's the control unit for the suit and what puts the 'chameleon' in ChamWare."

"Why is the control unit so heavy, Sergeant?"

"You seem reasonably smart *for a Flight puke,*" the armorer grinned, "so I think you can appreciate the massive energy required to make something disappear. The power supply is minuscule in size but so dense it accounts for half of the weight. Most of the volume of the control unit and the remainder of its weight is taken up by the heat sink. ChamWare wouldn't be nearly as useful if it made you invisible but left you shining like a beacon on infrared. The human body generates a ton of heat, and we've got to put it somewhere if we're going to keep you hidden. These units are rated to absorb enough heat to keep someone my size camouflaged for a week. It should be far more than adequate for your puniness over a two-day mission."

"Understood. Thank you, Sergeant."

"Good luck down there, cadet. The recon company you're traveling with is a pretty amazing team so I wouldn't worry about running into any trouble they can't handle. Just be sure you don't do anything to get in their way or piss them off."

Zax checked the time as he turned to make his way to the hangar. The chitchat with the sergeant had left him barely enough time to get there by 0700. He double-timed it—at least as much as the excess weight of the kit bag allowed. His desperate scramble was fueled by concerns over what might happen if he violated the armorer's advice and angered the Marines right off the bat by showing up late.

Zax reached the hangar dripping with sweat and gasping for air with secs to spare. He jumped into formation a couple of steps behind a group of Marines wearing their kit bags. Mikedo, standing next to Major Odon at the shuttle's entrance, acknowledged his arrival with a subtle wink.

"Good morning, Marines. Along with our usual drivers for the bus today, we've got a couple additional guests from the Flight corps. Standing next to me is Lieutenant Mikedo. Some of you may have had reason to work with her previously in her role as the Marine liaison from Flight. She is chaperoning a cadet who is standing over there."

One hundred pairs of eyes bore into Zax when the major gestured towards him—most with simple disdain but at least a few with outright malice. The major continued. "The lieutenant has assured me neither she nor her cadet will interfere with our mission in any fashion. If either do, you have my permission to do whatever is necessary to halt the interference. Please keep in mind, though, it would be better for relations with the Flight corps if we could at least *attempt* to get them back here in one piece."

There were quite a few chuckles among the Marines, though it sure sounded to Zax like the major was not joking a bit. One bell rang to warn everyone of the pending FTL Transit. "They're getting ready for the Ship to jump into orbit," said the major, "and we'll be off the boat three mins after it does. Load up!"

"Sir, yes, sir!" came the throaty response from one hundred Marines. They filed into the craft and Zax trailed behind. Mikedo did not board with the major but instead waited by the hatch for Zax.

"Good morning, cadet. You ready?"

Mindful of the Marines still within listening range, Zax replied both more formally and more loudly than he typically would have with Mikedo. "Ma'am, yes, ma'am!"

With another wink and a smile, Mikedo turned and led him inside the shuttle. The Marines were almost settled in and many of them had closed their eyes and appeared to be asleep. Mikedo steered Zax up a ladder to a second deck where there was a separate compartment for the two of them. As they sat down, he asked, "Are some of those Marines actually sleeping?"

"Yup. Learning to fall asleep instantly is one of the most important skills a Marine picks up during training. When you spend your life getting dumped into combat with no idea how long it might be until you get a chance to rest, taking advantage of every opportunity is a great strategy. By the way—you haven't been eating, right?"

"Not since breakfast yesterday, just like you suggested. I didn't even have any nutripellets this morning. I loaded a bunch into my kit and will eat once we're out of FTL."

"Excellent. I really don't want to spend the next two days ground-pounding in gear covered with your puke."

Zax started to protest, but the pilot's voice cut him off. "Welcome aboard, Marines. Flight plan today has us taking off three mins after the Ship completes its Transit. We'll be clear of the Ship ninety secs later. Thirty mins after that we'll be feet dry and within a min of touchdown at the first landing zone."

The pilot's voice was followed by the major's. "You heard the woman. Most of you should be asleep already, but if you aren't, you've got another twenty mins for shuteye so grab it while you can. Final mission brief and prep fifteen mins before we land."

Zax closed his eyes and breathed deeply in an effort to calm his nerves. The FTL Transit came and went in a blissfully puke-free fashion, and a few mins later his inner ear suggested the shuttle was moving. Zax gazed out of the window next to his seat as the craft departed the hangar. The pilot turned wide and a huge expanse of the Ship's surface came into view.

Zax gaped in awe as he could never escape being astounded by the simple existence of something so massive which had been forged by humans. His appreciation of the Ship was forgotten a moment later, though, when the shuttle's destination came into sight. The planet wasn't nearly as beautiful as the images Zax had seen of Earth, but unlike humanity's long dead home world, he would tread upon this one's dirt and breath its air.

A few mins later Zax's window glowed from the glare of superheated plasma as the shuttle burned an entry hole through the atmosphere of the planet. He closed his eyes and rested—basking in the good fortune which had led to this opportunity and giving only the slightest passing thought to how Kalare had been robbed of it.

CHAPTER TWENTY-SEVEN

These little guys can fly!

Zax slipped into his ChamWare with only a few critical, yet embarrassing, hints from Mikedo. The suit included biological componentry to handle the processing of sweat, urine, and feces, and Zax had a hard time getting the crotch bits aligned just right. The control unit proved hefty, but Zax started to forget about it once it was properly strapped to his back. He was particularly impressed by how the suit's visor made Mikedo appear in front of him as if she wasn't wearing the invisibility suit at all. He lifted the visor and she disappeared until he dropped the visor back over his eyes.

Once fully dressed and configured, Zax and Mikedo filed down to the main deck and listened to the major's mission briefing.

"You all know about our alien friends who beat us to this rock. Our primary mission over the next two days is to gather firsthand intel to help determine how we're going to clear them out. The Captain says we'll Landfall here come hell or high water, so the only question which remains is how quickly we can exterminate these bugs for her."

The major paused for a moment while a projection of the planet was displayed and zoomed into the smaller of the two land masses. "The bugs are centered around two settlements. The smaller one is marked LZ1 and the larger one is LZ2.

"Landing zone one is a half klick to the east of the alien's smaller compound. Scans and drone surveys have shown there are only twenty or thirty bugs at this location. There are a couple dozen structures and almost all of the alien activity is centered around three of them. Ship records show we've never seen this sort of population pattern from these aliens before, so the intel weenies are particularly interested in what we can learn around there."

The major pointed at various groups of Marines as he gave his dispersal orders. "First Platoon is going to head around the north side of the settlement while Second Platoon heads around the south. Third Platoon will head straight on in. You all know what kind of stuff we're looking for. Keep your eyes peeled and your helmet cams focused on what will be most valuable for the intelligence teams.

"One last thing." The major stood to his full height and raised his voice. "I know we've been told this planet only has worker bugs because no warriors have been spotted. The workers ignore humans, but we're still in our ChamWare for a reason. If I see any of you acting like this mission is a stroll through the woods, I'll kill you myself. Get the rest of your gear and be ready to hit the dirt in a few mins."

The major gestured for Mikedo and Zax to approach. "Against my better judgment I've agreed to the Flight Boss's request that you two join Third Platoon and go straight into the bug compound. Just remember—I was dead serious back on the Ship when I gave everyone permission to do whatever's necessary if you interfere with our mission."

"Understood, sir," Mikedo replied crisply. "You and your team won't even notice the cadet and I are with you."

"Unlikely." The major scowled and strode away.

Mikedo turned to Zax and opened her mouth to speak but stopped when a sergeant approached. It was the same one who had asked the question about the carnivorous trees during the mission briefing.

"Excuse me, ma'am. Sergeant Yolis, Third Platoon. My commander, Lieutenant Isoria, has asked me to shadow you two while we're down on the planet."

The sergeant was not quite as big a specimen as Zax's Marine instructors had been, but he wasn't far off. His jet black hair was cropped closely like so many of the other Marines wore theirs. While introducing himself, he had gestured over to a Marine lieutenant who Zax had already noticed on the other side of the shuttle. She was as tall as the sergeant though did not have anywhere near as much mass. She had stood out because her blond hair was pulled back in a long ponytail which Zax believed was against regulations in both its style and length. He needed to just give up on deciphering the unwritten rules of being a Marine if he wanted his brain to hurt less.

"If you wouldn't mind, ma'am, I'd like to perform a quick review of your gear." The sergeant's demeanor was as pleasant and polite as the major's had been disagreeable and rude. "I realize you've probably been part of a rodeo like this before, but I hope you can understand we'd rather be safe than sorry."

"By all means, Sergeant. I appreciate the double-check."

Mikedo slowly rotated as the sergeant gave her chameleon suit a quick once over. He then did the same with Zax. "Everything is fitted and configured properly, ma'am. If you two would please follow me, we're going to form up over here. Third Platoon will be last off the bus. We land in ninety secs."

Zax had lost track of the time and was shocked they were so close to the surface. For most everyone in the Flight Corps, the idea of landing on a planet filled them with terror because it meant they had gotten bounced out of the Crew and dropped into a colony for the rest of their lives. Zax, on the other hand, was about to experience the surface of a new world while safely encased in Marine ChamWare and with a guaranteed ride back to the Ship. He was participating in a recon mission which would scout out an alien encampment in advance of an extermination force. His mouth was dry and his hands were clammy, but the feeling in his belly was excitement and not dread. He closed his eyes and focused on his breathing in an effort to not be overwhelmed by the moment.

With a jolt, the shuttle touched down and an instant later the loading bay door dropped to the ground. A half dozen sergeants barked orders and Marines poured out of the craft. A sharp nudge in his back made Zax move forward to join them.

The natural sunlight was momentarily blinding, but Zax's visor quickly compensated and his view was soon unhindered. Two-thirds of the Marines had already disappeared into the jungle while the remainder, Third Platoon, were arrayed in a loose defensive posture around the landing zone. The shuttle door closed and the craft took off. Since these aliens weren't known to have any form of flying craft or detection technology, the pilots had the luxury of orbiting lazily around the rally point while they awaited rendezvous with the Marines in 120 mins.

Zax had ignored the background chatter on his suit's commlink, but then Sergeant Yolis' voice cut through. "Lieutenant Mikedo—you and the cadet will be sticking with me, and we're going to be near the rear of the formation as we head out."

Zax gaped at the massive trees. They towered above the ground like nothing he had ever imagined. He tried to locate the top of the nearest one and estimate its height but quickly gave up and stared back down at the ground when he was overwhelmed by vertigo.

The ground beneath his feet was only dirt, but it was *alien* dirt. Zax yearned to remove his gloves and run his fingers through the stuff. He wished he could ditch the suit altogether and immerse himself in the planet. In particular, he ached to experience the warmth of the sun on his face. Zax contemplated lifting his visor *just for a quick sec* until an excited voice shattered his reverie.

"Hey—watch this! These little guys can fly!"

Zax looked over at a Marine private who stood five meters off to his right. The Marine had picked up one of the small grazing animals and it sat docilely in his arms. Once he had an audience, the private heaved the creature through the air at one of the large leaves. Its panicked bleats were muffled when the leaf snapped shut around the beast. The tree sprang into motion and the creature was transferred from leaf to leaf until its journey, and its life, ended near the top.

The sergeant's voice quickly halted the laughter of the Marines who witnessed all of this.

"What are you thinking, Private? If the major witnessed that stunt, he'd have your head! All of you—the lieutenant is heading towards the settlement. Get moving! I'll take up the rear along with first squad and our guests from Flight."

The private smirked but turned and made his way west towards the settlement. Zax despised the Marine's gratuitous cruelty but appreciated the graphic reminder about the planet's dangers and the need to stay clear of the leaves. Mikedo turned to follow the Marines, and he fell into step behind her. They all disappeared into the jungle and left the landing zone vacant behind them.

CHAPTER TWENTY-EIGHT

Are you OK, cadet?

The alien settlement didn't look like much of anything. A large clearing had been carved out of the jungle and populated with a couple dozen buildings. 'Building' was probably the wrong word to use since it actually seemed more like giant dirt clumps had been randomly scattered on the ground.

Sergeant Yolis called the group to a halt. "We're going to break up and check each structure. You should note all of the bug activity at this location is focused on the handful of buildings which are on the western edge of the settlement. We'll check those last as we prepare to leave. That way we'll have gathered as much intel as possible if anything crazy happens and we have to hightail it to the rally point. Squad leaders—you have your assignments. Lieutenant Mikedo—you and your cadet are with me."

Mikedo and Zax fell into position behind the sergeant and followed him towards an empty structure. Zax had studied the construction techniques of this species after the mission briefing and learned their buildings were formed from partially digested biological material. He had laughed at the realization his first alien encounter would involve buildings made with alien puke. The ant creations were all curves and rounded edges with never a straight line to be seen. An initial handful of small buildings were typically expanded upon through the years until they all merged into labyrinthine structures.

They approached their target building and Sergeant Yolis signaled for Zax to halt. The Marine gestured for Mikedo to follow him inside and pointed for her to scan the right side of the entryway while he eyeballed the left. Zax waited just outside the entrance and watched the deserted area around them until the sergeant called "All clear" from inside.

Zax entered and was immediately struck by how the structure appeared even more primitive on the inside than it was on the outside. It was nothing more than a larger version of the ant mounds he had seen on the Ship. There were two small passageways which led away from the main entrance and Mikedo strolled out of one while the sergeant exited the other a moment later.

Mikedo grinned at him. "What do you think of your first alien adventure, Zax? Not very exciting to look at, huh?"

"Yes, ma'am. It's nothing but a giant pile of bug barf. Where do the passageways go?"

"Actually, it's just a single passageway which begins and ends here. No apparent reason for building it, but then I don't pretend to understand how these bugs think. If they even do. Maybe some day the exobiology team can explain why an alien race, which must be relatively advanced given how frequently we've seen them across the universe, can appear bereft of technology when we observe them up close." Mikedo turned to Yolis. "Sergeant—nothing much here. Shall we head to our next target?"

"Yes, ma'am. Teams have almost finished checking the newer buildings and all of them match this one—simple and empty. We're going to converge on the older structures where the drones have recorded all of the alien activity. Stay close and keep alert as we expect to run into workers once we reach the other side of the settlement."

Zax followed the sergeant and Mikedo as they exited the structure and weaved their way past various buildings towards the western edge of the clearing. He sweated profusely as the temperature climbed inside his suit. He had originally blamed the increased heat on being inside a building where it was even warmer than the jungle, but his discomfort did not abate once

Zax got outside. He opened a private channel to Mikedo.

"Are you hot? I'm starting to get uncomfortable inside this thing."

"A little warm I suppose, but nothing more than you would expect after walking around in a jungle. Give yourself a little longer to adapt, Zax. If you're still having issues when we get to the rally point, we can ask the sergeant to check out your suit."

Zax wasn't entirely convinced about Mikedo's plan but didn't want to make a fuss and nodded in agreement. A few mins later the group reached the western edge of the settlement and its three older structures. They gathered around Lieutenant Isoria along with the rest of the Marines, and Zax heard her speak for the first time.

"I've been here observing while all of you were checking the newer buildings. Very light bug action, but we've seen a few. All of them entered the westernmost structure. I want first squad to set a perimeter around that building while second squad goes inside. Third squad—I want you to split up and check out the other two."

The Marines dispersed to carry out their orders, and Sergeant Yolis addressed Mikedo and Zax. "I've sent the rest of the squad to check out the larger structure, and we can scout out the small one."

Zax found it a little odd how the sergeant scouted along with the two guests from Flight all by himself, but he assumed it was an indication as to how low pressure this mission was for the recon Marines. The three of them walked towards a building which seemed different than the rest. Whereas the other buildings appeared perfectly organic with no signs of right angles, this structure had a hint of straight lines deep underneath its outer shell. Once again, Mikedo and the sergeant entered first and Zax hung back until they announced an all clear.

Unlike the first building, this one was not entirely empty. There was a small mound inside which might have once been a table of some sort. It was covered with so much of the bug's construction puke it had become a nearly indistinct blob. Without thinking twice, Zax took the butt end of his blaster and smashed it repeatedly against the top of the mound. The organic material split and flaked as Zax pounded away.

The sound of Zax's banging brought Mikedo running back into the main room just as a final piece of material fell off and revealed what appeared to be stainless steel underneath. She did a double take and called out. "Sergeant—check this out."

The Marine was already walking into the room and he approached the mound. Before he got there, he closed his eyes for a moment and focused on his Plug. "We'll come back and check this out later. There aren't any aliens visible in the other buildings, but one of the structures includes an entrance to an underground tunnel system. The lieutenant is sending some folks down and I need to get over there."

Zax's heat stress had worsened after his vigorous smashing with the blaster, and he stumbled to the ground as they exited the building. Mikedo called out over the public channel.

"Are you OK, cadet?"

"Ma'am," Zax panted as he staggered to his feet, "it's so hot inside this suit I'm having a hard time breathing. It's way worse than when we talked about it earlier."

Sergeant Yolis hustled over to Zax. "You can cook your brain inside one of these suits if it malfunctions. Let's get you vented." He lifted Zax's visor and unzipped the front of his suit.

The fresh air on his face was glorious and Zax swore there were waves of heat emanating of his chest once the zipper was down. The raising of his visor, however, rendered the sergeant and Mikedo invisible.

"This is pretty freaky—I can feel your hands moving around on my suit, but I can't see anything."

The sergeant removed his own visor and his face floated in midair. He must have been down on a knee because his head was at the same level as Zax's as he smiled at him.

"Which do you think is weirder—getting handled by the invisible man or the disembodied one?" The sergeant started to laugh, but then stopped and focused on his Plug.

Zax gazed through the sergeant's transparent body and spotted an alien warrior running out of a structure behind him. The giant ant's red and green stripes were a blur as it moved even faster than the one in the briefing video. The creature raised one of its blade weapons as it charged towards them. Zax called out a warning, but Yolis was already spinning around. The Marine's reaction was too late, and a blade sprouted out of his back as the sergeant collapsed to the ground.

An invisible blaster fired directly in front of Zax. Mikedo must have jumped in front of him to shoot at the alien. It went down in a heap, and then Mikedo's visor was off and her face appeared in front of his.

"Run and grab some cover just inside the tree line over there! I've got to take care of the sergeant, but there's help on the way and I'll come find you in a min!"

Mikedo's face disappeared once again. She must have reached down and lowered the sergeant's visor because he was once again fully invisible as well.

Zax ran to the tree line and found a place to hide behind a fallen tree covered in moss and small vegetation. He caught his breath for a moment and then peeked out over the log. He didn't see anything back towards the buildings, and there was no noise whatsoever.

The empty landscape was transformed when Zax lowered his visor. He counted five Marines who had joined Mikedo. Four of them stood in a defensive formation while the fifth assisted her in tending to the sergeant's wounds. The suffocating heat returned as soon as his visor was down, so Zax quickly pushed it back up.

Zax settled back against the log and accidentally dislodged one of the bushes which covered it. The falling vegetation tore away dirt where its roots had previously found purchase on the log. The missing soil revealed something like transparent titanium or some other artificial material. Zax bolted upright and tore into the remaining plants.

After a few mins of furiously removing vegetation and brushing away dirt, Zax uncovered something which made zero sense. He had not been leaning against a tree, but it was instead some kind of fighter which had been knocked onto its side and subsequently swallowed by the jungle. The clear material he first spotted was part of the craft's cockpit dome.

The fighter wasn't the same model as those the Ship sometimes deployed during planetary expeditions, but it could have sprung from the imagination of the same designers. Zax peered into the cockpit and his discovery evolved from bizarre to incomprehensible.

The labels on the controls were unintelligible, yet recognizable. There were lots of strange, squiggly characters, but they were interspersed with plenty of E's and O's and M's and other letters which were exactly like those he had used his entire life.

Identifying writing which appeared human was strange enough, but then Zax spotted something which took his breath away. A plaque to the side of an instrument panel featured a picture of a planet. Zax instantly recognized the pale blue marble with its wispy clouds and distinctive landmasses—Earth.

CHAPTER TWENTY-NINE

Listen carefully to what I say next.

Zax's mind raced and his heart pounded. He was standing next to a *human* fighter which had been abandoned in the jungle of this *alien* world. A noise off to the side startled Zax, and he spun around to find Mikedo approaching with her visor up.

"The sergeant's in rough shape. They're moving him to the rally point for evac and we need to catch up ASAP. Wait a sec—what the hell are you looking at?"

Zax was at a complete loss for words so he simply pointed into the cockpit. Mikedo scanned the interior for a min, turned to him for a moment, and then stared back inside again.

"What is this thing?" Zax finally gasped. "Why is there a fighter with human writing and a picture of Earth inside its cockpit sitting here in the middle of this jungle? This craft isn't one of ours, but it sure is similar. The Ship's never been to this planet, right? You know what this means—there are other humans out here! We're not alone!"

Mikedo gazed at Zax as she took a couple of deep breaths. "I agree with you about what this looks like, Zax, but I want to warn you about throwing around the word *human* without considering the possible implications. Something as strange and potentially disruptive as this discovery—"

"But," Zax tried to interrupt and Mikedo waved her hand to silence him.

"Listen—we've had 5,000 years of history lessons which tell us the Ship is the only remnant of humanity. Our Mission to seed the universe with new colonies, our leadership structure, all of our traditions, everything we do is based upon that premise. If people hear there might be other humans traveling around, will they hope maybe Earth is still alive and sending out more ships? Or will they dream there is a new human home world somewhere which is technologically advanced enough for space travel?"

It slowly dawned on Zax where Mikedo was going with her concerns, but he was still surprised to hear the words come out of her mouth. He was even more shocked to recognize how she had transformed from her preternaturally calm self into someone who was nervous—maybe even frantic.

"You know what life has been like on board in recent years, Zax. Some days it feels like the Ship might just disintegrate all around us. They keep slapping together repairs, but eventually something critical will break which can't be fixed. We just went through all that time without a Landfall and even some Crew started to jabber about whether the Mission is feasible anymore."

Mikedo paused for a deep breath and then continued. "Of course, the civilian population is always ready to explode, and something like this could be the spark. If enough civilians heard about this, don't you think they might revolt against dumping people into new colonies? They'd start a wild goose chase looking for some mysterious human outpost. Right? Or even worse, force the Ship back to Earth."

Zax stood flabbergasted. In the span of ninety secs, he went from imagining himself on the newsvid being wildly celebrated for finding proof of other humans to learning that Mikedo felt his discovery was actually bad news.

"Here's what I want to do," offered Mikedo. "We need to get to the rally point. As soon as we are back with the Marines, I'm going to check with the Flight Boss. Sorting out what to do with all of this is above my pay grade. The Boss can figure out what's next. Do you agree?"

Zax wanted desperately to understand what was making Mikedo nervous, but the middle of an alien jungle didn't feel like the place where she would be likely to share much more. Instead, he nodded in agreement and promised himself he would force her to explain more fully once they were back on the Ship.

Mikedo took his face in her invisible hands and held him focused on her disembodied head as she spoke. "Listen carefully to what I say next. I think it's best if we act like you know *nothing* about this. I'm going to tell the Boss we got separated. I discovered this on my own and didn't tell you anything about it. He'll believe I would've kept this secret from you if I'd found it first because—well—I would have.

"I beg you to trust me when I say this, Zax. This is dangerous, dangerous information, and you don't want to be associated with it in any way. Do you understand? Promise me you understand."

Zax hesitated. The expression on Mikedo's face bordered on desperation. If she felt this strongly about what was going on, who was he to question her judgment? But at the same time, this wasn't something he could just blindly trust anyone about—even Mikedo.

"I'm sorry," he replied, "my head's spinning. Let's get moving and that will give me a few mins to process all of this."

Mikedo and Zax walked back to the rally point in silence and arrived just as the Marines had settled Sergeant Yolis and arranged a defensive perimeter around the landing zone. Lieutenant Isoria thanked Mikedo for acting so quickly to treat the sergeant and informed her the other two platoons would arrive within the next ten mins and the shuttle two mins thereafter. Mikedo requested the comms specialist and was pointed to the other side of the clearing. She gestured for Zax to follow and a min later they found her.

"Corporal—I need you to configure a private channel between my Plug and the Flight Boss. Maximum encryption please."

"Yes, ma'am."

Mikedo gave Zax a wan smile and walked a dozen meters away. She sat with her eyes shut and concentrated on her discussion with the Flight Boss. A few times the muscles of her face twitched and betrayed the intensity of the conversation. After a handful of mins, she opened her eyes and exhaled a deep breath. She gestured for Zax and whispered once he drew close.

"That did not go quite the way I thought it would, but I don't want to go into the details right now. I promise I'll give you some more details once we're back on the Ship. The part of the conversation which did go as I expected was when I told him you knew nothing. I think he was pleased about how I hadn't told you about the fighter, but it felt was like he was testing me since he asked three separate times in three different ways whether or not you knew anything about it. Each time I made it crystal clear the answer was no."

Mikedo extended her hand and Zax clasped it to help her stand. "Listen, Zax, I know this is almost impossible, but you've got to promise me you'll put this discovery out of your head for now. I don't want you sharing it with *anyone*. You and I probably shouldn't even discuss it again. The more you talk about anything like this, the easier it is to mess up and reveal something about it at the wrong time. This will be a painful secret to keep, but I need you to keep it nonetheless. I truly hope there'll come a time when we can figure out the right way for this information to be revealed so you can get full credit, but until then you need to forget it ever happened. Promise?"

Zax wanted to shout "no" with every fiber of his being. He had found evidence of other humans traveling the stars! Even putting aside how amazing it would be to get credit for the discovery, it screamed out as something which was important for everyone on board the Ship to know.

We aren't alone!

But then he reconsidered Mikedo and her pleading, near desperate expression. It came from the woman who had shown more care and compassion towards him in the last two weeks than anyone in the Crew had in his entire life. The woman who was so smart and talented and had already accomplished so much in her career. She wasn't trying to steal credit for what he found. She just wanted what was best and safest for him. He sighed.

"OK. I get it. I was never there. I never saw anything. We got separated after the warrior attacked the sergeant, and when you found me, we went straight back to the rally point."

"Good boy." Mikedo smiled, but her eyes betrayed great sadness. "I'm so very sorry about all of this, Zax, I really am. I'm touched you trust me enough to follow my instincts about what we should do. I promise I'll never abuse your trust or do anything to make you regret giving it to me. I'm going to work with the Boss, and we'll figure out what to do with all of this." She pointed to where the other platoons had gathered while the shuttle descended. "Let's get on board, find someone to check out that suit of yours, and figure out what's wrong before we hit the next LZ."

CHAPTER THIRTY

I have orders to do yours first.

The shuttle landed and they all filed on. The major approached and frustration was evident in his voice.

"Go ahead and get out of the ChamWare, Marines. The second leg of the mission's been scrubbed and we're heading back to the Ship. Since we've encountered a warrior, the Omegas want to re-evaluate our mission parameters before we recon the bugs' larger settlement."

The major's announcement elicited universal grumbling. Like everyone else on board the Ship, the Marines were nearly crazy after so much time without encountering a habitable planet. This group was clearly upset at the prospect of losing time on the surface and the opportunity to do their job and kill some aliens. The major held up his hands.

"Settle down, Marines. I know you're disappointed. I guarantee Charlie Company will be included in the final mission plan. We're leaving now, but I promise we'll be back soon enough to finish the job."

Mikedo and Zax returned to their compartment to undress and get strapped in for the trip back to the Ship. A few mins after takeoff, a medic appeared holding a transdermal injector in one hand and a tray full of vials in the other. Mikedo had gotten so involved with something on her slate that she didn't look up when the Marine entered their compartment.

"Excuse me, ma'am. I'm sorry to interrupt, but the Omegas have ordered that we all get immune boost injections since we had an encounter with the bugs."

Mikedo looked up with a quizzical expression on her face. "I'm sorry, Corporal, but I'm confused. This isn't some new, unknown species. We've run into these bugs a dozen times just in my lifetime, not to mention the hundreds of other times the Ship has encountered them. There has never been a single instance where there was any sort of infection traced back to them. Why are we worried all of a sudden about getting immune boosts?"

The medic sighed. "I'm sorry, ma'am. I don't know if maybe it works differently in Flight, but when Marine corporals get orders, we carry them out rather than ask a lot of questions."

Mikedo smiled. "Point taken, Corporal. I'm in the middle of something so please take care of my cadet here first."

The Marine seemed sheepish. "I'm sorry, ma'am. I have orders to do yours first."

The smile faded from Mikedo's face. "That doesn't make any sense, Corporal. Why should it matter whether you do me first or the cadet?"

"Perhaps you'd like to take it up with the major, ma'am?"

There was a long, uncomfortable silence. It didn't make sense to Zax why Mikedo was giving the medic such a hard time about following orders, but the expression on her face was impenetrable.

Mikedo finally turned towards Zax and smiled as she rolled up her sleeve and replied to the Marine. "That won't be necessary, Corporal. Go ahead and give me the injection. Better safe than sorry, I suppose."

The medic gave Mikedo her shot and then loaded a new vial into the injector before turning to administer Zax's dose. The Marine apologized one last time for the interruption and then exited the compartment. Zax rolled his sleeve back down and sensed Mikedo watching him as he did so. Her cheeks were flushed and she wore a pained expression.

"I need to send an important message, Zax, but I've got to tell you something first and you must promise me you'll always remember *these exact words*. I absolutely believe you will do great things."

Zax was clueless about how to react to such a compliment, so he replied with a simple "Thank you." Mikedo gave him faint smile and then sat back and shut her eyes. With nothing else to do, Zax closed his as well and attempted the Marines' trick of napping during downtime.

It could have been five secs later or it might have been five mins, but Zax was startled awake by the thud of something heavy hitting the deck. He discovered Mikedo crumpled on the deck next to her seat—unmoving.

Zax unbuckled his straps and jumped up yelling for help as he scrambled to check what was wrong. Mikedo's lips were blue and her body radiated heat like she was on fire. Her breaths were shallow and horrifically labored. Zax went for the hatch but found it would not open. He pounded on the control panel. "Help! We need help in here! Help!"

"Cadet—please calm down," replied a voice over the intercom. "Calm down! The biosensors show that Lieutenant Mikedo has taken ill. We've got medics donning isosuits who are almost ready to assist. We're worried it might be something infectious from your encounter with the bugs, so we can't let them in until you calm down and step away from the hatch."

Zax backed up to the other side of the compartment and stood over Mikedo's body. He was about to yell again when a soft hissing noise was immediately followed by the buckling of his knees. He collapsed with his body draped across Mikedo's and panicked about whether this was the first sign he had also caught whatever brought her down. The voice on the other end of the intercom spoke again.

"Don't be alarmed, cadet. For everyone's safety, we've doused your compartment with sleeping gas. It doesn't appear you're ill, but we've got to keep you quarantined until we know for certain. There's a team just outside the hatch, and they're going to help the lieutenant as soon as you're fully sedated."

Zax fought to resist but was unable to stave off the effects of the gas. His last thought before dropping into unconsciousness was one of tremendous desperation. Mikedo was no longer burning up, but her breathing had quit altogether.

CHAPTER THIRTY-ONE

It means you have a message waiting.

"Try again—don't let her go!" Zax heard the words, but they sounded like they came from somewhere far above him up a deep, dark tunnel. He opened his eyes and attempted to move his body, but discovered he was somehow restrained. He was still in the shuttle compartment and was staring up into the expressionless face of a man behind the mask of an orange isolation suit.

The figure reached for an injector which he applied to Zax's arm. The last thing Zax registered before everything faded to inky blackness was the major standing impassively just outside the hatch.

Clap!

"Cadet—wake up."

Clap! Clap!

"Zax—wake up."

Clap – Clap – Clap!

The clapping right next to his head grated on Zax. "Go away," he mumbled, his lids clamped tight against the bright light attempting to shred his eyeballs.

"That's no way to talk to an officer, cadet. Particularly one who has been taking care of you and is here to share some good news."

The female voice sounded familiar, and Zax was flooded with relief at the prospect of talking to Mikedo. He forced himself fully awake and blinked the sleep out of his eyes. It wasn't Mikedo in front of him but rather an unknown woman dressed in one of the orange isosuits. He checked his surroundings and concluded he was no longer on the shuttle, but instead in the medbay.

"That's more like it, cadet. You're still restrained so don't bother trying to sit up or move your arms. That's part of the bad news. We've got to keep you isolated here for another forty-eight hours to be certain you didn't contract anything hazardous on that planet which might make you or anyone else sick. The good news is the Flight Boss was down here this morning to check on you personally. When he heard we needed to keep you for another couple of days, he ordered us to go ahead and get you Plugged In right now. He said as long as you're stuck in sickbay you might as well get some benefit out of the time and use it to recover from implantation."

"Wait—what happened to the officer I was with? Lieutenant Mikedo. Is she all right?"

The medic smiled down at him benevolently. "I'm sorry, cadet, but I don't know anything about that. I'm just here to get you sedated. I know it's annoying I woke you up only to put you back under again, but we need to verify your neurological function is OK before we go cracking your skull open. The scans are all checking out normal and you seem fine, so we'll get you asleep again. The next time you wake up you'll be Plugged In."

"Wait! Stop! Please—I've got to find out what happened to Lieutenant Mikedo. I have to know!"

"Sorry, cadet, but it's too late. I've already applied the anesthetic. You're going to feel your eyelids getting heavy in a couple of secs. Don't worry about the lieutenant—I'm sure she's fine. Let's just worry about getting you completely sedated right now so they can take care of your Plug. Trust me when I say you don't want to wake up in the middle of this particular surgery."

Zax soon felt like his eyelids weighed a million kilos, and he ultimately lost the battle to keep them open. Once again, unconsciousness engulfed him.

Beep.

Beep Beep.

Beep.

Beep Beep.

The incessant electronic bleats dragged Zax into consciousness, and he found himself in what appeared to be a medbay recovery room. He blinked a few times and turned his head to discover Kalare beaming in a chair next to him.

"You're finally awake! Good morning! It's great to see you! I've missed you these last few days. You're not going to believe this, but you're actually in the same bed I was in when we last saw each other. What a crazy coincidence! How funny is it you came here to say goodbye to me and now a couple days later I'm here to say hello to you!"

Zax tried to focus on her words, but Kalare was hard to keep up with when he was fully conscious much less when he was just waking up with a sedation hangover.

"Whoa—too—many—words. Slow down—please."

"I'm sorry. It's just so exciting to see you again." Kalare sucked in a couple of exaggerated deep breaths before continuing. "I haven't had anyone to talk with since you went away, so I've been bugging the medics nonstop about when they were going to wake you up. And now—you're up!"

"I get it, I get it. Thanks. It's nice to see you too. How long have I been out?"

"You were down on the planet three days ago. Most of the time since you've been unconscious to recover from getting implanted. I can't believe how lucky you are to get Plugged In so much earlier than the rest of us!"

Zax had forgotten about the conversation with the medic where she told him he was getting put under for implantation surgery. Kalare's reminder made him aware something was indeed different inside his head. A red light flashed in his field of vision. It seemed at first to be attached to a piece of equipment past Kalare's shoulder, but as he turned his head the light moved as well. It was being projected by his Plug and was something only he could see. He was clueless about how to interact with it, but he was now Plugged In! Mikedo could teach him how to use it—wait—

"Where's Mikedo? How's she doing? Did they figure out what was wrong with her?"

Kalare's smile vanished. "You mean they haven't told you?" She sighed and dropped her face into her hands. The next words came in a whisper. "She's gone, Zax. She died while you guys were coming back from the surface. They disposed of her straight out of the shuttle rather than risk bringing her body back onboard the Ship. They were worried she was still infectious. The story led the newsvid broadcast the day after you came back."

Zax had somehow known this would be the answer, so his emotions were already primed and the tears came instantly. Massive, choking, gasping sobs. Kalare draped her body over his and hugged him as she joined in and cried softly. A min later the hatch opened and Zax recognized through his tear-stained vision it was the same medic who was taking care of Kalare when Zax had visited her. The man discovered yet another crying scene between the two of them, and this time turned and left rather than interrupt.

Kalare straightened up after a few mins and perched herself on the side of the bed where she stroked Zax's head while he continued to sob. Eventually he croaked, "Thank you" through the last remnants of his tears.

"I'm so sorry, Zax. She was so amazing, and it must have been so hard for you when it all happened."

It was hard. Zax's mind flashed back to his hopelessness as he pounded on the door of the shuttle compartment and screamed for help. He remembered the horrible panic he felt when he was lying across Mikedo's body and realized she was no longer breathing. The tears welled up again, but Zax fought to choke them back.

"Do they know what happened to her?"

"All I know is what they announced on the newsvid. Your recon mission went down to figure out the best way to clear out the bugs before Landfall. A group of you had a close encounter with a bunch of bugs. You all got immune boosts, but it must have been too late for Mikedo because she fell ill on the shuttle and died a short time later. Speaking of the newsvid, it's about that time." She walked over to activate the monitor embedded in the wall. "I heard a rumor there's going to be a big announcement this morning, so we should definitely watch."

The announcer appeared and the graphic behind his head featured a single word—Landfall.

"The Omegas have made a final determination as to the status of the planet we are orbiting. We shared with you previously that a member of the Flight Corps died of an infection sustained during a scouting mission to the planet's surface. She had been in hand-to-hand combat with a large group of bugs, and the Ship's medical staff has concluded this was the source of her deadly infection—not anything having to do with the planet itself.

"The original plan was for the Marines to remove all of the bugs before Landfall, but the discovery of this illness has shifted that thinking. The Captain has decided to instead remove the bugs by deploying a Planetbuster from orbit against their settlements. This will glass over the landmass where the bugs are located and make it uninhabitable for centuries, but the Omegas have wisely concluded this is a small price to pay in exchange for not risking additional infections among our Marines. There is more than enough high-quality land on the second continent to sustain a settlement. The loss of the other should not make a difference for the future of the colony.

"We will nuke the bugs in 172 mins and, unless there are any problems, Landfall will start tomorrow. The first wave of colonists will depart at 0700. Let's go to a report from the staging area where preparations are being made."

Kalare smiled at Zax. "Well, there's some good news for you. Cyrus is part of the Colonial Security staff, so he'll be off the Ship with the first wave tomorrow morning. Since the medic said you're in here for another twenty-four hours, you don't have to worry about ever seeing him again."

Kalare's words barely registered with Zax. Cyrus was the furthest thing from his mind. All he could think about was what had transpired down on the planet. How his recollections didn't sync with what he just heard on the newsvid. Kalare was still rambling about something related to Landfall when Zax interrupted her.

"Doesn't all of this sound a little weird to you? There are tons of historical records of the Ship encountering those bugs, right? We've *never* experienced any sort of infectious disease in our dealings with them before and that includes some furious, all-out battles where thousands of Marines experienced plenty of hand-to-hand combat. When they came to give us our immune boost shots on the shuttle, Mikedo was surprised and questioned the medic about it because she said we *never* bother doing that when we encounter the bugs. And speaking of Mikedo, the newsvid has it entirely wrong. She didn't have any close combat with a bunch of bugs—there was a *single* warrior and Mikedo took it down with her blaster from fifty meters away."

Kalare seemed bewildered, but Zax continued. "So now, rather than try to learn anything about this mysterious new infectious disease which killed someone within mins of exposure and is associated with aliens we encounter all the time, we're instead going to just nuke it all away. We're going to destroy half of the landmass on this planet the day before we drop a colony onto the other half. When was the last time a Captain even used a Planetbuster? Can you think of a single situation from the Ship's records where we've done anything similar to this? It's all crazy!"

Zax glared expectantly at Kalare and after a few secs she started laughing. "I'm sorry to react this way because I know you're being serious, but it's super funny how things have been flipped. You may not remember it, but I distinctly recall a conversation with you from a few weeks ago where I started questioning what I'd just seen on a newsvid and you got terribly upset with me. In fact, you were so angry you stormed out of the mess hall muttering something or other about my 'paranoid fantasies.'"

Kalare had a point, but Zax was certain she would share his doubts if only she knew what he had found down on the planet. He felt compelled by his promise to Mikedo, though, to withhold that critical detail. Zax was trying to figure out how little he could disclose while still getting her to appreciate his concerns when the medic returned.

"I'm sorry to interrupt, but I have to get you prepped for a Plug diagnostic." The medic turned to Kalare. "Time for you to leave, cadet. Your friend will be discharged tomorrow morning and you two can chat all you want after that."

Kalare stood to leave. "Bye, Zax. Hopefully, they didn't screw up your brain when they gave you the Plug and that's what's making you all crazy paranoid like me. We'll talk more tomorrow."

The hatch shut behind Kalare, and the medic appraised Zax with an expression of grave concern. "What did she say about you being paranoid? Are you having any strange thoughts? It's important I know if there has been any change in your mental state because it could signal a problem with your implantation."

Zax's mind had been flooded with all kind of strange thoughts since the newsvid played, but he was certain they had nothing to do with his Plug. "No, sir. Nothing out of the ordinary. She was just joking around. She's got an odd sense of humor, that one."

"Well, she seems to care an awful lot about you. She's been here pestering the staff nonstop about when you would wake up and she could visit you." The medic grinned. "I might even suspect there's something happening there beyond just friendship."

Zax blushed but quickly regained his composure. "You mentioned something about a Plug diagnostic, sir. There's a flashing red light I've been seeing in the lower right corner of my vision. Is that anything to worry about?"

"No, that's not a problem. It means you have a message waiting. The diagnostic is just a quick scan to be sure your neurons are properly melding with the Plug. The implant tech will be down here in a min and she'll check you out."

Zax was intrigued by the idea of a waiting message since he had no clue who would have sent him anything already. "How do I access the message?"

"Sorry, but you can't just yet. The Plug needs another twenty-four hours to meld before we can fully activate the neural interface. You're seeing some of the low-level notifications now because that functionality is the first to come online. Assuming there aren't any problems, you'll have an orientation session tomorrow afternoon. Your instructor will activate everything and teach you how to interact with the Plug. Don't worry, cadet—that message isn't going anywhere."

CHAPTER THIRTY-TWO

You said 'if', sir.

The next morning Zax awoke to enjoy one final meal in bed before he was due to leave medbay. He ate breakfast as the morning newsvid broadcast live coverage of the first two hundred colonists grimly marching into their transport. The former Crew members no longer wore their uniforms, but instead dressed in clothes which identified them as Colonial Security.

Zax caught a glimpse of Cyrus boarding the vessel and allowed himself a quick smile at the realization he had dodged that problem. Aleron remained on the Ship, of course, but Zax could deal with him. A giant psychopath with more muscles than brains and nothing to lose like his mentor, however, was better left far behind.

He received one final physical evaluation and was then discharged. The medic smiled as he wished Zax farewell and said he hoped to not see him again anytime soon—either as a patient or a visitor. Zax's assignment schedule for the day revealed only light duty with three commitments. He had to lead a class about Landfall for the Gammas in the morning and was scheduled for initial Plug training in the afternoon. Those two activities were sandwiched around a meeting with the Flight Boss which was booked right after lunch.

The thought of meeting with the Boss filled Zax with foreboding. Mikedo made it clear how she told the Omega that Zax had zero knowledge of the mysterious fighter, but the Boss might try to verify that for himself. The chain of events which occurred immediately after Mikedo informed the Flight Boss about the fighter suggested her concerns about the discovery might have been more than paranoia. Zax desperately wished to believe it was all a giant coincidence, but he refused to bet his life on it. He needed to be on top of his game if he sensed the Boss was digging for any reason to mistrust what Mikedo had told him.

Zax set his concerns aside and entered the training compartment full of Gammas. There was a buzz in the air as they were all following the news about Landfall with great excitement. It had been so long since the Ship found a habitable planet that the kids in Gamma probably had no memory of it ever happening. Zax barely remembered the last Landfall himself.

"Good morning everyone. Who watched the morning newsvid?" Zax knew it was a silly question, so he was not the least bit surprised when every hand shot up. "OK, good. I was busy and missed it so who can tell me what they showed?" All of the hands stayed up, and Zax chose a boy who sat in the front row and bounced with enthusiasm.

"Sir—they showed the first wave of colonists loading up for transport down to the planet."

"Interesting. Who typically makes up the first group?"

"Sir—the new Colonial Security staff goes first. They are former Crew members, so everyone has gone through the rigorous training we all experience. The same way the Crew has final authority on the Ship, Colonial Security has final authority in the new colony."

"Exactly right. Ten credits." A girl midway towards the back appeared puzzled and raised her hand. Zax pointed at her.

"I don't understand, sir. No one from the Crew ever volunteers to join a colony, right? So that means the only Crew members who are picked for Colonial Security are those who have been Culled. Doesn't this mean all of our colonies are being led by the very worst people from the Crew?"

A boy in the back row jumped in before Zax could answer. "That's a stupid question! Why do you think the rest of us worry about the Leaderboard so much? No one wants to get Culled because that's what happens—you wind up dumped off to some nasty colony."

Zax smiled at the girl who asked the question. "There are no stupid questions, only stupid *cadets.*" He smirked at the boy who had jumped in as he stressed the last word. "Ten credits for the cadet who asked a good question. For her classmate with the quick answer—ten credits for being right, ten demerits for calling a smart cadet stupid, and fifty demerits for speaking without first raising his hand."

The boy glared at him, but Zax smiled broadly back at him before he continued. "Though the cadet's answer was technically correct, I think there was a deeper meaning hidden behind the original question. I would rephrase it this way. Does it make sense for colonies to be led by the worst members of the Crew? I think this question has two distinct answers. Who wants to take a crack at it?"

A number of Gammas raised their hands, but Zax called on the cadet he punished for speaking out of turn. The boy answered smugly, "Because even the very worst Crew member is better than the best civilian."

"Spot on. That's the more obvious of the two answers, though, so I'm only giving you five credits." The boy glared at him even more fiercely than earlier. "Anyone want to take a crack at the second answer?"

All hands remained down around the room. Zax allowed the silence to linger for a few extra beats so everyone was good and uncomfortable before he expelled a dramatic sigh. "Do I have to do all of the work here, cadets?" Zax enjoyed being a trainer so his exasperation was fake and played for effect. He believed you had to needle the kids a little every once in a while to keep them on their toes.

"We all know the Ship's Mission is to seek out habitable worlds and seed the universe with as many human colonies as possible, right?"

Heads nodded around the compartment and Zax continued.

"If we represent the last remnants of Earth, we owe it to our ancestors who built this amazing Ship to continue that Mission and propagate our species far and wide. We *could* choose to maximize the chances of survival for any single colony by populating it with the best members of the Crew. Our Mission isn't to create a single successful colony, however, but to create thousands of them. Therefore, the greatest chance of succeeding at our Mission is to keep the best of us on board so the Ship can continue its journey. Since we know the worst Crew member is still far better than the best civilian, we can be confident even those who aren't good enough to stay in the Crew are well prepared to lead and develop our colonies. Make sense?"

Most heads were nodding, but the interruption boy raised his hand again. Zax pointed in his direction.

"You said 'if', sir."

"Excuse me?"

"Sir—you said '*if* we represent the last remnants of Earth' like there's some doubt about it."

Dammit, thought Zax, this was exactly the type of slip-up Mikedo was worried about when she warned him to push the discovery of the fighter far out of his mind. He hoped the lights were dim enough in the room the cadets wouldn't notice the flush in his cheeks.

"Thank you, cadet. Good catch as I obviously misspoke. There's no question the Ship and the colonies it has settled are the last remnants of humankind in the universe. Our ancestors realized almost too late the Earth had very limited time left. They were able to put aside their long history of destructive conflict to unite and pool what remained of the planet's meager resources to build this Ship—the one and only lifeboat for humanity."

He wasn't feeling enthusiastic about the standard Landfall lesson script given all his worries, but Zax knew it was important he deliver it convincingly. "The best and brightest of Earth were selected to be part of its one hundred-thousand-member Crew while a planet-wide lottery picked the civilians who got to come along and staff the less important jobs and provide a pool of future colonists. Ten million civilians were to remain conscious at all times and support the Mission while an additional one billion were put into the Ship's cryosleep holds. Look around the room right now and you see the descendants of that original Crew. We serve our Mission with pride once more by settling another group of humans who will represent a new outpost to prevent the extinction of our species."

Zax forced himself to smile at the boy. "So, I'm going to give you five credits for catching my mistake. I'll give you a chance at another forty which gets you back to even for the day if you can answer my last question. The colonists in the first wave are awake when they get sent down to start the new settlement. The other twenty thousand go down still packed in their cryotubes, though. Why is that?"

The boy was quiet for a couple of secs before answering. "Well, sir, I can think of two reasons. First, it takes time to set up and organize a colony. We provide them with enough bots and consumable raw materials for the initial buildout and setup, but all that stuff still takes time. It's probably a lot easier to get a colony up and running if you only have two hundred former Crew coordinating the initial work rather than twenty thousand useless civilians running around causing problems."

The boy pushed ahead without pausing for any comment from Zax. "The other reason for leaving the colonists in cryosleep is probably to prevent issues on board the Ship before they leave. Twenty thousand doesn't sound like a lot of people compared to the ten million who are awake on board, but I'm guessing they could cause an awful lot of problems if they were scared about getting left behind and wanted to fight back instead."

"Great answers. You've earned the forty credits." Zax acknowledged a raised hand on the other side of the room.

"Sir—I saw you on the newsvid the other day. You went down with the scouting mission. What did you think about the planet? Would you be scared about getting settled on it?"

Zax paused for a long moment and considered the question. He imagined living on a world where half of the landmass has just been roiled by the Ship's nukes. He remembered watching one of the herbivores getting eaten alive by a carnivorous tree. It was all pretty terrifying to him, but that wasn't a great answer for these kids to hear. After all, some of them had a decent shot of being at the bottom of the Leaderboard some day and finding themselves in a future first wave of colonists. He forced a smile. "It wasn't all that bad."

CHAPTER THIRTY-THREE

Look at me—I'm a blubbering mess.

After lunch, Zax visited Flight Ops for the first time since the mentorship contest started. He arrived as a CAP fighter launched and could be seen through the panorama streaking away into the void.

He desperately wanted to believe there was no connection between Mikedo's death and the information she shared with the Flight Boss a short time before it happened. Though he understood the rationale she had offered, it remained difficult for Zax to accept how the fighter's existence posed any risk. Ultimately, if Mikedo thought it was true, then Zax would put faith in her opinion. She believed the information was worth killing over, so it stood to reason she might be dead because she had shared it with the Boss.

Zax appraised the man who might have arranged Mikedo's death. He was convinced the Boss would attempt to ascertain whether he had any knowledge about the mysterious fighter. If the Boss had killed Mikedo over its discovery, then Zax was certain he wouldn't hesitate to do the same to him if the man harbored the slightest suspicion.

The Flight Boss rose once he noticed Zax's arrival. A cigar was clenched between his teeth as always and he grinned around it. "Cadet Zax—it's great to see you again! We've missed having you around these past few weeks!"

The warmth of the Boss's greeting disarmed Zax. He had walked into Flight Ops brimming with dread, as if he had just been Culled, only to be greeted like a long-lost friend. He quickly concluded the man's behavior should provoke even greater paranoia and pasted a smile on his lips. "Thank you, sir. It's great to be back."

"Mini-Flight—come join Zax and me in the conference room."

Kalare stood in response to the Boss's order and grinned at Zax as she approached. They fell into formation behind the Boss, and he led them to the small conference room attached to Flight Ops. He sat and gestured for the two of them to do the same.

The Boss took his cigar out of his mouth and rested it on the table before he spoke. "I have to tell you how fantastic it's been over the past few weeks to get reports about the amazing job the two of you have done with the mentorship contest. I heard nothing but high praise from the Marine instructors, and you can imagine how much it pains them to ever compliment Flight cadets. Sergeant Bailee, in particular, was blown away by your performance during the live fire exercise he crafted. He shared how his simulation was far too advanced for cadets your age and yet you nailed it."

The removal of his cigar allowed the Boss a smile far more broad than Zax had ever witnessed on the man. He jammed his fingernails into his palms in an effort to keep himself focused on the possibility of a trap. Zax refused to get caught off guard and slip up once the Boss started to probe for any weakness.

The Boss's smile faded as he continued. "Of course, we were all crushed by what happened to Lieutenant Mikedo. She was an amazing officer. Amazing. I remember her walking into this very same conference room for the first time like it was only yesterday. I picked her for my mentorship contest on a whim, really. I didn't think she had a chance against the other two cadets, but there was some undefinable spark about her which demanded attention. She stood before me and insisted she would win and I would be stuck with her for a good long while. She was correct about winning, though not about how long I'd be stuck with her."

The Boss choked up and his eyes brimmed with tears. "I'm sorry to get all emotional here, cadets. M-M-Mikedo's loss still hasn't quite sunk in. Look at me—I'm a blubbering mess. That woman left a huge impression on everyone she met, and I will forever be a better person for having had her in my life. I was supposed to be mentoring her, but there were plenty of times where I swear it wound up being the other way around."

The Boss turned away for a moment, and when he faced them again, there were tears streaking his cheeks. The knot of paranoia in Zax's stomach untied itself. It was clearly impossible for this man to have hurt Mikedo for any reason. The Omega took a couple of deep breaths and then continued.

"So, I'm going against my own instincts and have made a decision based on Mikedo's recommendation. I'm going to mentor both of you. Everyone reports you make an amazing team, so I've decided to keep nurturing your connection. I'm hoping we can prove that sometimes one plus one can be much greater than two."

Zax was struck dumbfounded by the officer's words and display of emotion. He walked into Flight Ops terrified about what might happen as a result of interacting with the Boss, and now his thoughts had been spun 180 degrees. This man could *never* have been involved with what happened to Mikedo. Zax desperately wanted to believe that meant *no one* was. He couldn't imagine a scenario where the second most powerful officer on board would be unaware of a decision to murder a member of the Crew. Bad luck happened sometimes, and Zax's mind worked furiously to convince himself Mikedo's death was just that—rotten chance.

His paranoia about the Boss had always been accompanied by enough disbelief that Zax was sufficiently primed to replace it with excitement provided with enough reason to do so. He was beyond thrilled to learn his career would be massively boosted by working with the man and even more so hearing it would happen with Kalare by his side. She was clearly insane and oftentimes drove him crazy, but he could not agree more about how they made a great team. He glanced at her expecting to find the same level of excitement but discovered she wore an expression of consternation instead.

"Sir—" Kalare hesitated. "I'm sorry, sir, but I don't quite know how to say this. Your offer comes as a tremendous surprise. I thought I was out of the running for your mentorship after I got hurt and didn't participate in the recon mission. I wasn't bothered because I knew how much Zax cared about winning, and I felt he deserved it far more than I did. That should be even more true when you hear I don't even know if I want to stay involved with Flight much longer. I respectfully decline your offer, particularly since you're extending it because you want me and Zax to keep working so closely together. He deserves better than a partner who isn't one hundred percent committed."

Zax expected the Boss to be angry, but the man smiled at Kalare instead. "I have to say, cadet, this is the first time I've ever had someone attempt to turn down my offer of mentorship. Anyone else in the Crew would gnaw off their arm for this opportunity. Your ability to speak your mind and make unconventional choices is precisely what I need in people I work with, however.

"I acknowledge you want to decline my offer, but I order you to hold off on making that final until we leave this system in forty-eight hours. I'm sending the two of you on a mission before then which I hope might influence your decision. Both of you meet me inside the hangar tomorrow after lunch. You're dismissed."

CHAPTER THIRTY-FOUR

You're the pilot.

Zax woke the next morning in a haze. He had wanted to spend time with Kalare after their meeting and convince her to accept the Boss's offer, but the Plug training which had immediately followed occupied him right up until lights out and their paths never crossed.

'Training' was a misnomer for what Zax had endured. He went into the session expecting instructions about how to accomplish amazing things with his new implant. What he got instead was seven hours of isolation in a pitch black room where he was forced to remain perfectly still while seemingly random images and noises were pumped into the headphones and goggles he wore. The room's temperature alternated between painfully hot and freezing cold, and once in a while his chair delivered electric jolts when he closed his eyes for too long or fidgeted too much.

The stated purpose of the session was the formation of various sensory pathways between his brain and the Plug. The actual outcome was the instigation of a crushing headache. The pain had receded by the morning, but Zax's brain still seemed to be operating a half sec behind the rest of his body.

After an extra long (twenty demerits) and extra hot (twenty additional demerits) shower, Zax headed to the mess hall. To his dismay, Kalare was not at their usual table and was nowhere to be found. He desperately needed a few mins with her to discuss the Flight Boss. Zax would never have believed it two weeks earlier, but he wanted nothing more than for Kalare to accept the Boss's offer so the two of them would be mentored together.

The morning newsvid droned while Zax ate. There was not a single mention of the new colony on the planet below. The first story announced an FTL Transit, which was scheduled the next day after lunch, but from there it went into mundane news about random happenings on board. It was as if the former Crew members and twenty thousand civilians down on the planet no longer existed, which Zax supposed was more true than not as far as most of the Ship was concerned.

Zax set out for another round of Plug training after breakfast. He dreaded what kind of torture was in store, but discovered instead the compartment was empty except for the instructor. The man stood as Zax entered.

"Good morning, cadet. I'm sorry, but we've been forced to delay the final portion of your Plug training. I was informed the Boss requires your participation in something later today and that will not leave us sufficient time to complete the session. I've already booked you a new appointment in two days."

Zax was not disappointed about skipping the session in favor of whatever surprise the Boss had in store at the hangar, but one thing bugged him. "Sir—is it possible for you to just tell me how to access the message that is waiting for me? The blinking red light in my field of vision is driving me crazy."

"I'm sorry, cadet, but that's impossible. We have strict training protocols, and I would incur serious demerits if I taught you how to access messages before you had completed the earlier lessons. Maybe this news will provide some consolation, though. I have a note here from the doctor that says I'm supposed to tell you not to worry about throwing up anymore. I have no idea what that means, so I hope you understand it."

Zax's face broke out into a huge smile. "Yes sir, I understand what the doctor's talking about." With all of his excitement about getting Plugged In, Zax had forgotten about the other benefits he had long been promised regarding his implant:

No more giving up food in advance of FTL jumps—

No more nutripellets—

No more cleaning up vomit—

No more Puke Boy!

His elation about the FTL news carried Zax through the boredom of hours with nothing to do before lunch, and he eventually headed to the mess hall with a bounce in his step. Once again, Kalare was nowhere to be found. He was forced to consider whether she was actively avoiding him because she had decided to decline the Boss's offer. He put aside the worries since he still had another full day to convince her to do otherwise. He grabbed a quick bite on his own and headed off to meet the Boss.

As he entered the hangar, Zax discovered Kalare had already arrived. The Flight Boss stood next to her with a silver case in his hand. He was speaking to Kalare, but her body language suggested she wasn't particularly engaged in the conversation. Zax feared if she wasn't chewing on the Boss's ear it was the best signal yet she would decline his offer. The Boss greeted him.

"Good afternoon, Zax. I'm sorry we had to delay your second round of Plug training for another day. Hopefully, you won't mind once you learn what I have in store for the two of you. Besides—it will give you another day to recover from all the fun of that initial session."

"Thank you, sir. And yes, I won't mind some additional time to try to forget about the first day of Plug training."

The Boss flashed a smile at Zax's reply and then turned to Kalare. "Sorry to be speaking cryptically, Kalare. You'll find out what we're talking about soon enough when you get your Plug. Mikedo convinced me to get Zax implanted early before she left for the planet. If you decide to let me mentor you, we'll get yours done soon too. Let's get today's adventure started."

The Boss strode off towards a corner of the hangar, and Zax and Kalare fell in behind him. Considering the massive amounts of work involved with transferring the settlers and their supplies down to the colony over the previous days, the hangar was surprisingly empty. There was only a handful of Crew performing various tasks. The Boss led them towards a small shuttle which sat prepped for departure.

"I need to have this case delivered to the head of Colonial Security before we leave the planet tomorrow." The Boss continued with a grin. "I figured since Kalare never got a chance to go down to the surface, and since your trip was cut short, Zax, you two would be the perfect messengers."

Zax was thrilled about another opportunity to visit the surface. Particularly one that wouldn't involve stomping around the jungle wearing ChamWare. "Thank you, sir! Where's the pilot?"

"You're the pilot. I royally screwed up and forgot to hand the case over before the colonists left. I don't want to get in trouble with the Captain, so I've kept the entire trip secret and only involved the bare minimum of Crew."

The Boss laughed at Zax's expression of confusion and concern. "Don't worry, cadet. The shuttle is configured to take off, land, and return on autopilot. It has all of my override codes preprogrammed so it can get off the Ship and return without triggering any alarms. All you have to do is verbally issue two commands—one to launch from here and then another when it's time to return from the surface. Do you think you can manage that?"

Zax nodded, though he couldn't help but wonder what in the case was so important the Boss would go through all of this subterfuge to have it delivered. If the shuttle was effectively configured as an automated drone and didn't require a pilot, it meant the Boss's decision to send Zax and Kalare along for the ride was his last attempt to convince Kalare how being mentored by him would involve interesting opportunities. Zax believed this strategy was working since Kalare appeared excited as she asked questions.

"Sir—how do we find the head of security? Will she meet our shuttle, or are we going to have to search for her?"

Zax's enthusiasm for the trip faded once he fully processed what Kalare asked. He had managed to avoid any encounters with Cyrus before his departure with the first wave of colonists, but now Zax was visiting the planet. What would happen if he stepped off the shuttle and the first person he ran into was a psychopath who had promised to kill him? He listened carefully as the Boss replied.

"You don't have to worry about any of that. The landing pad for the shuttle is right next to the main administration building and the chief will be working in there. All of the civilians are still in their cryotubes and everyone in security with the exception of the chief is away on an all-day recon mission. I wouldn't dare send you two down without a Marine escort if there was actually anyone around other than the chief. Most of Colonial Security would kill you on sight so they could hijack the shuttle and attempt to sneak their way back onto the Ship. Those former Crew got Culled for lots of different reasons, but none of them had it happen because they were too smart."

They shared a polite laugh at the Boss's joke, though Zax's was a little more genuine due to his relief about avoiding any chance meeting with Cyrus. The Boss gestured for Kalare and Zax to enter the shuttle.

"Good luck down there, cadets. I'll be waiting here for the shuttle when it returns."

Ninety secs later they were strapped in and Zax issued the command to launch. He glanced over at Kalare a short time after they departed the hanger. She stared out the shuttle window with a melancholy expression on her face.

"This trip had you excited at first," Zax said, "but it isn't changing your mind about getting mentored by the Flight Boss, is it?"

Kalare sighed as she turned to face him. "I'm sorry, Zax. I know how you want me to want this. I know I should want this. But, I just—don't—want—this.

The last few weeks training with you have been fantastic, but that's the only reason why I'm here at all. You look out this window and get inspired by the Ship passing beneath us and dream of flying around it all the time. All I see is my friend's face smiling back at me as her dead body floats by. I've realized I can't tolerate the whole idea of being outside in space and that makes me a very poor candidate for Flight, don't you think?"

Zax knew he would never change her mind after that explanation. In fact, it would be selfish to even try. He nodded slowly and Kalare continued.

"I can't thank you enough for everything. Two amazing things have come out of this experience. First, I got to train with the Marines. Even if I become just an average ground-pounding grunt, I've learned the Marines is where I belong."

Kalare reached over and took Zax's hand in hers. "The second amazing thing is that you and I are now friends. I haven't had many in my life—in fact, I think the last people who I truly considered to be my friends were those two girls who got vented into space. Something snapped inside me that day, and I decided I would be better off if I just kept my distance from everyone. I don't want to live like that anymore and I've got you to thank. Whatever else the future brings, I hope we stay friends."

"Thank you. I hope so too." Zax wanted to say so much more but recognized trying to do so would overwhelm him with emotion. Instead, he held Kalare's hand in silence as the view out the window filled with the fast approaching planet.

CHAPTER THIRTY-FIVE

He sent you here for this?

Their path through the atmosphere brought the shuttle over the nuked continent which only a few days earlier had held a thriving bug colony. They were too high and the clouds were too thick to see any of the destruction, but the shuttle's threat board barked alarms about the presence of radiation below. The spacecraft's shielding would protect them from any ill effects given their altitude, so Zax ignored the warnings and they subsided once the shuttle crossed the ocean.

As they got closer to the ground, the new structures came alive due to the mass of assembly bots which swarmed over them. Gauging the progress made since Landfall, Zax estimated the construction would be complete in just a few more days. The encampment would still be pretty grim even then, but at least the civilians would come out of cryosleep and find finished buildings rather than a tent city.

Seeing things up close like this forced Zax to really think about the civilians and their thawing process for the first time. The Ship optimized the people picked for each Landfall by considering both skills and genetic diversity. This meant the colonists were a mix of people who had been Culled and frozen recently, those who would be awake for the first time since the Ship left Earth, and everyone in between. How such a random group could wake up on a strange, hostile planet and be expected to immediately work together for the colony's survival was incomprehensible.

As the shuttle landed, it became clear why the Boss was not worried about them finding the administration building. It was four basic walls and a roof which appeared thrown together, but it was the sole completed permanent structure within a sea of tents and half-completed shells of new buildings.

Zax pressed the button which opened the shuttle's door. The heat and humidity assaulted his senses before he even stood up. He hadn't noticed it as much on his first visit since he had worn the ChamWare, but Zax could practically taste the jungle. The Ship's training rooms did a terrific job of replicating the experience, but now he had felt the real thing he would forever think about them differently. Amazing simulations, yes, but simulations nonetheless. Kalare gaped out the door and smiled from ear to ear.

"You seem excited—"

"This is wild, Zax! I sure wish I came down here with you and the Marines! It must have been incredible to walk through the jungle and experience everything up close. All we're going to see today is this nasty settlement, but just tasting air which hasn't already been breathed by ten million people is making me feel more alive than ever! I want to go running off into the jungle and climb the highest tree I can find and then just sit and soak it all in."

Kalare hadn't seen what the trees were capable of, but there was zero chance Zax would get in a word of warning right now. She bounced on the balls of her feet and continued to voice her excitement.

"Check out all of those assembly bots over there! Wait—is that an animal of some sort in the tree line? I can't tell from here. Nope, it's just another assembly bot. Those trees are huge! And the leaves—those are the largest leaves I've ever seen! And how about that sky? There's not a cloud to be seen. Do they have weather on this planet? Of course they have weather— every planet has weather—right? There's so much I want to soak in. I'm standing on a planet for the first and possibly last time of my life and I just can't believe it!"

Zax grinned at Kalare's exuberance, but his own joy about returning to the surface was tempered by the memories of what transpired here on his last trip.

"I'm very happy you got to come down here. I wish we could explore and give you the full tour, but, unfortunately, we've got a mission. Let's go find the security chief."

They exited the shuttle and walked into the administration building. Its unfinished exterior was echoed by the thrown-together nature of what was inside. Desks had been scattered around the space and partially assembled workstations littered every surface. There was a single desk which appeared like it was completely configured and that is where they found the security chief. She looked up as they approached and immediately looked frustrated.

"A couple of cadets—what were they thinking sending you two down here?"

"Good afternoon, ma'am. The Flight Boss instructed us to deliver this case to you personally." Zax handed the case to the woman. He technically didn't need to refer to the chief as "ma'am" since she had been Culled and was no longer part of the Crew, but it couldn't hurt.

The security chief opened the case and examined its contents. "He sent you here for this?" She slammed the case shut and tossed it onto a pile of trash. "I can't even begin to tell you how much I hate my life right now, but at least I know I'll eventually die without ever again having to deal with that man. Or the rest of the Omegas for that matter. I hope you don't find it rude if I don't invite you to sit down for a meal and some lovely conversation, but I've got twenty thousand damn civilians who're going to be thawed out in forty-eight hours and I need to be certain we're ready for them. Good luck, cadets—you need it even more than I do."

She turned her attention back to her work and acted as if Zax and Kalare no longer existed. They looked at each other quizzically for a few moments until Kalare shrugged her shoulders and turned to leave the building. Once they were outside, she stopped and waited for Zax to catch up.

"What do you suppose that was all about?" Kalare asked. "Seems pretty odd the Boss would send us to the surface to deliver something the chief would treat like so much garbage."

"I don't have a clue," Zax replied as he walked past her. "Let's get back to the shuttle and off this planet—that is unless you still want to go for a stroll in the jungle."

"Hah, hah—even I'm not *that* crazy!" Kalare laughed and followed Zax as they approached the shuttle.

Something crashed into Zax's skull as he walked through the shuttle hatch. He collapsed to the deck on his hands and knees and then heard Kalare get cut off mid-scream by a stunstik discharge. The thunder of the weapon was followed by the sound of her body hitting the ground. He had no clue what was going on, but it was clearly bad news.

Zax was flipped onto his back by the crushing impact of a boot to his belly. Zax saw stars as his breath left, but he finally glimpsed his assailant—Cyrus. He must have dropped the stunstik after using it on Kalare because the only thing in his hands was a knife with a blade which was almost half a meter long.

"Well, well, well—I never would have imagined this wish would come true." His eyes were dull and vacant, but the menace in Cyrus's voice was unmistakable. "I went to bed last night thinking the rest of my life would be spent on this damn rock. They told us on the ride down our Plugs were disabled, so you can imagine my surprise when I woke up and found a message."

Cyrus smirked. "It said you and your girlfriend were going to show up today. All I had to do was kill you both and then I could use your shuttle to get back up to the Ship. Sounds like a pretty great deal, right? I'll take care of you first and then I'm going to wake her up before getting rid of your friend. It wouldn't be as much fun to kill her while she's stunned, don't you think?"

Zax wanted to do something, anything. With all of the air knocked out of him, all he could do was gasp helplessly as Cyrus approached with the blade aimed at his throat. He shut his eyes rather than witness his impending death. A moment later a stunstik discharge was followed by the thud of body hitting the floor. Zax opened his eyes as Kalare administered a second and then a third stunstik blow to Cyrus's body in quick succession. She wore a frantic grin.

"I always knew my ability to withstand stunstiks might come in handy," she said, "but I never dreamed it would actually save my life. Help me get him off the shuttle so we can get the hell off this planet!"

Zax staggered to his feet and took hold of Cyrus' right leg. Kalare grabbed the left and together they dragged his unconscious body outside. For some absurd reason, Zax experienced a pang of guilt when Cyrus' head came off the shuttle and hit the ground with a sharp thud, but it passed once he caught another glimpse of the blade that was still clutched in his hand. Kalare stunned Cyrus one final time and then heaved both the stunstik and the knife ten meters away from the shuttle. Thirty secs later they were strapped in their seats, and Zax sent the craft aloft.

They sat without speaking for quite a while as they recovered from the shock and exertion. The only noise was their labored breathing. Slowly, their breath quieted and eventually Kalare turned to Zax and broke the silence.

"You're bleeding."

Zax put his fingers to the spot on his head where a dull ache originated and sure enough they came back tacky with blood.

"It's not too bad."

"How did that just happen?" she asked. "I thought the Boss said all of the colonists were out on a scouting trip. What kind of epic bad luck made Cyrus the one person who was still around?"

Kalare must have still been outside the shuttle when Cyrus mentioned the anonymous message he received. She didn't know it was a deliberate act of someone on board the Ship rather than random chance which put Cyrus in their path. Her question required a response, but Zax's head spun from more than just getting smashed with the stunstik. He had previously pushed aside the crazed paranoia which arose after Mikedo's death, but it had all come crashing back with a vengeance in the mins since the attack.

Had the Boss actually arranged Mikedo's death and then attempted to use Cyrus to get rid of Zax? The Boss said their flight to the surface was largely secret, but also said there were a few other people who knew. Maybe it was one of those other folks who sent the message to Cyrus. The Boss had appeared so crushed by Mikedo's death Zax could not imagine he had anything to do with it—but—the Flight Boss was the most obvious person to suspect as Zax considered all of the possibilities. That seemed even more true when you factored in the security chief's reaction to what the Boss had portrayed as a critical delivery. If nothing else, who but the Boss possessed the power necessary to follow through on any deal which would allow Cyrus back on board.

Zax wanted desperately to share everything with Kalare and see what she thought, but he kept flashing back to Mikedo's statement about how he must not tell anyone else about the human fighter. The attack revealed that Kalare was in danger too and deserved to know why, but Mikedo had been so insistent when she extracted the vow of secrecy from him. He needed time to think all of it through—more time than they had given how quickly the shuttle approached the Ship.

"I don't know if anyone's luck could ever be that bad, but I don't have a better answer for you right now." Zax took comfort in not explicitly lying to Kalare. He genuinely hoped to have a better answer later once he had a chance to clear his head and think things through. "The Boss is going to notice the cut on my head. What do we tell him?"

Kalare didn't hesitate. "We were checking out the colony construction and you tripped and hit your head. The Ship is leaving this system forever tomorrow, so Cyrus will be nothing but a bad memory. Why should we deal with any questions the Boss might bring up if we were to tell him the whole story?"

"What happens if someone finds him unconscious down there? Aren't they likely to report the incident to the Ship?"

Kalare snorted. "Are you crazy? What's Cyrus going to say—he tried to murder us and we got away, so he wants to be sure we get in trouble for having stunned him? Besides, you heard what the security chief thought of the Boss and the rest of the Omegas. You think she would bother to contact the Ship about some tussle between a couple cadets and one of her colonists? She's got far bigger worries right now. If anything, I bet Cyrus wakes up before the rest of the security staff returns and no one is ever the wiser."

Zax nodded his agreement. There was no chance anyone on the Ship would ever know about what happened down on the planet. He corrected himself because it actually wasn't true. Someone on the Ship had arranged for Cyrus to be there, so at least one person knew about it already. Zax needed to identify that person. What he might do with the knowledge was still a complete mystery, but he would figure that out later. In the meantime, he sat back and closed his eyes to think as the shuttle approach the Ship.

CHAPTER THIRTY-SIX

I said it before and I will say it again.

True to his word, the Flight Boss was waiting when the shuttle touched down. There might have been a trace of surprise on the Omega's face when the hatch opened and he saw who was inside, but if it was truly there it disappeared instantly. His eyes went to Zax's bloody scalp and he asked what happened.

"We were checking out the construction, sir, and I tripped and hit my head."

He paused for a moment, but the Boss's expression did not reveal anything other than complete belief of Zax's answer. "That looks like it hurts. It's getting late, so you should head to medbay and get that wound dealt with."

The Boss turned to Kalare. "You should get to your berth and get ready for lights out. I hope this little trip has caused you to reconsider my offer, but even if it hasn't I don't want to hear an answer from you until tomorrow. Take one last night to sleep on it.

"Both of you—report to the Flight Ops conference room immediately after tomorrow's FTL Transit. We'll finalize your mentorship decisions and get back to regular work. We've got to find our next Landfall. It better not take as long to find as this one did! Dismissed."

Zax and Kalare exited the hangar together. Zax reached for Kalare's arm before they went their separate ways. "I want to be sure we have a chance to speak before we meet the Boss tomorrow."

"OK—I promise."

Zax was frantic about what he might say to Kalare and how much he should share. His worries consumed him throughout the visit to medbay and then again during his trip back to the Zeta berth. Zax arrived as they announced lights out, so he crawled into his bunk in full uniform (ten demerits) rather than getting undressed in the dark.

The core problem which kept him wide awake was that Zax remained entirely unsure about what was happening around him. He needed someone to talk to about everything—a person who could hear him out and provide advice. He couldn't go to an officer or any other figure of authority. If he was mistaken about his suspicions, it would be an extremely career limiting move to accuse the Flight Boss of arranging the murder of one Crew member and conspiring in the attempted murder of two others. If Zax was right, he was just dragging more people into a life-threatening situation. Even though Kalare seemed to already be inextricably linked, the echoes of Mikedo's exhortation to keep the human fighter secret left him paralyzed at the thought of opening up to his only friend.

He was well accustomed to being alone, but this was the first situation where Zax recalled feeling so painfully lonely. It had been thrilling to share his recent highs and lows with Kalare and Mikedo after a lifetime of being on his own. The recent experience of having friends to fall back on made it that much harder to tackle this massive challenge by himself. Eventually, the tears poured down Zax's cheeks as utter despair and hopelessness took hold.

When Zax rubbed his eyes, he became aware once again of the little red light which blinked in his field of vision. Zax stared at the light and desperately wished he could read the message it signaled. It felt strange to focus his vision on something he knew existed only in his mind, but when he did a text prompt appeared.

Read message, yes/no?

Brilliant! Zax concentrated again on his desire to read the message and sure enough it opened up before him. When the header revealed it was from Mikedo, the excitement took his breath away. The message contained nothing but gobbledygook, though, so his hopes were just as quickly dashed. Random letters and symbols hung in the air before him in a giant mishmash of meaningless text. He stared at the message and wished it was understandable and another prompt appeared.

Decrypt message, yes/no?

Excellent! Zax wanted to decrypt the message, and when he thought about doing so, a tiny keyboard was displayed along with a prompt.

Enter passphrase:

Zax was clueless about what secret word or phrase Mikedo might have picked to encrypt this message. He pounded on his forehead and despaired about why she would have sent him something he had no way of accessing. Zax stared at the keyboard, but nothing happened. He didn't know how to interact with it and the first attempt where he concentrated on each letter proved fruitless. It soon dawned on him he shouldn't be so literal about considering each letter, but rather needed to focus on whatever words he intended to enter. This approach made the difference and the first passphrase he wanted to attempt was displayed on the screen.

passphrase

He assumed this was a silly guess with zero chance of success, but he figured he had to start somewhere. He focused his mind on submitting the text and got a response.

Invalid passphrase. Try again yes/no?

Zax racked his brain for any word or phrase he imagined Mikedo might have used, but every attempt resulted in the same negative response. What information hid behind the encryption of her message? It had to be something important or otherwise she wouldn't have bothered to encrypt it, right? Zax's hopelessness threatened to reappear so he turned his attention away from the message and breathed deeply with his eyes scrunched tight in an effort to will away another bout of tears.

Zax returned to the note and studied the header again. The message was from Mikedo and included a timestamp which detailed when she sent it. Something about that timestamp gnawed at Zax until he solved the riddle—the message coincided with riding back from the surface in the Marine transport. Sending this note was Mikedo's last action before she died!

Zax thought back to that fateful trip. They had gotten on the transport and the major told them to settle in for the ride to the Ship. Zax and Mikedo went back to their compartment and she focused on doing some work before the medic came in with their immune boosts. After the weird back and forth between Mikedo and the medic, she finally accepted her injection and then Zax received his. He wanted a quick nap, but Mikedo said one final thing to him before he closed his eyes. It felt like a weird, random compliment at the time, but he recalled now how she had been insistent he listen and remember exactly what she said.

I absolutely believe you will do great things.

He focused on the encrypted text and submitted that as the passphrase. Success! The garbled text shimmered as the letters and numbers rearranged in his vision and transformed into Mikedo's final words.

Zax,

If you're reading this, it means my fears were warranted and I'm dead. What hurts even worse than knowing I'm about to die is the fear my decisions and actions have put you in danger as well. There's nothing I can do now to protect you other than share what little information I have to help you chart a better course of action than what I chose.

Almost as soon as the medic injected me, I understood something was wrong. The injection was normal at first but then burned as it made its way through my veins. I would have stopped her from administering your dose, but she had already done so by the time I figured out something was wrong with mine. You are sleeping peacefully in the chair next to me and it appears you're fine, so I'm guessing it was only my injection that was tampered with.

When you found that fighter I was at a loss about what we should do. I'm so incredibly sorry I failed you when you needed me most. I was convinced any information revealing there are other humans traveling the stars was dangerous—both for the Ship and for us as individuals. I know you didn't accept my rationale when we were back on the planet, but I've got three pieces of information to share which I hope will convince you.

The first two come from the bizarre conversation I just had with the Flight Boss. I expected him to be shocked when I described what I found, but he wasn't. He calmly asked for details about what I had seen, and then shared information which made it clear why he wasn't surprised by my report.

It started with our visit to the last white dwarf and the battle we had there. I know you were in Flight Ops that day, so you probably remember how the Boss consulted with Alpha about the origin of the unknown fighter when Vampire relayed it might be human. Alpha confirmed it was, but advised the Captain and the Boss they should not share this fact with anyone. The AI was worried the news would cause problems on board.

A few days later Alpha's concerns were proven correct. A series of full-blown civilian riots were triggered by rumors the Ship had encountered a human spacecraft. You might remember how this disrupted tube service one day during training. The AI had accurately predicted these riots, but more importantly had gone even further and asserted they would evolve into an outright revolution if there was ever definitive proof of other humans.

Zax was surprised to hear the story about the human spacecraft had reached the civilians, but he shouldn't have been. Since the rumor had made it all the way down to younger kids like the Gammas, it had clearly spread far and wide. He didn't understand why anyone would riot over it or why Alpha thought it might be so disruptive as to start a revolution. He attributed his lack of understanding to the fact he'd never stepped foot in any of the civilian parts of the Ship and had zero clue about how those people actually lived. He wished Mikedo was still around to answer his questions and help him make sense of it all. He focused on her final words once more.

You already know the third piece of information, Zax, but I'll say it again to reinforce its importance. I'm dying.

What did I do wrong? I told you to keep the discovery a secret. I told you we shouldn't share it with the Marines or anyone else, but instead I would tell the Flight Boss. I did and now I'm dying. The Boss was insistent with his questions about your involvement, and I think I convinced him you don't know a thing, but I don't think you should trust your life to my instincts any longer. If the Boss or one of the other Omegas was willing to kill me over this, then I'm guessing they won't hesitate to get rid of you too if they ever have reason to believe you know anything.

The only way you can be truly safe at this point is to make the information public. Alpha believes knowledge of these humans might be dangerous to the Omegas' control of the Ship, but there's no way it's reasonable for you to sacrifice your life in exchange for maintaining their status quo. We all signed up for the Mission of saving humanity—not for allowing the Boss and the other Omegas to retain command through any means necessary. Once everyone on the Ship knows about the human fighter, there won't be any reason for you to be seen as a threat. I wish more than anything I had called the Marines over when we were on the planet. With their helmet-cams transmitting to the Ship and being viewed by dozens of people in real-time, it would have been impossible to hide any of this.

I've attached video footage from my helmet-cam to this message. It shows the human spacecraft and has detailed shots of the cockpit—including the picture of Earth. I didn't know why at the time, but I lied to the Boss when he asked if I had any video or pictures. There's no sound and I kept you out of the frame at all times so you can maintain the story you were never there. The only way to guarantee your safety is to figure out a way to get this evidence spread far and wide.

One last word of advice for you Zax—don't try to carry this burden on your own. I know you like to be independent, but I think it would be a mistake for you to try to solve this predicament all by yourself. I told you earlier not to share this information with anyone, but I'll amend that now and suggest you tell one person—Kalare can help you think this through. That girl thinks the world of you and will do anything she can to help. Together you two are an amazing team, and if there is any hope of finding a way out of this situation then it rests with the two of you working together.

Goodbye, Zax. I said it before and I will say it again. I absolutely believe you will do great things.

Tears streamed down his face and Zax's heart beat like crazy, but now it all stemmed from gratitude and excitement rather than his earlier despair. He had received exactly the help he needed from a most trusted and yet unexpected source. He still didn't have any final answers, but at least now he would be able to enlist Kalare to help shoulder the burden of all the questions.

CHAPTER THIRTY-SEVEN

What I'm about to tell you will sound insane.

Zax woke the next morning to an abnormally quiet Zeta berth. He sat up and discovered it was empty. He checked the time and was shocked by the realization he had overslept (one hundred demerits). Not only had he missed breakfast, but he was also going to miss out on lunch if he didn't hustle. He had to skip the shower (fifty demerits), but a short time later he walked into the mess hall and spotted Kalare sitting in their regular spot. He filled a tray and sat down across from her as she acknowledged him with a grin and spoke.

"Good morning there, sleepy-head! I was going to wake you up, but I know how stressful things have been for you these past few days and figured if you managed to sleep through reveille then you deserved some extra rest. You look like you just woke up. Did you just wake up? That would be amazing! Do you know what time it is? Have you ever heard about anyone sleeping all the way until lunchtime? I'm surprised they can't send electric shocks to our bunks to make sure something like that doesn't happen, though I should probably—"

"I'm sorry, Kalare, but I need you to be quiet." She seemed a little hurt but stopped talking and waited while Zax took a couple of deep breaths before continuing. "What I'm about to tell you will sound insane. I'm sorry I haven't told you any of it already, but Mikedo made me promise I wouldn't share the story with anyone. I'm only telling you now because I got a message from her last night saying I should."

Mikedo's name had the desired effect and Kalare became intensely focused on Zax. He checked their surroundings again to be sure no one was nearby and quietly launched into his story. "I discovered a human spacecraft on the planet during the recon mission. Mikedo was afraid the Omegas would be upset if the information became public and convinced me she should tell the Flight Boss she was the one who found it and I knew nothing about it. A few mins after she had that conversation with the Boss, she was dead."

Saying the word "dead" caused Zax's voice to catch, but he fought off the emotion as he knew it was critical to remain calm. "I was afraid the Boss had done it at first, but you told me I was being paranoid. I saw how torn up he was about her death and decided his involvement made no sense and everything had just been a horrible coincidence. Then we went back down to the planet and got attacked by Cyrus.

"It was not bad luck Cyrus showed up when he did—while you were still outside the shuttle, he shared how someone from the Ship sent him a message and told him we would be there. That pointed the blame in the Boss's direction again and my worries were all but confirmed in a message from Mikedo I finally opened last night. She sent it to me right before she died. She knew almost immediately after they gave her the immune boost she was being murdered and believed it was most likely the Boss."

Zax stopped to gauge Kalare's reaction. She stared at him with her mouth open for a moment until her jaws started to move like she was attempting to speak. No sound came out and she soon gave up and instead gazed off across the mess hall with her brows knotted in concentration. Zax took advantage of the pause in their conversation to take a few bites of lunch. He was famished and it was his favorite—noodle day.

Finally, after a few mins, Kalare managed to speak. "I have a million questions and don't quite know where to begin. You're right—this all sounds insane. I guess I should start at the beginning of your story. What makes you so convinced the fighter you discovered was human?"

The disbelief was evident in Kalare's voice, but Zax couldn't blame her. "Mikedo's note included some video she took which I can show you later. In the meantime, here's what I saw.

"If you glanced at the spacecraft you would think it was one of ours. It was roughly the same size and shape and the design was extremely similar. The real key for me was the cockpit. The writing inside it was human. I couldn't decipher it because the alphabet included some different characters, but a lot of the letters were the exact same as ours. Finally, there was a plaque inside the cockpit which had a picture of Earth on it. A fighter which is similar to ours but actually comes from an alien race—maybe. An alphabet which looks very much like our alphabet but actually comes from an alien race—maybe. An alien race with a picture of Earth displayed inside one its fighters—maybe. All of those things found together but actually from an alien race—impossible."

Kalare nodded. "OK—I buy that. Now, I'm not sure I understand why discovering more humans would be such a bad thing, but let's just trust Mikedo and put that aside for a moment. If the Boss wanted her dead, how would he manage to do it when you guys were still on the shuttle?"

"When the medic came into our compartment she was very insistent Mikedo get the first shot. She said she had orders from the major. The injector was already loaded so it's possible she might not have even been aware of what was going on. Maybe the major loaded up the shot himself and then told her to be sure to do Mikedo first. Marines don't argue with officers when it comes to orders. She would have just said 'Yes sir' without question even if he had handed her an injector and told her to apply it to herself."

Zax paused for a moment to reconsider what he just said. "Now that I say this out loud, there's a chance the major might not have known about it either. When I was in the medbay after my Plug was implanted, I observed how injectors are often filled automatically by the computer. It would have been super easy for the Boss to send a command to the transport's medstation to fill up an injector with whatever he used to kill Mikedo. Again—if the major got an order from the Boss the first dose was specifically to be used on Mikedo, you can bet he would make sure it happened. As soon as there was any worry about an alien infection, the Boss knew the decision would be to get rid of her body before the shuttle returned and there would be no investigation into how she died."

Kalare took another min to think about everything as Zax worked on finishing his noodles. Eventually, she spoke again.

"So let's pretend for a moment it's the Flight Boss behind this—how would he know to get Cyrus involved and why would he go through all the trouble of sending you down to the planet? Wouldn't it have been easier to somehow arrange for you to get killed on the Ship? And why would he find it necessary to include me too? Wouldn't he just send you down there by yourself if he wanted to get rid of you?"

Zax smiled. "Of all the crazy stuff in this whole situation, those bits are what makes the most sense to me. Mikedo would've told the Boss about what was going on with Cyrus. He said he was getting constant reports about our training, and the details about why Cyrus would intentionally shred your knee sounds like the sort of thing Mikedo would've shared."

Kalare nodded in agreement and Zax continued. "As for sending us down to the planet to get rid of us, I think that's easy to understand too. There's no way he would risk killing me himself. Every unexpected death onboard is investigated to make sure we never have an infectious outbreak or someone roaming around who has snapped. He could try arranging a training accident of some sort, but that would require getting at least one other person involved. Nothing is a secret if it's known by more than one person, and I bet the Boss wouldn't want any loose thread hanging over his head.

"With Cyrus, he knew it wouldn't take any convincing to prompt action. All of the evidence would be down on the colony and no one up here would ever care about it. If Cyrus succeeded in using the shuttle to get back to the ship, the Boss would've simply killed him on sight for having escaped the colony. No loose threads."

Kalare nodded again as Zax drove to his conclusion. "The reason behind killing you is the easiest answer of all. He knows we're good friends and would've assumed I'd share the discovery of the fighter with you. I regret that I didn't."

Kalare beamed. "I think that's the first time I've heard you refer to me as being a friend, Zax."

Zax blushed. "I'm sorry. This friendship thing is new to me. You had practice when you were younger— I've pretty much been on my own my whole life."

"That's OK, I'm just teasing. It makes me really happy you're sharing all of this with me. I don't know what we're going to do about it all, but I'm honored you think I can assist somehow. I'm even more touched since I know you never ask for help."

Zax didn't know what to say so he went with his default, "Thank you."

"You're welcome. Here's the first step. After the FTL Transit—hold on—FTL Transit?" Kalare paused for a moment. "We've got a Transit here in a little while and you're eating real food?"

"I know—isn't it awesome! The instructor told me they programmed my Plug to fix my problems with FTL. It's so great to not worry about Transits anymore. If I never again taste a nutripellet, it will be too soon!"

Kalare smiled. "That great, Zax. OK—back to the plan—after the Transit we're going to head over to our meeting with the Boss and I'm going to tell him I'm super excited to accept his mentorship. After that—"

"Wait—what? You've changed your mind? Are you crazy? You've made it clear to the Boss you weren't interested in his offer, so you're in the clear. I've just told you it seems like the man has reason to kill you and most likely has already attempted to do so. Obviously you're going to do the most logical thing with that information—you're going to pass up your chance to get as far away from him as possible and instead take him on as your mentor. I'm stuck in this situation, but you're going to jump into it willingly. I just wanted help thinking all of this stuff through—I didn't expect you to stick your neck out!"

Kalare grinned. "There's an ancient Earth saying I read about a long time ago that's always stuck with me. *'Keep your friends close and your enemies closer.'* Sticking with Flight and letting the Boss mentor me lets me do both of those things at once—how could I say no?"

Zax paused for a long moment and considered his good fortune. The sadness of losing Mikedo would always be there, but he was incredibly grateful some of that hole would be filled by Kalare. "You are insane, but I'm guessing that's why you're willing to be my friend."

"You got that right, Zax—both parts!"

CHAPTER THIRTY-EIGHT

What are you doing here?

Zax and Kalare finished lunch and agreed to connect after the FTL Transit to inform the Boss about their acceptance of his mentorship. Zax's intention to enact a different plan before then without Kalare's knowledge aroused some guilt, but he was determined to do whatever he could to protect her. If she heard his plan in advance, she would insist on helping even if it meant both of them getting in trouble—or worse.

The Tube opened and Zax stepped out towards Flight Ops. The lights were still broken and the area around the junction remained dark and dank. It only served to reinforce the feelings of dread that battled the noodles for space in the pit of Zax's stomach.

The compartment hatch opened, and Zax was surprised when the Flight Boss was not present. He approached the cadet working Threat.

"Good afternoon, Threat. Where's the Boss? Isn't there a Transit coming up soon?"

"Hi, Zax. He needed to step out but should be back any min. Why are you here? I could've sworn I checked the duty roster and saw you're not on for another day."

"No—you got that right. I need to check something though. What do you say you let your mini take a break for a few mins and let me borrow his station?"

"Of course. Be my guest."

The cadet at the Mini-Threat station stood and walked away. Zax sat down and used the console to put his plan into motion. A few mins later the Flight Boss entered the compartment and Zax caught his eye.

"Good afternoon, Zax. What are you doing here? I wasn't expecting you until after the Transit."

Zax's heart threatened to burst out of his ribcage and his mouth had gone bone dry. He paused for a deep breath and then spoke.

"Hello, sir. There's something I need to discuss with you, and I figured it was best to come right away rather than wait. I received a message from Lieutenant Mikedo with some weird stuff in it."

Most of the Flight Ops staff were hard at work prepping for the FTL Transit, but a couple of nearby Crew looked up from their workstations in reaction to

Zax's statement. A private message from the Boss arrived via his Plug.

"Zax—what's going on? What do you mean you got a message from Mikedo?"

"I'm sorry, sir, but I'm thinking it would be better for us to have this conversation verbally. I'm still getting the hang of all of this Plug stuff, and I would hate to be in the middle of this discussion and mess something up."

"Cut the crap, Zax. I can see your face turning red from here. There's clearly something that has you worked up, so please do me the courtesy of dropping this game. What did Mikedo's note say? I have to tell you the medics believe she wasn't particularly lucid before she died, so I wouldn't put much faith in anything she sent towards the end of your visit to the planet."

Zax's face burned even hotter with the Boss's observation. He noted the statement about Mikedo's mental state. It was amazing how the Boss was already laying groundwork to discredit anything Mikedo might have discussed in her message.

"You see, sir, she found something strange down on the planet when the two of us got separated. We never had a chance to talk about it before she got sick and died, but she sent me a note via my Plug which I've just now been able to open."

More Crew were now paying attention to what Zax was saying out loud. The Boss continued to gaze at him impassively even while their private communication became more heated.

"Zax—I have to warn you that what you're doing here is extremely dangerous. Let's head into my conference room and we can discuss this privately. It would be a shame for you to cause a lot of disruption and panic over nothing more than the ravings of a feverish individual. We both cared for her deeply, and neither one of us wants her reputation sullied by something she wrote while her mind wasn't working right. Let's figure this out together."

Appealing to his desire to protect Mikedo was a wise move by the Boss, but Zax charged ahead regardless.

"I know this sounds crazy, sir, but Mikedo told me she found a human spacecraft from Earth when she was down on the planet."

All activity ceased in Flight Ops. Every head turned and stared at Zax in response to the words "human" and "Earth." The Boss finally spoke out loud.

"You're right, cadet. That does sound crazy. The medics believed she had been ill for some period of time before she collapsed, so I'm guessing anything she thought she saw was nothing more than feverish hallucinations."

"I would have thought the same thing, sir, but she included some video with her note."

Zax's field of vision flashed red as the Boss's latest private message arrived marked with the highest level of urgency and importance.

"*Cadet—do not say another word! THAT IS A DIRECT ORDER!*"

Zax kept his expression neutral, gazed at the Boss straight in the eye, and pointed at the panorama. The officer checked the screen and the color drained from his face.

Mikedo's video had started and every person in Flight Ops stared at it intently. Whispered conversations which began at the sight of the fighter morphed into a much louder buzz as the camera panned into the cockpit and revealed the human writing. Flight Ops finally erupted in absolute tumult when the footage ended and a close-up of the mounted picture of Earth remained on the giant screens.

"*Eight thousand demerits, cadet! You're lucky you didn't violate my order about speaking or you would've found yourself challenging Cyrus' record for demerits. I'm hitting you with the maximum I feel I can justify right now, but rest assured I'll be watching you closely and will enjoy every opportunity to pile on more! Needless to say, my mentorship is no longer available.*"

"Calm down, everyone. Calm down please." The Boss's spoken tone was cool and calm in marked contrast to his private communication with Zax. He waited for the noise to fade and then continued. "That is a very interesting piece of video, cadet. I will ask Alpha to evaluate its content and will want to discuss it with you further. Until then, please return to your berth and prepare for the Transit. Dismissed."

The Boss turned away. Zax stood to leave the compartment but paused for a moment and considered the situation. He followed Mikedo's advice and made the existence of the human fighter public, and based on past experience he expected the information would be dispersed around the ship within days if not hours.

What was the cost to Zax? He lost everything he worked for over the past few weeks of the intense training. Not only the extra credits from the emergency panorama repair, but also the Boss's mentorship. Zax slowly realized this cost paled compared to what was truly lost. Mikedo was dead. Zax owed his life to her since she died trying to protect him. Revealing the existence of the fighter was a down payment on that debt, but it wasn't enough.

"Sir—there's just one more thing."

The Boss's head snapped around. The fury in his eyes was clear for all to see, and it was acknowledged by shocked gasps from more than one person.

"It appears to me, sir, that Mikedo's death was not an accident. I believe she was murdered by someone to hide the existence of the human fighter. Most likely the person who attempted to kill me yesterday with the same goal in mind. All of the evidence points to that person being one of the Omegas."

Time froze within Flight Ops. Zax could practically see the echo of his words as they reverberated around the compartment. His pounding heartbeat filled his ears as everyone held their breath and waited in the absolute stillness.

The silence was finally broken by laughter—hearty, rolling guffaws from the Boss. The man's expression a moment ago had primed Zax to expect rage, so the laughter came as a complete surprise. The longer it continued, however, the more it became clear that anger would probably have been a safer reaction.

"Thank you, son, but I haven't had a laugh like that in a long time." The Boss chuckled one last time and took a deep breath before he continued. "It never ceases to amaze me how young people can possess such amazing imaginations. The Ship really benefits when all of that youthful exuberance is harnessed which is why we get you all involved in such important jobs so early in your careers. I almost hate to stifle your creativity this way, but, unfortunately, you've crossed a line that should not have been crossed."

The Boss paused for a couple of beats as he stared at Zax. The laughter had drained from the man's eyes and they were once again stone cold. Zax fought to keep his knees from buckling under the weight of the steely gaze. After an eternity, the Boss spoke.

"Fifty thousand demerits. Get out of my compartment."

Zax wanted to run out of Flight Ops, but it seemed as if his legs were momentarily paralyzed. A final private message arrived from the Boss.

"It's a real shame, Zax. I don't know what you were thinking, but things could have been so different

if you had just come to me privately with Mikedo's message and your concerns. I should send you straight to cryosleep for making such an outrageous accusation, but doing that might make people think I was actually trying to hide something. I hope you achieved whatever you were after, though I can't imagine it being worth throwing your career away. Now get out of here without another word before I change my mind and decide it should be a trip out the airlock instead of demerits!"

Zax was finally able to move his body and flee the compartment. He paused once the hatch closed behind him and bent over with his hands on his knees. A series of deep breaths fought off a wave of nausea. He started to walk again and was immediately flooded with self-doubt. What had he done?

If he had stopped after playing the video, he would have succeeded in announcing the existence of the human fighter with the only cost being a relatively small number of points and the loss of the Boss's mentorship. Instead, he announced that someone among the most powerful people on board the Ship had committed murder with nothing to back him up other than a bunch of assumptions and coincidences. It was almost certainly the Boss behind it all, but Zax had zero proof and the man was surely aware of that fact. No wonder he laughed in the face of the accusation.

In the end, Zax had traded getting laughed at by the Boss for a staggering fifty thousand points. He started high enough on the Leaderboard that getting hit with even that many demerits wouldn't guarantee him being Culled, but he was just barely in the safe zone. Something as simple as a botched exam or a stupid injury could send him to cryosleep.

Even if he did avoid being Culled, Zax now faced a lifetime with nothing for a career. At the bottom of the Leaderboard, he would wind up working somewhere in the bowels of the Ship doing something horrifically distasteful. If he was lucky, he might someday rise up to the level where he could manage the sewage system or something similarly depressing. In the span of a few short mins, he had dropped himself from the absolute pinnacle of Crew life almost all the way to the very bottom.

Should he have found a different way? He had exposed the existence of the fighter, but should he have just stopped there? Maybe if he could have kept his job in Flight Ops and stayed close to the Boss, he would have found a way to make the man pay for Mikedo's death as well. Was that a realistic scenario, or was he just flailing at anything that might have led to better self-preservation?

Zax finally shocked himself with the conclusion he didn't care about himself or his career any longer. Contrary to 5,000 years' worth of history and tradition, the Ship was not the only human presence in the universe and soon everyone on board would be aware of that incredible fact—for better or worse. Mikedo died because of this discovery, and Zax had just made sure her death wasn't in vain. The sacrifice of his career was a small price to pay when compared to the sacrifice of her life. He hadn't come close to exacting revenge for her death, but at least he had guaranteed it would have some meaning.

He reached the Tube and requested the Zeta berth just as the FTL bell sounded. He sighed in relief knowing it meant he would have time to digest everything that had happened before he had to face Kalare and share the story with her.

CHAPTER THIRTY-NINE

Hello, lunch?

The sour, gag-inducing smell hit Zax the moment the bells woke him. He recognized the odor but was dismayed by its presence. He opened his eyes and the source swirled around him. Hello, lunch?

What the—? Wasn't it bad enough he had just tossed his career into the trash, but now he couldn't even catch a break with his Plug? The medics said he was fixed—they had adjusted his implant so he would never barf after FTL again. What happened?

Zax was even more out of luck because he had not positioned any cleaning supplies nearby since the problem was supposedly cured. He looked up and desperately hoped the voluminous puke would stay in orbit directly above him and not come splashing down on anyone else. Right at that moment Kalare flew across his field of vision, vomit bucket in hand. She smiled that big beaming smile of hers. The typical chants of "Puke Boy!" echoed through the berth, but Kalare's voice cut through them loud and clear.

"Hey there, friend—how about I help you out?"

If you liked Zax and Kalare and would like to read more about their adventures on the Ship, send an email to Zax@theshipseries.com and we'll send you the first 5 chapters of Volume 2.

Acknowledgments

About three years ago I was going through some particularly khrazy times in my life. My therapist (thank you R.G!) suggested that a great way to get myself more grounded would be a creative, right-brain activity that would balance all of the left-brain work that dominates my professional life. The seeds of this story had been bouncing around in my head for a while so I decided to take the plunge and write a novel.

Me being me, I actually decided that I would not write just one novel, but a series of SEVEN. Thankfully, I managed to talk myself off that particular ledge and you are holding in your hand book one of what will be only (!) a five volume series.

There are many people who played a role in getting this book published. The first is Owen Egerton. Owen is a creative polymath of the highest order who I am fortunate enough to call a friend. The degree to which he is wildly talented is surpassed only by the generosity with which he shares his talents. I remember how terrified I was the first time I talked to Owen about this project. He could have easily patted me on the head and said "nice try, kid", but instead he gave not only warm encouragement but also invaluable advice.

I was also lucky to benefit from my friendship with the other half of the talented Egerton duo when Jodi became my first editor. I'm tempted to go back and read some of the early drafts to see how far the story (and the prose) has come in that time, but I'm not sure I really want to subject myself to that kind of abuse. Jodi gave fantastic guidance and support when this project teetered between an absolute lark and something I really wanted to pour my heart into. Her encouragement pushed it forward into the form it is today.

Jodi eventually handed me off to a new editor in Stacey Swann. Stacey's guidance has absolutely made a huge difference in where this book wound up—both from a plot perspective as well as the writing style and quality. Her contributions were endless and will be eternally appreciated.

Outside of the professionals, I also benefited tremendously from the input of early readers among my friends. Kathleen Trail gave a couple of gentle pointers in the very early going that stuck with me throughout. Michael Lee was not only willing to read multiple drafts, he was also tremendously supportive and encouraging throughout the entire process. I will state here for the record that his life debt owed to me is discharged in light of his service to the Ship.

As the story got more and more refined, I was brave enough to share it with a larger group of friends who all provided encouragement and feedback. Huge appreciation for Laura Parrot Perry, Amy Nylund, Clayton and Tisha Havens, Scherry Sweeney, Scott Hyman, and Zachary W. All of those folks took the time to read and provide some great input.

Many thanks to Bryan McNeal for the cover concepts and art. I am honored that my book and Gatti's Pizza have both benefited from Bryan's artistry.

Finally, I want to express tremendous gratitude for my family. My lovely wife Kerry has provided constant encouragement and exhibited fantastic restraint about the number of Saturday and Sunday mornings I've spent typing away at Starbucks. My eldest, Parker, was super enthusiastic about reading the very first draft of volume one, even though he probably should have been begging me to refine it before unleashing it upon him. My youngest, Wesley, had book one read aloud by Kerry, and still managed to remember it a year later when I read volume two to him. The whole family provided great feedback and inspiration–even if Kerry still rants about the pronunciation of Kalare's name.

Made in the USA
San Bernardino, CA
31 January 2017